# Praise for
## *Jimmy's Girl*

"Most people think of teenage romance as fleeting, but Stephanie Gertler's *Jimmy's Girl* is a perfect reminder of how strong first love can be. . . . When Emily (who is married with four children) looks Jimmy up on the Internet, we're excited about their reunion but anxious about the repercussions of unearthing their lost love. *Jimmy's Girl* is definitely a page-turner, but perhaps the best thing about this novel is that, as you race toward the end, you're not sure what you want the outcome to be."                         —*Redbook* (editor's picks)

"An engaging tale of first love . . . polished by Gertler's smooth prose and her good sense of detail and structure. *Jimmy's Girl* is believable, and it is not impossible to see how married people such as these might want to return to their more intense first love. . . . Gertler manages to raise important issues and describe the process of the decision to act, on both sides, with humanity. . . . A promising debut."                         —*Chicago Tribune*

"*Jimmy's Girl* is a sharp-eyed, impeccably detailed novel about a harried mother/wife/artist who trades reality for a little romance."                         —*Marie Claire*

*continued . . .*

# Jimmy's Girl

## Stephanie Gertler

A SIGNET BOOK

SIGNET
Published by New American Library, a division of
Penguin Putnam Inc., 375 Hudson Street,
New York, New York 10014, U.S.A.
Penguin Books Ltd, 80 Strand,
London WC2R 0RL, England
Penguin Books Australia Ltd, Ringwood,
Victoria, Australia
Penguin Books Canada Ltd, 10 Alcorn Avenue,
Toronto, Ontario, Canada M4V 3B2
Penguin Books (N.Z.) Ltd, 182–190 Wairau Road,
Auckland 10, New Zealand

Penguin Books Ltd, Registered Offices:
Harmondsworth, Middlesex, England

Published by Signet, an imprint of New American Library, a division of
Penguin Putnam Inc. Previously published in a Dutton edition.

First Signet Printing, February 2002
10 9 8 7 6 5 4 3 2 1

For my parents

# ACKNOWLEDGMENTS

My appreciation to Tom McCullough, veteran (United States Marine Corps) of the war in Vietnam, whose recollections and reflections helped me understand what I hadn't known, and to Ray Hackett, veteran (Air Force) of the war in Vietnam who explained an era through journalistic eyes.

Special thanks to Judi Coffey, for endlessly listening and reading; Ellen Udelson, for always being there and making me laugh until I ache; Emily Coffey, Nancy Drexler, Timothy Dumas, Robin and Billy Game, my brother Jonathan Gertler, Judy Halden, Gigi Hayes, Alan Kannof, Andrea LaFazia, Roseann Spengler, Kerri Topalian and Joan Salwen Zaitz for the votes of confidence; Bruce Barnet, Leslie Garisto Pfaff, Bill Parish, Nick Peters and Nancy Schoenfeld Wettstein for jogging their memories.

For advice and fact checking, thanks to artists Marilyn Cohen and Nancy Stock; Ilene Donin, Ph.D.; Tom Campbell, program analyst, Washington Headquarters Services, Directorate for Information, Operations and

Reports; Lieutenant Andrew S. Landau, Operations officer, Marine Police Unit, Mamaroneck, New York; Liz Tate, mortuary affairs specialist, Department of the Army; the National Park Service rangers and volunteers at the Vietnam Veterans Memorial; and the United States Marine Corps.

My never-ending gratitude to Marcy Posner, my agent and dear friend, who told me right from the start that this could be done and always had faith in me. And then she kept me going, minute by minute, with reassurance, honesty, selflessness, love and great humor.

My deep appreciation to Carole Baron, my editor and publisher at Dutton, who called one glorious day to say she was in love with *Jimmy's Girl* and took me on this journey with warmth, sensitivity, friendship and an amazing eye for detail.

Thanks to Susan Schwartz, managing editor at Dutton, for holding my hand in the final phase.

To Ronni Berger, assistant to Carole Baron, and Alexia Paul, assistant to Marcy Posner, thanks for being so gracious and willing to answer a million questions.

To my children, David, Ellie and Ben: Thanks for suffering through all those cold dinners. See? I told you I was writing a book.

And, finally, thanks with love to my husband, Mark Schiffer: still the one.

# 1

I am Emily Hudson. I live in an old stone house in Connecticut. My yard is fenced with broad white pickets, lined with pink azaleas and blue hydrangeas but, still, it's not the best yard in the neighborhood. The shrubs are old. The lilac tree looks weary. The garden is strewn with soccer balls and old pails and shovels. There is a basketball hoop at the bottom of the gravel driveway embedded in a square of cracked pavement. Two of my sons are shooting baskets, perspired, shirtless, red-faced. My third son sits at the kitchen table studying his biology book, a pencil stuck behind his ear, a can of root beer too near the book. My daughter, the youngest, is upstairs. She is on the phone. Even though I can't see her, I know she is tipping back in her chair, bare feet up on her desk. I can hear her laughing.

The kitchen is deep green and blue with wide-planked oak floors. I am chopping green peppers and tomatoes on the cutting board. The radio is playing low, a golden oldies station. The late-afternoon sun is sinking in the sky, hidden behind the pine trees out-side the bay window. I can't see the sun setting but I know it is because of the way the shadows dance on the wall and the counters are spotted with gold drops.

I have become a quintessential suburban housewife, mired in school schedules, orthodontist appointments and bake sales. All this in between working at my painting. Lately I paint oils from a perch on the bluff at Tod's Point. I write words to go with my paintings. Short texts that tell a story, not believing that only pic-tures paint a thousand words. I drive the half hour's drive from New Canaan to Tod's in Old Greenwich every day. It was there at that beach where my parents rented a house each summer from the time I was an in-fant. It was there I disobeyed my parents for the first time when I walked with my friends to the pond.

"We told you never to go to the pond," my parents said. "The pond is thick and slimy and had you fallen in you could have drowned."

I felt so surefooted, though, even at the age of eight when I was small. Sneaking off to the pond. Climbing the rocks on the beach. The rocks were slippery with lichen but I never feared I'd fall. Digging furiously in the sand, convinced that I'd reach China. Determined. Until recently I was afraid to dig too deeply into any-thing, to venture anywhere remotely perilous. Though lately I navigate my way to places in my past where I probably shouldn't go. Looking back has come to give me solace. It is easier than looking ahead to a future where the crystal ball I once felt in my hands is now filled with blue fog and uncertainty. I am filled with a sense of reality. An awareness of middle life when something tells you that you have come to a fork in the road and you have to choose which path to take. I know all too well that looking back is a sure thing. The memories are trustworthy. They are faithful. Dependent only on the way I remember. And I am grateful that the past is etched with certainty since the future sometimes seems so hazy.

There was something else at Tod's as well. Something that until the last few months I tried not to think about as I looked across the horizon where it's hard to tell where the sky stops and the sea begins and they fuse into dubious infinity. I remember the summer of 1967. I think about the boy I loved who said he was a Cherokee. That might have been the only lie he ever told me. I was sixteen and he was seventeen. I had known him and loved him for merely four months but it seemed like forever. He stayed with us in the summerhouse for the week before he went away. My mother gave him the guest room next to hers. Ever-watchful. Ever wondering aloud why he was with us and not his own family.

Has he told you why he's here? she would ask me.

I've never asked him, I would say.

I thought it was so obvious. It seemed so right that he was with me. We stood on those rocks where I now sit with my easel and paint and I remember that boy who was tender and tough. That summer, when we stood on those rocks overlooking the horizon and I leaned my head on his shoulder while his arm held me so tightly, I was certain that he and I would be endless. But as the summer wore on after he left, I felt differently, not quite so sanguine. It was a sense that maybe the feeling I had for the boy who said he was a Cherokee would simply be one I would never have again, not with him or anyone else. It was a sobering epiphany I dismissed with denial that only adolescence can capitulate.

I go to Tod's now in winter while my children are in school and in summer, when they are at camp. I set up my easel, a wooden folding chair, the palette of oils and I paint the beach. I paint the lighthouse and the sand sculptures, the people picnicking on the dried-out redwood tables that have faded to a dusky gray.

In the summer, the air smells like hot dogs and cotton candy. The beach is filled with little girls in ruffled bathing suits, the kind I wore when I learned to swim. Mothers kneel at the shoreline beside naked babies carrying heavy pails of water. Older women sit together in groups, coated with oil. The straps of their bathing suits hang down their shoulders, tops drooping with the weight of their bosoms. I see the teenage girls in their bikinis, their bodies so smooth and firm, their even tans glistening the color of toast. They lie on sandy beach towels with their boyfriends whose stomachs ripple, a radio crackling beside them, their fingers entwined tightly as the sun beats down on them.

In winter, the picnickers are older people, wrapped in rough wool sweaters drinking steaming coffee from thermos bottles that serve as weights for the day's newspaper, eating sandwiches wrapped in foil. An old man tries to light his pipe in the wind.

But there's something that isn't quite the same now despite the sameness of the seasons and the same sweet smell of the cotton candy. The snack bar is old now. Its Formica counter is pitted and discolored. Signs for Fresca and Tab are worn and peeling. The town has taken away the old phone booth. The one with the seat and the black dial phone where you'd put in a dime, shut the door and the fan goes on inside. The one where you stepped in barefoot and felt the wet sand on the floor. There are three phones now, gleaming stainless steel, hanging on a wall with a sign that warns you of the fine for vandalism. It's just not the same. Sometimes I sit there on my folding chair and feel like a ghost lording over what used to be. Watching my memories the way I used to watch my children play at the shore. "Come back," I'd wave as they ventured too deep into the water. "Come back. Don't go above your head."

I paint mostly from my memory of summers. But when I go back there in the winter I see the beach for what it is, empty and untainted. The winters let me start with a clean slate, a white canvas. Memories undisturbed by time. By progress. Memories can be what I want them to be. Though sometimes I question them, wondering if perhaps some of them aren't merely dreams.

It is spring now but just quite spring. The air no longer has that edge of winter. Somewhere within the cool breeze there is a pocket of warmth, a portent of what is to come but still, I need my cardigan over my shoulders. The beach still holds that November sparsity. It's hard to tell where winter left off. The water swirls thick like mercury. It is still the color of charcoal. The sky is still more opal than turquoise. But lately when I go there, I am courageous as I look back. I picture the boy and myself sitting there. I can see his face so clearly, his long, shiny black hair, his hands jammed in the pockets of his blue jeans. White T-shirt. The way he walked with his head down as though he was afraid to look up at the sky, afraid to see how vast it was. Everything must have seemed so vast to him back then and riddled with doubt. Eternity and mortality. But suddenly he'd lift his head and smile at me and his eyes would blink and, looking back, I wonder if he was blinking away tears, but again, I am not sure what is memory or fancy. We were the only certainty for each other back then. This I know. This I clearly recall. I grip the cardigan that has slipped down past my shoulders, I check my wristwatch and push the images away. I pack up my canvas and oils, rinse my brushes in the sea and head back home.

I throw everything into damp brown cartons that sit in the back of my old Volvo station wagon. The car is pale blue, old and rusted through in little patches, but it holds my children and my paints. It reminds me of the one my mother drove when I was a girl. It makes me feel attached. Connected. It is continuance. We drove the boy to the train station in my mother's Oldsmobile wagon, a relic of a car like mine. That was the day I realized there could be something other than happy endings. The day I was no longer certain.

I have been married for nearly twenty years now to someone else. Years where lately I believe there have been too many long and silent nights ending in angry dawns. There are mornings when I awaken and find the bed empty beside me. Scrawled notes ("Had to leave early, see you later") on the mashed pillow where my husband Peter's head has slept have become all too familiar. There were the nights when I watched my youngest baby cradled in an eyelet bassinet next to my toddlers who smelled of talc and baby shampoo. They were swaddled in furry pastel blanket sleepers in little beds with crib sides, foamy beads of milky spittle around their soft mouths. Shallow breaths, little sighs. And I watched them alone. Grateful for them, but alone.

There were too many nights when the white wine on the kitchen table grew tepid while I waited for Peter to come home. Nights after long days alone with babies who barely spoke. Days when I longed for a pipe to burst so the plumber would come over for conversation. I chatted while he banged away, metal on metal, pinging and clanging, allowing me to hear my own voice, the man answering with an occasional, distracted "Uh-huh." He was a man with broad shoulders who made some repairs.

There was the man who polyurethaned the kitchen floor. He held a bag of ice on my hand after I burned it on a short-circuited sconce. I had turned on the switch and the light exploded like firecrackers, the baby in my arms shaken by the eruption. The man shook his key chain to calm the baby who sat on my lap and cried. Call the electrician, the man said. I'll stay until he gets here. A knight in shining armor with an ice pack.

I tease Peter sometimes. He says the teasing is really accusation. You missed the day we moved, I say. The day the light exploded. The day Jack took his first step. And except perhaps for Jack's first step, Peter doesn't feel he's missed too much. He doesn't see the importance of the mundane as I do. But with Jack's steps, he ached. "I was working, Emily," he said. "I know. I know. You think it wasn't worth it."

There were so many days when I looked in the mirror, longing for a reflection to gaze back at me for a brief moment and tell me I was worth seeing. Worth looking at. So many times I wished the reflection in the mirror spoke to me. I often longed to talk to someone other than my children. I could see my shoulders, sculpted still, no longer from youth or dance classes but rather from carrying babies on my hip, baskets overflowing with laundry, pails of trash. Lifting babies into playpens, catching them as they hurled down the slide in the park, pushing their swings, first one, then the other.

Every night, I stood at the picture window, a glass of wine in my hand, looking out at the dead-end street where the streetlamp flickered every few minutes to remind me that it wasn't the moon. Sometimes I cried. Not flowing tears, but hot tears that stayed trapped and burning. I stood and waited while the babies slept, their narrow chests rising and falling. I stood by the window, cracked open, blowing blue cigarette smoke into the cool night air, waiting for Peter to come home. I would listen for the crackle of the gravel in the driveway and I would light the candles on the kitchen table and hope for conversation. I would hear his key open the door. The house was so quiet. Babies sleeping. The warm wine waiting.

We would sit at the kitchen table and I would ask him about his day: What happened at the office? Where did you have lunch? Any interesting new cases? And he would be too tired to speak: Nothing happened. I had lunch at my desk. You know I shouldn't discuss my cases. So I would fill in the blanks: A new word uttered by a child learning to speak. We need more sand for the sandbox. Perhaps we should replace the gutters this year. Repoint the bricks in the fireplace. And after dinner, Peter would read the paper in the den. I would listen to the sheets of paper turning and shaking as I cleaned up the dishes. I would turn on the dishwasher and flick off the lights and then I would hear Peter fold the paper and drop it on the floor beside the arm chair. I would leave the kitchen, peek my head into the den. He would step into the hall. We would crack open the doors to the rooms where the children slept and stand for a moment, listening to the silence. We would leave the doors ajar. Good night. Good night. Another day was done.

People say to me, "You are so lucky. Your husband is charming and handsome." Yes, yes, yes. Successful and intelligent, well-respected, sought-after. But I often feel that my husband does not belong to me, nor I to him. Then there are the times when I am not sure I want to belong to him or to anyone.

My husband joked and said, "I do not beat you, drink up my paycheck or run around with other women. What is it that you want?"

And I wanted say, "Talk to me. Listen to me. Answer me. It's not a joke." But I would have felt foolish. Sounded like wives on the soap operas. I thought of the early days before we were married. When Peter and I would sit across from each other in a pub and I saw paradise every time I looked into his eyes.

So I tried to explain how I wanted to sit over a glass of wine and dream the way we used to before we had children. Before we were married. Remember how we used to picture who our babies would look like and we argued?

"I hope they look like you," he'd say.

"No, they should look like you," I'd say.

I longed for the times when we were sights for each other's sore eyes and sometimes questioned if those times were ever really there. Instead I asked him why he read the newspaper after dinner and he asked why I couldn't leave the dishes until morning. And then I'd ask him why it is that he looks the other way when I speak to him and he'd say that I am too demanding.

"But sometimes, lots of times, you barely even answer me," I'd say, feeling as though I were reading a laundry list, telling myself to stop as the litany of what he takes as criticism tumbled out.

Sometimes he'd protest, "I do answer but you don't hear me" or "I guess I don't say what you want to hear" or "Can't you simply understand that I am tired?"

People say that I should seek salvation in other places. That this is the way life is.

"Women friends are good enough companions," my sisters and my mother say to me. "Volunteer work, your painting, your children. These are the things that should fulfill you. Make your own life." I think they are so simplistic, my mother and my sisters. They have what they always wanted: the house, the kids, the husband. It is the way it was when we were little and my sisters and I played house: Even then the husbands weren't home. Daddy is working late, we said to the doll in the pink plastic high chair, spooning make-believe peas into her mouth. The Daddies were off working. We were diapering dolls and having tea parties and pushing prams. My sisters can be happy with all that still. I cannot.

My sisters say I am unrealistic. Your expectations are too high, they say. They tell me nothing is perfect. I know all this, but it doesn't matter. They tell me I am insatiable and I wonder if they're right. Maybe I just like the chase. Maybe if I caught the brass ring I would only try to catch it again. Maybe nothing would ever be enough. My sisters say that no one has everything. My sisters are twins. Cookie cutter wives who preach to me. My mother sits behind them like a silent echo nodding her head up and down as though to say, "Listen to Sara and Catherine. No one has everything. You are impractical. Unrealistic." It's not that I want everything. It's simply that I want enough.

Maybe this is why I started thinking again of the boy I loved in that summer of 1967. Not that I ever really stopped thinking about him but, until recently, I managed to push him out of my mind. He is the one I think about still when I paint on the beach. The one I had longed for and yet, until recently, could not paint.

My best friend, Jennie, stayed with us that summer of 1967. Jennie's parents had divorced two summers before. Her mother took off for the Himalayas. Jennie got a postcard and read *Lost Horizon*. So Jennie came with me. Jennie's father didn't quite know what to do with Jennie, still reeling at the notion that he was wifeless and left with a teenage daughter. We were right there in Connecticut. The house was across the street from the beach at Tod's Point. I pass the house each day when I drive to the beach but it doesn't look the same. For one thing, it is painted gray now and the shutters have been removed. My parents rented that house in Old Greenwich, so close to the water you could listen and count the waves hitting the shore in the middle of the night. So different from our apartment in Manhattan where the night was pierced only by sirens and concrete skyscrapers muffled the wind. The Old Greenwich house was pale yellow with blue shutters, peeling and weathered by sea spray. It had a front porch with columns so wide my younger brother, Robbie, could play hide and seek with Jennie and me and hide behind the columns. Robbie was the baby born when I (the youngest then of three) was ten. I was old enough to know how he happened, sickened and baffled at the thought.

The house had a cobblestone driveway, long and narrow. Jennie and I pulled Robbie in his Radio Flyer, back and forth, bumping over the stones, until the lightning bugs came out at night. Robbie captured the bugs in jelly jars, holes humanely punched into their metal lids. Jennie and I ran through the yard behind Robbie, slapping at mosquitoes that stuck to our arms and legs.

Jennie and I wrote short stories and poems and read Rod McKuen aloud to one another that summer. Jennie and I wore purple granny glasses and love beads. We baked in the sun, walked barefoot in the rain and burst into a wild dance on the beach when "Light My Fire" made number one on the hit parade. The days were so hot and humid that summer it was as though the air stood still and dared you to take a breath. We sprayed lemon juice in our hair and ironed it until it was stick-straight. We fanned ourselves with paperbacks and *Seventeen Magazine*. Jennie had a crush on Jean-Claude Killy.

The room I shared with Jennie had two pink canopy beds with a sunporch off to the side. The sunporch was wrapped in glass around the treetops, upholstered chintz cushions on carved-out window seats. The rain pounded down at night relieving us for a little while from the heat of the day and you could smell the salt and the strong stench of clams washed up on the shore. Jennie and I would open the jalousies on the porch and feel the breeze on our bare arms. Curled up on the seat cushions in lacy baby-doll pajamas, we listened to the breakers slapping the sea wall. The treetops glowed like silver and shook in the lightning only to be black a moment later. Wind swayed the branches against the house. Dramatic backdrop for the poetry and the strumming of my guitar.

I wrote in my diary and Jennie wrote in hers. And every night, I wrote the boy a letter telling him how much I missed him, how much I loved him, how I waited for him to come home. While my sisters went to movies and parked their Mustangs at the lover's lane on Tod's Point, Jennie and I sat at home pulling Robbie in the Radio Flyer. Watching him chase fireflies. She was the dutiful friend; I was the dutiful girlfriend.

That was the summer Jennie and I made origami fortunes and stuck our slender fingers in their enveloped sides and turned and counted numbers until the fortune answered our deepest questions. That was the summer I wrote Jim's name in all different variations with mine beneath it. James, Jim, Jimmy, James Robert Moran. I'd cross out the corresponding letters, counting "Love, Marriage, Friendship, Hate" and going on and on until I got the right combination. I'd write my first name with his last name over and over to see how it would look: Emily Moran. Emily Hudson Moran. I never dreamed that one day I would shun any man's last name as my own.

"Mrs. Walters?" the voices ask now when I answer the phone.

"No, I am not Mrs. Walters. I am Emily Hudson," I say. "I am Mr. Walters' wife."

Jimmy Moran was seventeen when he joined the Marines. His parents signed his enlistment papers because he was failing in school. The other boys who failed at his private school went to boarding schools in New England. Their fathers bought their way in. Legacies of the affluent. But Jimmy's father opted for the military. Not just some academy but the real thing.

That summer, Jimmy wrote me a letter every day from boot camp in Parris Island, South Carolina. Jennie and I would run down the stone walk to the mailbox every morning. My hands would shake as I searched the mail for the pale blue envelopes with the military insignia and then I would sit on the ground, my knees bent, buttocks resting on my ankles. Jennie sat silently next to me as I read the scrawled notes. Jennie made sure not to look over my shoulder. She busied herself by picking up clovers, muttering how there never were any with four leaves. Then I would read the letters to her, sometimes leaving out a line here or there. Like the part in one letter where he said he missed kissing the curve of my neck. I wasn't sure what Jennie would say. I was afraid she'd roll her eyes, say something giddy or maybe squeal so loud it would make it all seem too much, too silly. And it wasn't silly. It was all too private to share even with Jennie.

Jennie would look into my eyes when I finished reading the letters. It became a ritual.

"Jimmy loves you, Emily," Jennie always said.

"Are you sure?" I would ask.

"I am positive," she would say nodding her head in one short affirmation, bringing her chin down but not back up, and then she would clasp my hand in hers.

And then Jennie and I would walk slowly up the stone walk to the house, Jennie still looking down for four-leaf clovers and me with my hand over the letter in my pocket. We'd go inside the house and sit at the kitchen table, flip on the television, drink juice from glasses with painted-on oranges, scrape butter on English muffins that by then were cold, and scoop out cottage cheese since we were "dieting."

In between the game shows, we took off our jeans and peasant blouses, revealing bathing suits underneath. We spread Johnson's baby oil on our bodies.

The bulletins came over the old black-and-white television with the reporters standing at the battle lines. News reports glowed with gunfire that summer. Bombs burst in midair and cameras panned to sad-eyed children with dirt-streaked faces. Maybe the dirt was blood. It was hard to tell in black and white. Helicopters whirled around the reporters as they crouched in front of a jungle. My breath would catch in my throat. I could feel myself swallowing hard and my eyes would dampen and sting. Salt mixing with mascara.

"I'm turning it off, Emily," Jennie would say angrily. Then she'd slam the button on the television and pull me by the hand and we'd run down to the beach, towels bunched under our arms. Jennie carried the radio. I carried the paperbacks, pens, crosswords, a deck of cards.

Jimmy left on July 5, 1967. My mother and I drove him to the train station. My mother had a strange look in her eyes when she said good-bye to him. Godspeed, she said. An expression I had never heard her say before and haven't heard her say since. And then she even kissed him on the cheek and I think she looked at him for a moment as if she wanted to remember him. As if she was memorizing his face.

Jimmy walked me behind the ticket booth, away from the Oldsmobile and my mother's sight. He placed his arms around my waist and his lips to my lips. He whispered in my ear that he loved me. He ran the back of his hand down my cheek as he always did. The train came too quickly down the track. We saw the shiny dot in the distance becoming closer, brighter, glaring. My ears were still moist from his whisper when the train roared in. And Jimmy was gone.

I had my ears pierced later that day because I made a bet with myself that no one knew about: If I pierced my ears, Jimmy would come back, although deep-down inside I already knew he probably couldn't come back to me. Jennie knew that, too. I wrote in my diary that day after Jimmy left. Words that could only belong to a sixteen-year-old: "Loving him and know-ing it will end wears away at my innocence. He leaves an indelible stamp on my soul." I never showed that part to anyone. Not even to Jennie.

My sons throw the screen door open with a pop and it bangs on the metal frame. My oldest, Jack, puts a sweaty arm around my shoulder and steals a pepper from the cutting board. The middle boy, Sam, is fifteen. He swills Gatorade from the bottle. My fourteen-year-old son, Charlie, closes his biology book and stretches. Julie, who is twelve, comes downstairs and I can tell it is two steps at a time. Her feet are bare. Her hair is gathered on top of her head in a bright blue elastic.

I set the table for dinner. For six, even though we all know one place will not be used.

"Mom, hey! Look at you! Where are you now? Your eyes are very far away," Jack says to me.

I notice that he is wearing blue jeans and a white T-shirt. It hits me that Jack is seventeen.

I smile at him but I am barely here. I am on the beach with Jimmy Moran. I am waiting for someone to come home.

# 2

My name is Jim Moran. I am forty-eight years old. I live in Mobile, Alabama, with my wife and daughter. Our house is built from dark cedar and sits by a stream that my daughter, Clancy, calls the river. I watch my daughter from the living room window, skipping rocks and dancing on her tiptoes. Clancy is seven years old. She wears a cap turned backwards on her head that has a New York Yankees emblem embroidered on the brim. Her pink seersucker shorts are too big and hang down over her skinny, pale, little legs. She throws the rocks and watches as they fly, clasping her hands together and standing higher on her tiptoes each time one splashes and skips across the stream. She picks up a small container of blueberry yogurt she leaned against a weeping willow tree. She takes a taste from the plastic spoon and places the container down again, making sure the spoon doesn't fall or tip it over. Clancy is meticulous, righting the spoon, balancing it here and there, until she is certain it will stay. She looks over at the window and waves to me from time to time.

"Daddy! Daddy! Look at me!" she cries. She picks up a rock and hurls it into the stream. Big lift, backwards arm. A grunt. To her, it's like a boulder. To me, it's just a stone.

It is important that I am here to wave back to Clancy.

My hair was black at Clancy's age. My skin is copper-toned and dark. My mother used to tell me they adopted me from a tribe of Cherokee Indians. It took some time before I stopped believing her. Before she confessed the truth. My hair is gray now. My middle is thick. But the rest of me is thin and smooth. Maybe too smooth. Before I went to Vietnam I had hair on my chest. It's all gone now. I look at myself in the mirror and for a second I think of thick and thin and how some things never change.

Clancy is adopted, too. But unlike my wife, Mary, or myself, she is delicate, red-haired and blue-eyed. Her little body is tight and firm. She is my daughter.

"Mr. Moran, this is your daughter," the nurse said the day she put her in my arms.

Mary was with me that day seven years ago in Longview, Texas. We sat side by side in the waiting room outside maternity. Mary's hands twisted in her lap. Our shoulders touched but we just sat staring straight ahead. I held a quilted yellow diaper bag on my lap, filled with cloth diapers and paper diapers and a white stretchie, bottles of sugar water and a white crocheted blanket that Mary's mother made. It wasn't quite the way Mary and I thought it would be, yet our child was about to be born. The irony of that day struck me even then: The mother of our child was giving birth to her fifth, finally admitting there was one too many. The doors to delivery swung open after hours that felt like eternity. The nurse stepped outside carrying Clancy wrapped in a pale pink blanket. And for some reason the nurse handed the baby girl to me. Maybe she could see me swallowing really hard, my Adam's apple going up and down, looking like I might cry at any moment. Maybe she saw that Mary's hands were shaking. As I stared into the blanket, I had this vision that the woman who was giving birth to Clancy would change her mind at the last minute. Maybe that's because all my life I wondered why the woman who gave birth to me didn't change her mind at the last minute. I took my daughter into my arms, balancing her tiny body, holding her like she was made of glass. Counting her toes. Running my finger along her ear. Hold her head, the nurse said. And, as I placed my hand behind Clancy's head, I thought, Now I am a father. And Mary's voice came out of nowhere, almost startling me, asking to hold our baby. The next day we took Clancy home.

It wasn't until I was just around twelve that my mother finally told me the truth (laughing because I'd believed her for so long) that I was half-Spanish, half-Italian and there were never any Indians in my blood. I always wanted to think it was my biological mother who was Italian but no one ever told me for sure. I asked my mother once but she said she couldn't remember and then she turned her eyes away. I wanted to think I had my mother's dark eyes and dark hair, something of hers. They say that boys look mostly like the mother. I tried to picture what she looked like. I wondered if she ever held me even for a moment, the way I held Clancy.

When I was a teenager and even in the service, I still told the girls I was a Cherokee since it seemed a hell of a lot more romantic and exotic than any half-Spanish,

half-Italian kid whose mother and father for some reason couldn't keep him. Wouldn't keep him. Didn't
want to keep him. Of course, if Clancy's parents had
kept her then Mary and I wouldn't have her. Clancy is
my life now. Our marriage is still no love affair but
Clancy makes us a family. On this I rest my bonds. For
this reason, I could never leave.

Mary and I have lived in Mobile for the last twenty-
two years. Mary works in a roadside store, The Stitching Post, that sells pottery and Afghan blankets and
souvenirs to tourists and local people who are buying
gifts. There's a sign outside saying the store has fresh
coffee and clean rest rooms. There are pine benches
and azaleas in moss-covered baskets. I stay at home
with Clancy. It wasn't always like that. When Clancy
was two, I walked in the door one afternoon and she
barely knew who I was. She looked at me and
screamed when I held out my arms to her. So just like
that, I quit the hotel where I worked double shifts on
the desk for next to nothing and Mary got the job at
The Stitching Post. I do the grocery shopping and the
cleaning and the cooking in between my part-time
work in a liquor store now. I take Clancy to school and
pick her up at the end of the day. Lately I notice circles
underneath Mary's eyes and streaks of gray in her hair
that used to be so black like mine. This is not the way
Mary thought things would be. I know.

When I was a kid, my father was always home when
I walked in the door from school. The funny thing is, I
felt like I barely knew him. He was a writer. If he
wasn't pecking away at his typewriter, he was drowning in a glass of gin. Maybe it was really me who just
felt invisible to him. I'd toss my books down on the
kitchen table and go inside my father's den to say

hello. He'd lift his head, his chin up in the air. He'd peer at me over his half glasses and he'd nod. Home so soon? he'd ask. And that was all. Home *too* soon, perhaps he meant to say. Each day when I said hello I thought maybe this will be the day when he stands and walks over to me or beckons me over to him. Maybe this will be the day when he tells me I should sit and talk with him. It never happened. I never want it to be that way with Clancy.

My old man died about a dozen years ago, long before Clancy was ours. After the memorial service, the estate lawyer sent me his ashes in the mail. They came in a tin box, taped up in a padded carton. I peeled off the brown wrapper and the tape, took out the box of cinders and held my father in my hands. I was never quite sure why they sent them to me. But in my father's will, he requested that I receive them.

I loved my old man but I hated him. I hated him because every time I walked through the front door he was sitting in that big leather desk chair, all done up in his silky white shirt and that paisley Ascot. His face was all mottled with streaks of purple and his eyes were rheumy and almost fixed. Like I said, he'd call my name out sometimes and I'd come running in, thinking maybe this time it would be different but it never was. Get your dad some ice, would you Jimmy? That was all he would say. One day it was different though. It was February 1967, a bleak day when the sky was white and the air was so still and you just knew it was about to start snowing. I remember it so well. I took my work boots off in the vestibule and heard my father's voice call me into the den. Sit down, Jimmy, he said and gestured to the sofa in his office. My hopes were high for a moment. And then he blub-

bered about how I didn't know right from wrong and
said he couldn't figure out why I was failing in school,
the whole time holding his glass so tightly in his hand
that I couldn't stop staring at his knuckles because they
were so white. It was always about me. He never
talked about him or why he was drinking. And I never
found the courage to ask him.

"You're a failure, Jimmy," he said through his gin
and tonic, the ice hitting his teeth as the glass went dry.
"You'll never amount to anything, I swear. I'm tired of
paying tuition. Maybe the Marines can make a man
out of you." The enlistment papers were in his hand. I
was under eighteen so his signature was already on
the bottom. He handed me a fountain pen. Go ahead,
he said. Sign by the X.

I bet he never even had a thought that maybe it was
his penchant for gin that made me almost want to fail.
For sure it had been the thing that made me lie in bed
at night and stare at the ceiling, focused on the cracks
and the reflections from the traffic outside. Finally the
emptiness and the shadows would hypnotize me. I'd
close my eyes and fall asleep. Even as a kid, I slept fit-
fully. Same as now.

I'm not sure what it was that made me take my father's ashes back north. I packed the tin in a leather zipper case and caught a plane from Mobile to Atlanta to
New York. It was March 20, 1986, when my dad died.
His ashes came in April. April first to be exact. And I
couldn't help but wonder which one of us was the April
fool. I took my rental car and drove up to the Mamaroneck Harbor, the ashes on the seat beside me. When I
was a kid, we had a summerhouse there right on the
beach. We stayed from the middle of June when school
let out until Labor Day. You could fit ten of the house I

own now into that summerhouse. My family owned a
sloop called *Melodrama*, a name I never understood at
the time, but clearly it was an allusion to my father's
line of work. It was a beautiful boat, teak deck, the name
gilded and scripted on the stern. My dad wrote scripts
for soap operas like *Thunder Road* and *Heart of Passion*.
The sloop's name makes sense to me now.

When I got to the harbor, I asked to see Tubby the
harbormaster. But there was a new harbormaster:
Frank DiPalma. He sat in Tubby's old, white Adiron-
dack chair on the porch of the maintenance hut by the
dock. Inside, a small refrigerator was tucked under a
metal table. The refrigerator and the Mr. Coffee were
the only modern additions to the hut along with the jar
of Cremora, packs of sugar scattered around, coffee-
stained Styrofoam cups. In Tubby's day, there was just
an old percolator sitting on a hot plate and a cracked
china mug.

"Tubby died about five years ago," Frank said.

"I used to come here when I was a kid," I said. "I
came here with my dad. He had a sloop called *Melodrama*."

Frank wasn't much older than me. He said he'd been
there since 1975. I knew Tubby, he said, Tubby taught
me all I know. But Frank didn't know the *Melodrama*.

"*Melodrama*'s long gone," I said. I brought out the tin
from the zipper bag. "These are my father's ashes in
this box. I want to sprinkle them over the Sound."

Frank pointed at a barge in the harbor. We're dredg-
ing, he said. Too much silt's collected from the streams
and brooks nearby. He went into a lengthy explanation
too technical for me to care about. He was all fired up.
My face must have looked blank.

"I want to toss the ashes," I said.

"Boats can't go out there," he said. But then I think he thought again, looked at my face, saw me holding the box of cinders in my hand. He said he'd lend me his outboard.

"Don't go too far, though," he said. "Just take a ride past East Basin. Throw them toward Connecticut. On a clear day, you can see Greenwich from here. Too bad it's so overcast."

I wanted to sit down and talk to Frank the way I would have talked to Tubby if he'd been there. I wanted to tell him how my dad's liver finally gave out but there were two things he loved: the sea and his booze. Frank wouldn't have been interested. Tubby would have remembered with me. He would have understood.

It took a few pulls on the cord to get Frank's little boat going but then I was off. I wished I had the guts to take it out to Louie's, across the Sound in Port Washington. But I took my father's ashes and sprinkled them over the water and sat in that skiff, crying like a baby. Talking to my father for the first time in my life when I felt he was listening. It sounds really corny, but I told him how Mary and I were trying to have a baby.

Dad took me on *Melodrama* exactly twice. Mostly he went with his friends and a giant cooler. But one day dad took me across the Sound to Louie's. I remember it so well even though I was there only once: a one-story white building with blue trim. Louie's blue, they called it. That was the day my dad taught me how to eat oysters, cover them with hot sauce and tip the shell into your mouth. The little sucker slid down my throat the first time. No chewing, my boy, my father said. Just swallow. Let it sit in your mouth for a few minutes so you feel the hot sauce burn your ears. And even though the oysters pretty much made me gag (I was only around eleven at the time) I ate every one just to please him.

Truth is, I waited for him many times when he got off that boat hoping one day he wouldn't be too tanked up to take me out for a spin. I waited for him, always hoping maybe one day it would be different. It never was, really. He'd walk off the dock and he'd tousle my head like you would the son of a friend you'd just met for the first time and I'd hop back on my bike and head home. But, in all fairness, I do remember that one time he came up and put his arm around me and walked me to this hot dog stand on the beach. Walter's, it was called. He bought me a hot dog smothered in relish and ketchup and a Coke. It's one of those memories I hold onto along with him buying me ice cream at a Knicks game and taking me to a doubleheader at Yankee Stadium, where he taught me how to place a bet. Mostly I remember him sitting at his desk writing those sappy scripts for the soap operas. He'd sit at his desk, the drawer half open; the bottle of gin peering out, a glass of ice waiting for a fill-up right near his IBM Selectric. Mostly I remember him drunk.

Sitting there in the middle of that harbor with those ashes I thought of the day I walked through the door when I came home from Chou Lai. It was January 1970 and I was shivering but probably not just from the cold. My father looked so much older to me when I saw him sitting on the couch in his office that day. He looked weary. His eyes were even redder and more watery. I stopped in his doorway and knocked on the open door. I could feel how straight my back was. I could feel the pumping of my jaw as I ground my teeth. And he stood up, walked over and kissed me in the middle of my forehead. Then he lay his head on my shoulder and sobbed. I could feel myself tense when I smelled the gin on his breath. At first, I stood with my hands at my side as he sobbed on my shoulder and then, as though it was slow motion, I reached one hand up and placed it on his back and shut my eyes. But my hand just sat there. It didn't stroke him and it didn't press too hard. It stayed so still. I didn't know what to do with him. He didn't know what to do with me. I often think that maybe if my father hadn't been drunk his whole life, we both might have done things differently. Maybe I would have told him all the things I want to tell him since I got Clancy.

My father never got to meet Clancy, which might be just as well. I think about my father more than I should lately and every goddamn time my eyes well up with tears, and if I squint too hard they fall on my cheeks and I find myself shaking my head back and forth. Trying to pretend the tears aren't there. If only he had listened.

Before Mary and I settled down here, I was in the Marine Corps. I traveled from South Carolina to Memphis to California, back to my hometown of New York City and back to the South again. Somewhere in that blur there was a liberty in Bangkok, stockyards in Camp Pendleton and the trenches in Chou Lai. Coming home from Vietnam, there had been no ticker tape parade. Instead the vets like me were called names like "baby killer" and people sang out "Johnny Get Your Gun" when I told them I was a Marine. I spent years looking for familiar faces and dialing phone numbers that were disconnected. Sometimes I reached people who didn't remember me or said they didn't. '

"Jim Moran? Jim Moran? You'll forgive me, I re-

member the name but I can't place you," they'd say.
Then they'd hang up the receiver. And I'd stand there
holding the phone and staring at it like someone was
going to come through the wire.

I think of this while Clancy skips rocks and I wash
organic lettuce and arugula for tonight's dinner. I
cover the pot of water waiting to boil for risotto while
I run the broom along the pegged maple floors. I push
things out of my head with every sweep. I don't want
to think how I went from that private school in New
York City to humping whores in Thailand. There are
many things I try not to think about now.

My mother lives in Arizona since my father died.
Scottsdale. When he died, she stopped drinking and
she stopped crying. She plays golf every day with her
women friends and mah-jongg when it rains. She
takes those senior buses and goes to the Orpheum
Theatre in Phoenix. She's finally happy. Doing all the
things she wanted to do and never could. I'm not exactly sure what my parents were thinking the day they
signed me over to the United States Marine Corps. I
think they figured the Marines would give me the kick
in the ass that I needed. I mean, there was no way I
was going to graduate with my class. I think my father
really believed the military would make a man out of
me and I watch Clancy and can't understand why anyone should hurry up a boy into manhood. A child to
adulthood. Maybe they were sick of spending money
on my education. Most likely my old man was too
drunk to realize there was a war in Vietnam and my
mother just threw her hands up in the air and then she
poured them both another martini.

I grew up in New York City. A long way from Mobile and a long way from anywhere I might be right

now. We lived in a town house on a street they called
a lane in Greenwich Village. Someone once told me
that Edgar Allan Poe lived on that street. Our house
was built of brick, painted gray. The windows had
black shutters. I went to one of those ritzy private
schools in New York City. I played football and sang
with a band called Siddhartha and palled around with
other guys in gray flannel trousers and crested navy
blazers but somehow they kept getting by and I didn't.
I smoked a lot of pot and poured out bottles of Coke
and filled them with stolen rum from my parents'
liquor cabinet. The other boys did the same things I
did, but somehow they never got caught. They managed to keep up their grades. They managed to move
forward.

We've given you every opportunity, my father
would say to me, shaking the report cards with Ds and
Fs in my face.

It seemed I did everything my father told me not to
do. But who did he think he was to give me advice?
The pot calling the kettle. God love him. Jesus, I never
said that in my life, "God love him."

Maybe if he hadn't been my father, I would have
said he was a great guy. My mother always said he
looked like Gary Cooper. He was tall and lean. What
folks called strapping. Funny thing is, except for the
fact that I was so much darker, I could have been his
natural son. I was built, still am, a lot like him.

One day when I was maybe not quite thirteen, he
was driving me in his new silver Jaguar XKE. We were
racing down the highway. We must have been doing
ninety. The top was down and I could feel the wind in
my hair. I saw my father check the rearview mirror
and just as he said, "Oh boy, Jim, my boy. We've got a

little problem," a siren got really loud behind us. A red light swirled its reflection on the dashboard. We heard the trooper's voice boom over the bullhorn, Pull over. The trooper came up to Dad's window. License and registration, sir. Please step out of the vehicle (looking in at me in the front seat, slumped down with my arms crossed over my chest). And you know what? My father stepped out of the car and while he motioned to me, keeping his voice low down, he talked the cop out of the ticket. He ended up telling the guy to call him if he ever wanted tickets to the World Series. My dad reached into his wallet (by then the two of them were buddies) and the trooper joked, "Easy, easy, now" and my father handed him his card with William Moran printed in bold across the middle. Then my dad asked the trooper if he was married and when the guy nodded his head up and down, my father told him the next episode of *Heart of Passion*.

"Tell the missus what happens and she can be one up on all her girlfriends," my dad said. "And I'll talk to Howard about those World Series tickets. Don't you worry."

My dad winked at him and then the two of them shook hands. The trooper slapped my father on the back and opened the door to the car for him and we just hit the road. My dad peeled out, burned a little rubber and the trooper stood there shaking his head with a grin on his face. A real man's man, my dad. A lousy father.

I can see Clancy running up the path from the stream now. She holds the empty yogurt in her hand, wisps of red hair have escaped under her cap. Her cheeks are flushed and she is smiling. I think to myself how it is nearly spring and I remember the feeling I had when I was Clancy's age and spring was finally around that corner everyone talked about in the dead of New York winters. She opens the screen door, leaves her sneakers in the mudroom and skips over to me. I wipe my hands, damp from the vegetables I am rinsing, on the sides of my jeans and hold her next to me. And despite the dark thoughts I'd been having, the memories of battles real and battles perhaps imagined, her smile and the words uttered, "Hi, Daddy," take my breath away.

# 3

Jack was right. My eyes were miles away. I started, wondering whether reaching back in time wasn't simply more reliable than a future that seemed all too close and all the while untenable. Part of me felt, well, almost embarrassed at the notion that I was dreaming of the days when I was sixteen while Jack stood there before me. What could I have known at sixteen? Was this what I had come to? Gathering emotional salvation by reaching back thirty years? And yet it was precisely at that moment when I realized how much I wanted to find Jimmy Moran. I told myself it was a sort of closure but I knew that wasn't true. Part of me wanted to hear his voice and another part feared that if I did, it might not be quite enough. Part of me was dazzled by the thought of searching for someone who the years had made into a stranger. And yet even though thirty years had gone by, Jimmy still didn't feel like a stranger to me at all.

I tried convincing myself that the paintings at Tod's could no longer be done merely from a memory and that was the reason I needed to find him. Deep down inside I knew this wasn't true. Suddenly I saw Jimmy's face as clearly as though he stood before me. I could practically smell the Canoe he splashed on his neck and the way his hair smelled sweet like, okay, now this sounds really crazy, but it smelled like honey. But more, I remembered what it was like to be in love that first time.

I remembered every nuance of his gait as he walked toward me from the car he leaned against, waiting outside my school. How with just the simplest "Hey, Emmie" I could feel my knees weaken and my heart pound. How I picked up the phone so quickly when he called, trying to answer before my mother or twin sisters did. How he would say in a voice that struck me as so deep at the time, so undeniably masculine, "That you, Emmie?" And I would hear the sigh and a *tsk* on the other end of the receiver when my mother or my sisters hung up with a loud click of disapproval.

When I thought of him, the sense of secrecy and defiance I felt at sixteen came over me in a wave that made me shiver. Like the night when he was kissing me outside the screen door to the summerhouse in Old Greenwich. We were kissing before I joined Jennie in the room with the canopy beds. Before he would take the guest room next to my parents. Glancing up, we saw my mother's shadow at her bedroom window. And then my mother pulled up the shade with such ferocity it rippled and rolled again and again, flapping so loud that we jumped apart, our heads tilted up, our bodies now apart. I tiptoed up the stairs to my room.

My mother cornered me on the landing. "You know it all starts with a kiss and leads to other things," she said, standing with her hand gathering the collar of her silky beige robe close to her throat. Her hair was undone. A long braid down her back. Her mouth set grimly. And I just shrugged my shoulders, angry that she was so invasive, muttering under my breath "How would you know?" Thinking how it wasn't possible for her to remember, less possible to understand. Uncomfortable that my life was reduced to a passage in that book she bought me when I was twelve and got my period: *Love and Sex in Plain Language for Teenagers.* Cut and dried. Now I wonder if maybe it wasn't envy that made her pull the shade up so audibly, so angrily. I wonder whether she, too, wasn't satisfied with car pools and supermarkets and her volunteer work. I wonder whether she looked at my father in his study at night, poring over legal text, as she clicked around him in those slippers with the twisted wooden heels and the champagne pompoms on the front. Maybe he paid no attention. He called her "dear" but was she really? I mean, was she really so dear if they spent all those evenings sitting in matching chairs on either side of the fireplace in silence? So who was she to tell me not to kiss Jimmy? Someone who doesn't know what she's missing. Someone who never felt love like this where the world stood still as the boy you loved looked into your eyes. Someone whose main purpose in loving was merely procreation. After Jimmy left that summer, my father often slept in the guest room.

The timer on the oven went off. I called the children to the kitchen for dinner, almost relieved to stop thinking. My children and I sat at the kitchen table and I tried not to appear entrenched in my thoughts. I was uncharacteristically quiet and distracted. I am too transparent. I suppose, because they are my children, they become fearful when I am not myself. Their fear evolved into anger and they bickered relentlessly that night. Usually I insist they help clear, but this time I suggested they go outside. The night is so beautiful, I said. But Jack opted to go to his room. Charlie and Sam went to the basement to play Ping-Pong and Julie took a shower. Funny how they all preferred to stay around me.

I opened the kitchen window and took a deep breath, purposefully downshifting back to reality. I wiped the counters down and even hauled out the vacuum. I was not cleaning, I was cleansing. Reminding myself that this was my home.

But the night breeze came through the kitchen window and I was back again in that summer. The breeze was not like the ones of that summer with Jennie. This one was crisp and cool, not laden with heat and sea spray. We live inland. New Canaan is quite far from a beach. The weather report was windy for spring and promised rain. I took the stout blue candle from the kitchen table, placed it on a saucer and carried it upstairs to my studio.

The studio was once the attic. It was filled with cobwebs and dust but all it needed was a good cleaning out to turn it into the place that became my sanctuary. I spent weeks sanding the floors, scrubbing, washing the walls with a seafoam green paint. I painted and spackled every inch of the eaves. I rubbed the old beveled glass on the windows until it hardly looked to be there at all. Peter said, Hire someone to do it. You're wasting your time. But I wanted to do it myself. This was mine.

I had always felt that I had no place to go in our house. Everyone had a place where a door could close and shut out the others for a while. Everyone had a place to hide except for me. Until I finished the studio, my easel and paints were in a corner of the kitchen. Peter had his den. The kids had their rooms, their phones, their stereos, their own beds. I needed a place to go where phone conversations were private and I could paint without children and their friends walking through as though I wasn't there. I loved their laughter but at times it made me feel invisible. Sometimes their laughter resonated in my ears because I knew how empty the house would be when the day came that they were no longer there. Peter could talk about them going off to college so glibly. I could not. He could think about where they might want to go and whether they would need cars and what they should major in. All I could think about was the emptiness.

The attic eaves in my studio hang low, angled in certain spots so the windows sweep from floor to the ceiling. The floors are bleached wood and the color-washed green walls are barely visible through all the memories tacked upon them like a collage. The walls are papered with pictures the kids finger-painted in kindergarten. Pot holders and bookmarks they crafted at summer camp. Photographs when they were babies posing with Santa and the Easter bunny. Alongside charcoal sketches I made of the children are notes they have written to me and a Best Mom Award covered with hearts and stars and blue and gold glitter that Julie made for me just last year. There is a shelf filled with painted clay dishes (they used to call them ashtrays) and pastel ceramic tiles embedded with little handprints, a date etched with the child's name to the side. There are Mother's Day cards with embossed bouquets of violets next to bottles of lilac bath salts that I saved because I couldn't bear to use them up.

Gifts that the kids bought at the five-and-dime while I pretended not to look. Notes of apologies for messy rooms and talking back, signed with hearts and "Xs" and "Os."

There are no letters on the wall from Peter. Peter stopped writing to me a long time ago when he stopped leaving notes on his pillow. When it got to the point when he no longer had to explain that he had "left early" or would "see me later" because we just knew. Though there was a time in the very beginning when Peter wrote love notes to me. Sometimes he left them in the refrigerator or stuck to the bathroom mirror and one time he left one in a bouquet of tulips on the table where I kept my paints. They were printed in small, neat writing, sealed in envelopes, not scrawled and rushed like the ones left on his pillow. There is an envelope, filled with dried yellow petals (pressed in Janson's *History of Art* on my bookshelf) left over from very long ago.

The canvas leaned against the paint-splattered easel in the center of the room. It had been painted at Tod's that morning and the dampness of the oils still glistened. The young man stood at the shore, his jet black hair blowing back in the wind, hands shoved in the pockets of his jeans. I touched it, and the wet, dark paint became evident, staining the tip of my finger.

I hadn't looked at the painting since I packed up my oils and palette and loaded the canvas into the back of the car when I left the beach that morning. It was the first time I allowed myself to put memories on the canvas in front of me. It was clear to me who the young man was although I didn't show his face. I glanced at it only briefly as I loaded it into the back of the station wagon. I heard the cries of the gulls above my head. They squawked almost violently, swooping down in a frenzy on the garbage a picnicker had left behind. The painting was empty except for the young man and the Sound in the background. The Sound. I always thought it was the ocean. The beach was white and vast and infinite the way it used to be with the boy. He faced toward the sea, staring straight ahead.

"Time for a romantic evening, Mom?" Jack had asked with a grin as he passed me going up the stairs. "Only one candle? Ah, scented. Is that lavender I smell?"

Jack. My first-born. Jack who is reluctant to say precisely what's on his mind. He will gloss over the obvious, preferring to joke the problems away. Jack longs for everything to be in order. He is the one who would shoot dagger eyes at Peter when he walked in hours after dinner had been served. Peter would shake his head and walk into his den, briefcase bulging, and I would stand there wondering who is right, who is wrong, if there is a right or wrong. Jack is the child who tired early on of Peter's excuses that there was so much work to do. And to this day, sometimes I feel sorry for Jack and sorry for Peter and sorry for myself and wonder where the road forked and Peter turned one way and I turned the other.

"Dad, you're never here for dinner," Jack would say accusingly even at the age of ten.

"But, Jack, I tried. I got so bogged down," Peter would say. Floundering for excuses. Flustered when Jack uncharacteristically became confrontational.

And, still, neither man nor young man understands the other. Jack, sit with your father while he has a drink, I will urge. Peter, tell Jack you're going to have a drink and ask him to sit with you, I will say brightly.

But, instead, they go their separate ways. Doors shut. No words. Jack saying aloud that he doesn't get it, slamming his door, drowning my calls up the stairs with the volume turned up on his stereo. There was a time when Peter would ask me what he did wrong as though he were a child as well. There was a time when I offered explanations, weaving a tale that balanced the scale for both father and son. Making suggestions that would offer solutions. For a time, I was the peacemaker, the dream maker. And then, very simply, I became weary. The irony is, when Peter walks in brandishing tickets to a Yankee game or plane tickets to Aruba, he emerges as a hero. And I take my place again: The disciplinarian. The mother. The impasse that stands between the kids and a good time. I am the one who is here making sure the homework is done. Did you make your beds this morning? Are you wearing your retainer? Could you be on time for dinner?

"When I was a girl, I always took candles to my room in the summer," I said to Jack as he smelled the lavender too dramatically. "There were so many thunderstorms and just in case the lights went out, I wanted a candle. They were better than flashlights. The flames made silhouettes on the walls and danced with the wind."

Jack rolled his eyes at me. He put his arm around my shoulder and squeezed.

"I think the lavender's gone to your head. You're a crazy lady," he said and kissed my cheek. "Are you expecting a thunderstorm, Mom, or will you paint one?"

"The weather report said rain, Jack," I laughed, realizing the dialogue was a bit theatrical, lavender candle and all. "And one day your eyes will get stuck in your head."

I heard Peter come in the door. I heard him take the bottle of Scotch from the cabinet.

"There's no ice," I called down to him from the middle of the stairs. "Someone accidentally turned off the ice maker."

"I drink it straight up," he said.

My feet stopped on the stairs, "Since when?"

"Since I have a client who's a dietician and she says I'll drink less if I don't dilute it," he said.

"You're hardly a drunk," I laughed, thinking of Peter's low tolerance for liquor.

"No, but she says it's a good lifestyle. I like it this way," he said.

I walked back down the stairs, the candle teetered on the dish. "What does she look like?" I asked.

"What does who look like?" he asked.

"The dietician," I said.

"A redhead," he said.

"A natural redhead, Peter?" I said, a smile trying to play on my lips.

"I wouldn't know," he said. And with that he took his Scotch and walked past me to the den.

I could hear him sigh. I had provoked him. I was only trying to have some fun. I wanted us to laugh again. I wanted him to defend himself and maybe even say he was sure she was most definitely a natural redhead and then he could tease me as I asked what made him so sure. He didn't have to be so serious. I wanted him to sweep me in his arms and tell me I was the only one the way he used to. There were times I almost wished he had someone else because then it would explain why I felt there was so little time for me. I poured a glass of wine and walked back up the stairs to my studio. I heard the newspaper shake out and open deliberately. Soon Peter would call me as he climbed up the stairs. "Ready for dinner?" he would say as he'd tap the open studio door. But he didn't ask me to sit with him downstairs. Maybe because at that point he feared that I might turn him down.

A few weeks before, Peter and I had gone to a dive near our house with a red neon sign in the window that blinked Budweiser. We've lived in this area for fifteen years, passed by there a million times and never ventured inside. The boys were at a basketball game and Julie was baby-sitting. The house was so empty. We tried to stay home alone but the solitude was thick with the tension of our presence one on one. We got into the car and drove, deciding the neon sign was a good last minute stop.

The waitress in the bar (called simply Town Pub) wore a white décolleté T-shirt and a backwards baseball cap. Her T-shirt was brimming over and pulled tight across her breasts, her nipples jutting out and obvious. Her lipstick was thick and painted on red. She leaned over deeply when she took Peter's drink order, bent from the waist, legs straight, her rear jutting out at just the right angle, her cleavage at Peter's eye level.

"I'll have a Bass ale," Peter said, never raising his eyes.

"Did you see that?" I asked, laughing as she walked away. "Or were you afraid to look?"

"See what?" he said.

"She leaned over just for you," I laughed. "Some cleavage."

And Peter said he didn't want to get involved in such nonsense and why didn't I just cut it out.

I wondered sometimes what Peter was thinking and preferred not to say. If there wasn't a side to him that he kept from me. It was the type of thing when I tried his beeper and he didn't answer me for hours. I almost wanted to think he was in the arms of another woman. Just for some excitement. For the hint of something less benign. But I always figured either his battery was dead or he was.

The summer before last there was a girl named Amy. She was a summer student from Pace College who clerked in his office. Peter spent many nights that summer working late on a case. I wondered if he laughed and smiled and took Amy to dinner and listened to what was probably mindless chatter. He swore up and down there was never anything between them. And then he stopped trying to convince me because, with annoyance, he said I could not be convinced. He said he was tired of defending himself. That it was no longer funny. I wanted to feel there was still something to fight for. I wanted to win Peter over again, ignite the passion that we had when we first met and couldn't keep our hands off each other. Even if it took another woman. At least that way I wouldn't keep thinking that it was I who had simply become tiresome.

I longed for the kind of night where there could be a kiss below a bedroom window like the one I remembered from a lifetime ago. For years, I felt as though Peter denied me. For a while it was like a constant hunger, but then hunger pains die down and one day you look in the mirror and realize you are looking perhaps just a little bit wan and perhaps you need more sustenance. I thought it was me: The babies that came so quickly, pacifiers scattered on our bedroom floor, yellowed milk stains on my blouses, the scent of antiseptic from the diaper pails. I felt like an island,

scented with sour milk, drowning in apple juice, stepping over Legos strewn about the living room like
land mines.

Peter is handsome. He is tall and well-built. There
were mornings when he left, dressed in his three-piece
suit, smelling like cologne, his hair slicked back, still
damp from the shower, and I wished that things were
different. I thought of the days when his shirts were
drip-dry and not Egyptian cotton and his trousers
were the kind without the obvious crease. I remembered when he sang love songs to me and played the
piano. Sometimes I'd think he was on the brink of
sweeping me back into his life and then suddenly he
would pull away from me, burying himself under
legal briefs, rushing to dinners and meetings, hiding
behind the computer screen in his den. He hasn't
touched the piano in years, though I always have it
tuned.

I was, again, deep in thought when Jack came into
the studio drinking orange juice from the carton, covering his eyes with his hand the way he used to when
he was a little boy and thought if he didn't see me, I
wouldn't see him. I laughed at him.

"You're too old for that, Jack," I said.

"You're never too old for anything, Mom," he said.

I think Jack just said that because he had heard me
say it before, but I took it to heart.

Peter came up behind him. "Ready for dinner?" he
asked.

I sat with Peter while he ate. I wondered what was
worse: being lonely or being alone.

# 4

It was one of those days in late April when people living down South thumb their noses at the North. I still say "down South." Sometimes I feel like I don't really live here. Sometimes I feel as though I'm just passing through.

The weather was just about the mildest we'd had any winter and the spring came even earlier. Jonquils (they call them narcissus up North) were starting to push through the dirt and the sun was hot enough for me to sit outside on the deck. I had my book and a long-neck bottle of beer. It was around four o'clock in the afternoon and I had just gotten back from Long's where I work part-time in the wine department. I'd already picked up Clancy from school. I pulled up the lounge chair, took off my T-shirt, dusted the dirt off the cushion with it and hung it over the back. I took a swig from the cold Corona in my hand and looked up at the sky. It was so blue and there wasn't a cloud for miles around. Tarheel Blue we called that color sky when I was in the Carolinas.

The sun was hot but that kind of sun that appears toward the end of the day when you can almost stare right into it. Clancy was playing down by the stream again. This time she held a makeshift fishing rod she made from a twig, some string and a safety pin with bacon on the end. She could stand for hours not catching anything. I'd gone to work at Long's that morning and talked to Mike Long himself about what kind of wines I thought he should buy and which ones he ought to sell. I'd worked there about six months and like with everything I ever do, I go all the way until it's over. And usually, it's over too soon. I get so enthusiastic and then something happens. Like with Mike a few weeks before when he stood there as I spoke to him but I got the feeling he wasn't really listening. And then I felt like nothing was worthwhile or going to go anywhere, so why was I even bothering. There are no gray areas with me. Things either are or they aren't. I have this need to know. This need to find out. Sometimes I think it works against me. I overdo things. Mary says it's overbearing. She says I am relentless as a hound. But I'm never able to do anything halfway.

Mike Long is a real short, bald guy who wears a pinkie ring with a great big ruby in it. He must have been listening even though I felt like he wasn't. He said, "Since you seem to think you know so much about wine, Moran," that I could buy the wines for the store. And I bristled because I don't like it when people call me by my last name without a Mister in front of it. I had asked everyone I knew and read every book I could get my hands on and I learned about wines. I learned about grapes and vineyards and years and regions in Napa and I felt like I could hold court with anyone anywhere because, damn, if I didn't know what I was doing. The only thing I didn't bother with was the imported stuff, because I couldn't pronounce the names. They don't sell the imported stuff at Long's anyway.

So it was that day when the jonquils were poking through the earth and I got home from Long's and went and sat on the deck when the phone rang. I didn't answer the phone. I figured it was probably Mike going back on what he'd said about me doing the buying. I figured he'd say it was best if I kept to stacking the shelves and unloading the trucks. I didn't want to deal with him right then. I have this tendency to always think the worst. For a moment or two I felt guilty not answering the phone. There I was reading *A Separate Peace* and retreating back into my childhood through someone else's words. Jesus, how that guy could write. John Knowles. You'd think he had a perch somewhere inside my adolescence where he saw all that turmoil and that jealousy and then he sat down and said he was writing a book for Jim Moran who ended up okay despite it all.

There was a time in my life when reading a book was like looking at hieroglyphics. It wasn't until they gave me that physical in the Marines when I found out that some part of my eye is upside down inside, astigmatism, and that's why I could never sit too long and focus on a book or schoolwork or anything. They gave me these square, black plastic glasses, military-issue, real ugly like the kind that Buddy Holly wore except he looked kind of cool. And then with my glasses on, they sent me off in my underwear feeling like a geek from the North next to all those strapping southern boys with tattoos on their biceps. Half-Spanish, half-

Italian punk from a swanky town house in Greenwich Village who screwed up so bad his fancy daddy booted his ass out and now the kid was a Marine with four eyes.

The guys in my bunk called me Weasel from that day on after I got those glasses. Skinny kid with a shaved head who looked like he was wearing binoculars. The guys back home always thought I was so cool. I've got contact lenses now. I couldn't wear contacts in Vietnam and I couldn't afford them until a few years ago. And now I wonder if maybe one day my folks had been sober enough to take me to an eye doctor, maybe I wouldn't have failed in school and ended up in Chou Lai at eighteen. Maybe if they'd cared enough. But now I read books like crazy and watch movies like I'm afraid I might miss something. I can recite you lines from movies and tell you who wrote them and directed them and what year they were made.

So late that afternoon when the sun was going down behind the trees and I was stretched out on that lounge chair, the phone was ringing again. I still didn't answer it. When my beer was done, I went inside the house to the kitchen and saw the light blinking on the answering machine for two messages. Now I was sure it was Mike Long calling and this time he was probably pissed off because I didn't answer the phone the first time. Funny thing was, right before I pushed that button I was just thinking how I wished that day could be more special than it was. It wasn't enough to have the jonquils, the sun and a cold Corona. It wasn't enough that I had the money to buy those aluminum lounge chairs with the green and white striped cushions they had on sale at the garden shop. I needed something more. I felt kind of guilty that it wasn't even enough to watch Clancy fishing in the stream. I wanted something that told me it was okay to have just turned forty-eight and that I still had time to make my life different. Sometimes I feel like I'm running on a treadmill and getting nowhere. Like it's all some crazy, convoluted dream.

Clancy was supposed to be the thing that gave Mary and me that push. She was the thing that was supposed to take us to that new plateau Mary reads about in women's magazines and yeah, sure, I always heard that you don't have babies to make relationships fly, but did I pay attention? No. Something else I did wrong in my life. Like not going to college and making something of myself. Not saving money. Not having my own business. All the things I want Clancy to have.

I figured Mary wanted to have a baby and I couldn't and I wanted to be a father and I couldn't and so maybe adopting this baby would be just what we needed. And then I shuddered the way I always do when I go where I shouldn't and my mind races way ahead of me and I need to bring it back again.

So I was just about to get another beer from the refrigerator when I stopped to hit the button on the answering machine, waiting to hear Mike Long's nasty southern drawl, ready to feel the rug pulled out from under me. The first message was from Mary.

"Jimmy, pick up the phone," she said. "I know you're there, Jimmy." And then I heard her mutter "All right" and I could hear her tell someone else I wasn't home. She hung up the receiver as though she dropped it about midway before it hit the cradle. The clanging annoyed me. I was walking away from the machine, my hand was opening the refrigerator door to grab another Corona, when the next message came over the speaker. It made me grab the door of the refrigerator and hold on like maybe I was going to tip over.

"My name is Emily," a woman's voice said. "If you are the James Robert Moran I knew in 1967 who went into the Marine Corps, please give me a call. I got this number through the Internet so it may be wrong. My number is . . ."

My hands were shaking while I listened to her voice and my heart was pounding so fast I thought it would bust through my chest. I hit the button and I played the message again. And again and again and again. I swallowed real hard and I had this image of a girl, suntanned and blond, looking at me that day at the train station and holding onto my neck like she would never let me go. I took the old stubby pencil that Mary keeps by the phone and grabbed a napkin off the kitchen table (from that napkin holder that has daisies on either side) and wrote down the number. Then I dialed and the phone rang four times until I got a machine.

"Hi, this is Emily Hudson," said the voice on the machine. "I am either away from the studio or on the phone but please leave a message after the tone and I will get back to you."

Emily sounded so businesslike and official on that message. But I was sure it was her voice. She rounded her vowels and pronounced *either* like it was *eye-ther*. And I don't like machines. Christ, I don't even know how to use a computer or a copy machine at all. And I hate the way my voice sounds on a tape recorder. But I called back and left her a message. I spoke real slow and rounded my vowels and told her I was the James

Robert Moran she was looking for. I said I remembered her very well.

I called Clancy up from the stream and she came running up the hill. She held her sneakers in her hand, her feet were bare and muddy and her face was smeared with dirt. She smelled like a wet puppy. Clancy threw her sneakers down on the kitchen floor, and where usually I'd tell her to hose them off on the deck and put them where they belong, I picked her up in the air and twirled her around and kissed her on the side of her neck.

I made dinner for Mary and me. I grilled a leg of lamb and some vegetables. I opened a good bottle of red wine that I "borrowed" from Long's. Mary asked me what the occasion was and I just said I thought it was time that we celebrated and she just smiled. She didn't ask any questions. She never asked why.

I vacuumed the whole goddamn house that night and I watched some movie with Clancy and when she tugged on my sleeve and asked me if I saw this or that, I realized I hadn't been paying any attention. I just waited for Emily to call.

I was in boot camp that first summer at Parris Island, South Carolina. My girlfriend sent me her picture. She was wearing a yellow bikini. She was only sixteen. Emily Hudson. She went to a private school, too, and wore those plaid skirts and navy blue blazers. But she wasn't like the other girls who were willing to hike up their skirts and let you do whatever you wanted. And Lord, there were plenty of those. Emily was different, a little quirky and too sensitive. And Christ, did I love her. She wrote to me every day that summer. The sergeant picked up everyone's mail in the morning and opened all the letters. One morning I was standing in my underwear, folding that military issue green blanket that covered my cot and I heard the sergeant yell out, "Moran! Get your scrawny ass over here NOW!"

"Yes, sir." I ran over and tripped saluting in front of him.

"Put on your glasses, Moran, and look at this hog! We're putting this hog's picture right up here where she'll cheer up everyone, Moran, not just you," the sergeant said.

A hog. Sixteen-year-old Emily was reduced to a hog. The name for a girl who had a body to die for and the bad luck to be a pinup. Emily was queen of the hog board. She was never called a hog by me. She was barefoot with straight blond hair parted down the middle that smelled like lemons. I remember lying underneath the Ping-Pong table with her in the basement of her big old Connecticut house the summer I left for boot camp. We'd make out under the table, me lying right on top of her, feeling as though the zipper on my jeans was going to pop open. And all the while I'd try to bounce the ball so her mother would think we were playing Ping-Pong. Her father was British and used to call her "pussy." One day I asked her if that name didn't bother her and she looked at me with her head cocked to one side and asked me why it should. That was Emily. Innocent. I kissed her on the forehead and realized she didn't have a clue and I wasn't going to tell her. But when I burst out laughing after her father said, "Emily, come here, pussy," her dad looked at me a little sideways.

What I'm about to say is the God's honest truth. There were years when not a day went by that I didn't think about that summer day when Emily and her mother drove me to the train station. It was July 5, 1967, and the sun was beating down so hard you could actually see the air hanging like smoke by the train tracks but I was shivering. I got out of the Hudsons' big Oldsmobile station wagon and Emily walked me to the depot. I'm not sure if either one of us knew what was going on. Maybe we didn't want to know. Maybe we didn't want to admit it. Emily's lips were coated with a pink gloss and her eyes and nose were red from crying. She wore a peasant blouse and bell-bottom jeans and those strappy brown sandals that were all the rage then. I took her behind the ticket booth where her mother couldn't see us. I held on to Emily that day at the train station until the train came roaring in and then I got on, all aboard, just like in all those war movies I watch on television now.

The whole time I was in the service I held on to Emily. The only thing that kept me going was remembering her. Kissing her face, her neck, tangling my fingers in her hair. I never got to tell Emily any of this because after that day by the tracks, I saw Emily one more time and then I lost her. I lost her because she was still a girl and I came back with my neck a size bigger and one thing on my mind. Making out under the Ping-Pong table didn't feel like enough anymore. I scared her to death, asking her to do things she wasn't ready to do. Looking back, I wonder if maybe she just wasn't ready for me. I was scared, too, but I loved her so much. I still think about her, especially on days like this, when Clancy's playing by the stream and you can feel the springtime. Until Clancy came along, Emily was the last thing that was really mine. She was the last time there was any innocence in my life until Clancy came along, barefoot and skipping stones.

# 5

It was really quite chilly for spring. Sometime after midnight I awoke with the fleece robe over my shoulders and a fleece blanket over that to give me warmth. It came upon me like a flash, making my breath come up in quick short inhalations followed by a deep sigh. I was lonely. The fleece wasn't the warmth I longed for. Peter and I used to sleep like spoons. But suddenly we slept on either side of the bed, Peter facing one way and me facing the other. In younger years, I'd joke with Peter as we slept entwined in one another that if he ever planned to leave me, to please do so before I had to be maintained on hormone replacement therapy. Now the joke was becoming too real. Peter was aging with that characteristic maleness that gave him a distinguished look with salt-and-pepper hair and a small potbelly that any sane woman would view as sexy. I asked him just the other day, how many women do you know with gray hair and little potbellies whom men find most appealing? My years are numbered, I said to him. You can start a second life, a second family. I, on the other hand, have become far less of a hot commodity: a middle-aged woman with four children. He laughed and said that I was becoming too strident a feminist or else I wouldn't say such things. He didn't tell me what I wanted to hear.

When I looked in the mirror, I clearly saw the tiny lines around my eyes, which appeared less blue than they used to. The rest of me was still fit. Nights of working out at the gym in our basement, runs with the dog, a million trips up and down the cellar stair carrying baskets of laundry. My arms were strong from carrying canvases, mixing paints, sweeping floors. My hair was not gray, but had become a far mousier blond than it had been. Still, I was keeping. Staying. Considering that bathing in formaldehyde may not be the worst idea after all.

But more, I was tired of living for tomorrow when part of me felt that I still wasn't through living for today. I didn't want to hear about life insurance policies and retirement plans. Conversations with Peter were rare and when they happened at all they were about the children and his job. The electric bill is too high. The car registration expired. Should we take out a second mortgage. The kids need new shoes. Charlie needs braces.

I wanted to be back in the days before Peter Walters and I started and begin again. The question was, was it Peter I wanted to begin with again? Some days I thought I did. Other days, I didn't know where to begin or if I could forget enough to be able to go back to the beginning with Peter and start over.

And then further justifying the longing, the searching for something to awaken my middle years and make me feel alive, I wondered why I thought Jimmy

Moran held the answer. Why didn't I just turn over in my bed and place my arms around Peter's waist the way I did when we were first married?

Was I considering infidelity or was Jimmy just a diversion? Someone once said to me, whether it's first degree murder or manslaughter, the victim is still dead. I longed for someone to hold me close but I didn't want any victims.

It was almost territorial how I justified my search for Jimmy Moran. It was something that was mine, I told myself. Like the studio in the attic. The children. It was my art. Incentive for the paintings. A quest for closure. Picking up the pieces from a lifetime to finish a life that had turned into a puzzle. I gave it many names. Part of me feared perhaps I was opening Pandora's box. Jimmy would be forty-eight years old. For all I knew I was dreaming of a dead man. He could have been in a car accident. Dead from a heart attack. Dead from an overdose. He could have been one of those bodies that came home in flag-draped coffins and no one knew to tell me. He could be in prison, a drug addict, homeless. Or maybe I would find him and he would say "Emily who?" because the four months we spent together had gotten lost over the years. Maybe they weren't as significant to him. And then I would be shattered. Perhaps I'd crossed that fine line between what we remember and what we dream. I mean, once I thought the Sound was really the ocean.

As all these thoughts distilled in my head and the deep middle of the night brought on monsters that retreat into their caves with the dawn, I decided that somehow I would find this boy. Careful to remind myself that he was a man now. It brought back that sense of the old Emily to me. The one who was filled with

courage and optimism. The Emily who was so decided
and usually ended up having things her way through
sheer determination.

I placed my hands on the earrings in my ear, my tal-
isman. It had started to rain. The rain tapped down
against the window and I could see the trees bending
in the wind that tore across the lawn. The gusts made
the wind chimes on the porch jingle with such fury
that I wondered whether they wouldn't fly off and
spin somewhere into oblivion. I fell asleep again,
dreaming of seagulls swooping down on me as I stood
on the beach with a canvas covered with a splotch of
black paint.

I awoke again with a start and went up to my studio. It was three in the morning. I lit the blue candle,
digging around for the wick that melted into the wax,
and looked at the canvas I had painted that morning. I
took a sip of the half-drunk glass of wine left over from
the night before. I pulled up the lace shades and sat on
the windowsill with a sketchbook and my writing
tablet. I'd hoped I would hear the rain beating hard
and furious the way Jennie and I heard it that other
summer. But it was only the wind. Feelings, rummaging around my head all day, filled me to the point
where I thought I would explode. You get to a point in
your life where you have nothing to lose and even if
you end up losing, at least you find comfort in the fact
that you tried. Pretty much what I had thought thirty
summers ago when I knew the odds were stacked
against everything. Unlike middle age, youth has
courage, though the last few days with Jimmy were
tempered with a sense of dread and a lost sense of im-
mortality. The strange thing is, thirty summers ago
when Jimmy left me at the train station, I remember

thinking that I felt so very old. But it was easy to shake that feeling at sixteen.

I had spent the day before that sleepless night on the Internet, leaving messages for James Robert Morans around the country in towns where I thought he might be. I had run into his friend Chris on the street in New York City sixteen years ago. Jack was in his stroller. Chris had turned on his heels as Jack and I rolled by. Chris called after me, Aren't you Emily Hudson? I recognized him after he told me his name, though he was wearing a pin-striped suit, had a mustache and less hair on his head. Chris worked at Shearson, he said. He was a trader. I told him about Peter and where we lived on the Upper West Side of Manhattan and how we were going to move to Connecticut. And then I asked him if he ever heard from Jimmy Moran. At first, Chris laughed, remembering perhaps.

Jimmy Moran, he said twice. I wonder what ever became of him.

He said the last he heard Jimmy was down South. But that was five years ago, Chris said. Who knows?

I thought of that encounter as I searched the Internet. Maybe I didn't remember the exchange correctly. I was so involved back then with a new baby. Maybe I was just dreaming.

I heard footsteps coming up the stairs as I sat in my studio. It was Peter.

"Emily? Why are you still awake? What are you doing?" He walked into the room, tightening the tie on his maroon terry-cloth robe.

"I am writing and painting, Peter. I am fine," I said.

"You look so pretty by candlelight, Emily," Peter said. And with that he rubbed his hands down my shoulders, rested his hands on my hips.

There was a time, a very long time ago, when I would have responded. I would have turned my head and kissed him and with that we would have locked the studio door and pulled the futon open in the center of the room. We would have been lost for hours. Now there was too much to bring to the bed. At least for me. There had been too many years when I felt alone. Years when conversations and lovemaking were interrupted by a telephone ringing from someone at Peter's firm who seemed to think my husband worked for them day and night. Too many nights when Peter ignored the scent of my perfume or the new way my hair was combed. When I wore a new nightgown and he paid no attention. I couldn't seem to let go of those times. When I told him I missed him back in those days, he retaliated by saying he was working for us. What do you want from me? he would say angrily. Find someone else to pay the mortgage and I'll be home more. And I knew the "us" was being corroded by mortgage payments and tax returns and I couldn't help but think that Peter was allowing the consumption, hell-bent on having a bigger house and a better car. Maybe that's another reason why I have held on to the old Volvo. There is an edge to Peter that wasn't there when I met him. But there is an edge to me as well. I'm not sure who drew the edge first or whose was more acerbic.

Before we were married, Peter used to slip into his blue jeans with the ease of someone curling up on a sofa. He'd open a bottle of champagne and take two glasses from the kitchen cabinet and pull me down on the sofa next to the piano that took up the entire room in our studio apartment. He'd throw his head back like Ray Charles and croon to me like a singer in a nightclub. He made me laugh, singing Cole Porter's "It's

All Right with Me" and making up the words. There were conversations over bottles of wine until the sun came up and we heard the garbage trucks chuntering below the bedroom window, and we laughed about how tired we would be come noon in our offices but we didn't care. If I were to be perfectly honest, I would tell you that I don't quite know when it happened, but one day the silence was so loud it became deafening and the time spent apart made time together feel uncomfortable and uneasy. Except for the house and the kids and the bills with both our names on the windowed envelopes, Peter and I were at best roommates and at worse strangers.

Why was it that whenever I was in the mood not to be touched, to be alone, to be solitary, Peter seemed to want me the most?

"Not now, Peter," I said. "I need to think. I'm not done with this painting yet. Not now, Peter."

"Who's the boy in the painting?" he asked me.

"A boy I used to know," I said.

And with that he walked away as he always did at those times. He didn't ask any more questions about the boy. He didn't ask me when I painted the boy or where it was or why I did it. He really didn't want to know why I was awake at three o'clock in the morning. He turned on his heels but then he walked back into the studio, stopping at the door, one hand leaning against the frame.

"You think I'm a Philistine, don't you?" Peter asked with his chin jutting out at me. "I'm just the guy in the gray flannel suit reading *Barron's.*"

And as I began to protest, he walked away again, angry and sulking. I felt frigid and punitive. But maybe if he had stayed awhile longer. Maybe if he had

asked a few more questions. Maybe if he had insisted
on knowing why I was awake and why I painted
strangers and if they really were strangers. Maybe he
could have cajoled me just a little. Maybe he could
have hummed a verse from Cole Porter. But then,
maybe nothing would have made a difference. Maybe
it was too late.

I stayed in the studio until I knew Peter was sleeping and then I slipped the fleece blanket over my
shoulders again and got into our bed.

When I awoke, it was only 5:30. I got out of bed,
trying not to creak the floorboards, walking with an
exaggerated tiptoe. The sun was still crouched behind the trees on the side window of the kitchen. I
love that I can see the sun both rise and set from my
kitchen. I scooped the coffee into the metal percolator. I poured the coffee into my favorite mug, the one
with the pastel tulips and the big ceramic handle that
lets me grip it without fear of dropping it. My hands
are swollen, embedded with oil paint. They are
marked with scrapes and veins and dark spots.
Whenever I can, I curl my thumb into my fist. They
are so dry from detergents and turpentine. Peter used
to call them "working" hands when he attempted to
hold them.

I poured the coffee and looked at the magnolia tree
outside the window. I could see the tiny buds getting
ready to bloom. It reminded me of cherry blossoms. I
sat at the kitchen table watching the sun rise.

I remembered when Peter and I took the children to
Washington, D.C., many springs ago. Cherry blossom
time. We ended the day at the Vietnam Memorial.
Lines of people walked solemnly past the wall. Some
stopped, and taking thin sheets of paper and pencils,

etched the names of those who died, placing wreaths and single flowers on the ground below. Some wept. Some fell into each other's arms, still inconsolable after all those years. I stood off to the side with Julie in a stroller while Peter and the boys walked the length of the Memorial. I had this sickening feeling in my stomach that if I saw Jimmy's name etched on the stone, I would either collapse or have to pretend it didn't bother me at all and I knew I could do neither. I didn't look. I wasn't ready to know. I didn't want to know.

Peter came into the kitchen and took my clenched hand. "Such working hands, Emily," he said. "Good peasant stock."

He kissed the back of my head and then he walked away. Why did he do that now? I wondered. And because he caught me so off guard, and perhaps because I felt a twinge of guilt for my thoughts, I never turned my face away from the window.

Peter Walters is a simple man. He is a decent man. He is honest and practical. I am more complicated. He says I am rebellious though I don't see that at all. Someone once told me I simply had a restless heart that couldn't be stilled. I long for someone to still my heart and for some reason, Peter's attempts had become powerless.

The school bus came down our street that morning. The kids jumped from the kitchen counter, all of them surrounding me at once, kisses on the cheek. Bye, Mom. Don't forget to take back the library books. Jack making a last pitch to borrow my car. See you later. The bus has such a distinctive sound of braking as it stops near our driveway. I often wondered, if we still lived in this house after the kids graduated, how I would feel when I heard the bus rumble in. I pictured myself standing on the porch that first September morning when Julie was off to college. I imagined a young family moving in next door. I pictured a young mother with her jacket thrown over her pajamas, standing on the lawn, waving good-bye to a little girl with a knapsack too big for her back. And I worried that it would all seem too sad. Peter would be at work already and I would have to bear the scenery alone. Or maybe I would invite the young woman over for coffee and she would listen sympathetically while I reminisced.

The house was quiet with the kids at school. I sat down at the computer and called up *Yahoo!*, the website with the advertisement that says you can find lost loves. I typed in the name: James Robert Moran. There were hundreds of them up and down the east coast of the country alone and more on the west coast and in the middle. It seemed hopeless. I ignored the ones in Florida, thinking for some reason he would never be somewhere where people retired. I focused in the South, remembering way back when Chris said he thought he heard that Jimmy was in Alabama or Tennessee or Kentucky. But then Chris said he wasn't sure if Jimmy even came back and I wasn't sure if I remembered correctly what Chris had said. It was all so long ago. I began in Alabama. Start with the As. I started dialing phone numbers.

"My name is Emily Hudson," I said. "I am looking for a James Robert Moran who left for Parris Island on July 5, 1967. If you are the right person, please call me at . . ." and then I left the private number in my studio. Over the next few days, as I left the messages, sometimes I got a machine and sometimes I got a person and the whole thing seemed an exercise in futility. A crazy lady, maybe Jack was right. A crazy lady who was trying to conjure up romance. I wondered how I would feel if I couldn't find him. Would that mean he never came back? And though it made me squirm, I knew not finding him would be easier than not having him remember me.

A few calls came in that afternoon and over the next few days. Men with voices that sounded too old to be men in their forties and others with voices too young. Two calls came in from women who said James Moran was dead. I am his widow, each said, and asked who was I. An old friend, I said, and asked how old their James Moran would be. And then I tried not to sigh too visibly with relief when I heard one would have been sixty and the other eighty-two. Sorry, I said. Wrong James Moran. I had almost given up. I began to feel so foolish on this quest. Who was I to think you can find someone thirty years later? And then what do you say? What's new?

It was nearly a week later. I had spent the day doing chores, deciding to forgo the beach since it was drizzling outside. I went from one to the other of the children's rooms. Replaced CDs into their jewel cases. Stacked books and magazines. Straightened the beds they made a vain attempt to make. Picked up laundry strewn all over the floor. I sorted the darks, the whites, piled the clothes into the machine. Threw away socks with holes in the heels. I gathered Peter's shirts into a plastic grocery bag (he likes them to go to the French laundry) and copied the food list from the wipeable board in the kitchen. I pulled into the lot at the supermarket. When would the day come when I wouldn't have to buy oversized boxes of Tide and family packs of American cheese? When would Julie stop eating sticky Fruit Roll-Ups? When would Charlie stop drinking root beer for breakfast? And then I thought of the bus stop and how they ran out the door with kisses to my cheek and I threw an extra box of Roll-Ups into the cart.

When I came home I heard the phone ringing through the open window in the studio but my knee was holding up a paper bag already tearing at the bottom. I couldn't get my key into the lock in time. I put away the perishables and walked up the steps to my studio. The message light was blinking on the machine. I pressed it and walked across the room to put the top back on the turpentine. But then I stopped and listened.

"Emily Hudson. James Moran. Yes, I am that young man who joined the Marine Corps on July 5, 1967, and, yes, I remember you very well."

# 6

Emily called back the next morning. I had just come from taking Clancy to school. Normally I would have been at Long's, but Mike had called at dawn and asked me to work the late shift instead. When the phone rang, I knew it would be Emily.

"Jimmy?" Emily said. "Is it really you? Do you remember me?"

Oh, yes, I remembered her and with every word she spoke, more and more came back to me. But even though I kept saying it was really me, it wasn't until I gave her details that she believed me. I told her my father's middle name and my sister's name and where I had lived in Greenwich Village and where I went to school. And then I told her how I remembered lying with her under the Ping-Pong table and bouncing the ball so her mother wouldn't know we were kissing. That was when Emily said she believed it was really me. But as I told her about the Ping-Pong table, I pictured us there so vividly that I felt almost guilty talking about such things with someone other than Mary.

But then Mary and I hadn't talked about such things in years, so what did it matter? Mary and I sat rigidly next to one another when we watched a movie where people were making love. When I told Emily I remembered kissing her under the Ping-Pong table, well, maybe it was just my imagination but I thought I heard her breathe in softly and then breathe out deeply and then she said, "Yes, you do remember. I think you really do remember." Then there was a silence and with a breath that was almost a sigh she said, "Oh, so do I."

Then Emily just went on and on. She was breathless again, reminding me of our neighbor, Molly, who's sixteen and sits for Clancy sometimes. Molly comes over some nights just for conversation and goes on and on, rambling about this one and that one and how her teacher sent her to the principal and how her mama took away her phone privileges because she got home too late the other night. Sometimes Molly talks so fast and so much it's like she'll never come up for air. Well, that's what Emily sounded like. She sounded like a girl is how she sounded.

Emily told me about her summer in Old Greenwich when I was in boot camp. How she woke up every day and couldn't wait for the mail truck to get there. She told me how she and Jennie would take the stone path down to the mailbox and they'd sit there until the postman rolled in and she'd read my letters over and over again. Jennie. To be honest, I had forgotten Jennie's name. I could barely picture what Jennie looked like. Emily told me she lost every letter I ever wrote to her but she remembered almost every one of them. Emily told me she especially remembered the letter I wrote her one night when I was on maneuvers. Suddenly I could remember sitting outside a tent, writing that letter to Emily by the moonlight, not wanting her to worry if I missed a day of writing.

"Your handwriting looked like chicken scratch," she laughed.

"It still does," I said.

When I asked her what I said in all those letters, she asked why I had to know. I told you that I loved you, didn't I? I said. And I think she felt uncomfortable. Then she admitted that she'd thrown the letters away, something she said she does with many things once they have ended. I was afraid to tell you they were thrown away, she said. Now I wished that I had kept them. But I still have your ring.

I remembered the ring. We were sitting on the beach, high on the rocks, when I gave it to Emily. We could see the lighthouse in the distance. The moon was a crescent over the water.

Take this, I said and placed the ring in her hand.

She slipped it on her finger and it rolled around.

I need to wrap a Band-Aid on the back, she said. I don't ever want to lose it.

She remembered the name of the band I played with. Siddhartha. Christ, how did she remember that?

"You were the lead singer," she said.

"The only singer," I laughed.

I used to hold the microphone high in the air and hold the wire in my other hand. Thought I was Mick Jagger. We played at dances and one time at a party for the son of a Congressman who went to my school and I remember Emily standing in the front row and looking at me like she literally had stars in her eyes.

"You sang 'Under My Thumb,' " she said. "I always thought you were singing it to me. And 'My Girl.' "

And I said that "Under My Thumb" was really a pretty chauvinistic song if you think about it but Emily said she never thought about that at the time.

*"A Siamese cat of a girl"*? I said, and she laughed.

When I first spoke to Emily she said she heard the hint of a southern accent but after a while she said I was slipping back into that New York speak. I heard my own voice like it was coming to me from the past. She called me Jimmy. Mary was the only other person who called me Jimmy but somehow when Mary said it, it didn't sound the same. And I knew that wasn't fair to Mary because there was a time when she called me Jimmy in that southern accent of hers that used to sound so sweet to me and I loved it.

Emily knew the exact date I left for boot camp (though she said she wasn't sure what day of the week it was but she was certain it was midweek) and she remembered my address in Greenwich Village (though she called it a street not a lane and had the number of the building wrong) and, well, she just remembered me. I never thought that anyone, let alone Emily, would remember me. My mind flashed back on all those times I picked up the phone after Vietnam: "Who? Jim who? Sorry, the name is familiar but I really don't remember you."

So many thoughts started going through my head as Emily and I spoke. I started to worry that maybe Emily was depressed and calling old friends for what they call closure. There are so many reasons people take certain directions and it made me sad to think that maybe something was wrong with her. But when I asked her (I said, You're not depressed, are you, Emily? You're not getting your affairs in order, are you?), she laughed and said how she could see why I

might think that but no, not at all. I was embarrassed
that I'd even asked her. I could tell by the way she answered me that I was worrying for nothing.

"But there never was closure, Jimmy," she said.

I was hoping it wasn't closure that she wanted now.
Closure is too final.

I told Emily about Mary and Clancy, and my dad
dying. I told her how I wanted to put my father's
ashes someplace where he loved to be and that was
why I went to the Harbor and how I wished the *Melodrama* and Tubby had still been there. I told her how it
felt so good to throw those ashes into the sea and how
it was so intimate.

"It was the first time I had ever felt so close to my father," I said. "Even though at the time he was just dust
sifting through my fingers."

Words were pouring out of me, talking to Emily. Just
the way they did in the old days on the beach when I
felt like she was the only one in the world who seemed
to know me and didn't mind at all what she knew.

Emily asked me where I worked and what I did
and I never wanted to hang up the phone. She just
kept asking me questions. Every time I told her one
thing, she asked me something else. I don't think I
ever made an impression on anyone in my life and
the fact that Emily Hudson remembered me and
went to such great pains to find me lifted me higher
than anything had since the day the nurse placed
Clancy in my arms. For the first time in a long time, I
didn't feel like just another fucked-up vet from Vietnam. It was the first time in a long time, probably
since those days I sat with her on the beach in Connecticut, that I didn't feel like debris. There are so
many times, except for Clancy, that I feel like my life

has been a waste. Talking to Emily made me want to
go back and start all over again. Those days when I
sat with her and she'd lay her head on my shoulder
and we'd look out at the horizon. But I didn't talk to
her about Vietnam other than to say, yes, I was there.
I never talked to anyone about Vietnam. I was afraid
of what I might remember.

There were things I told Emily in just that first call
that I couldn't even tell the therapists I've seen over
the years. Mary was the one who told me to go to the
therapists but I hadn't gone in ages. Mary said I
seemed depressed and it wasn't normal for a man to
be awake half the night. I told Emily about all the
women I met and was so afraid to get close to after she
and I were over. About how I'd buy nickel bags of pot
on the street corners in Manhattan after I got back
from Vietnam and go down to my parents' apartment
and back to my old room and lie on my bed and smoke
and how I felt so alone. I told her how I called all those
old friends from my school and how they either pretended not to know me or had already forgotten me. It
was the first time I admitted to anyone, including myself, how much it all just hurt.

"Why didn't you call me when you got back from
Vietnam?" Emily asked, so simply as though it would
have made perfect sense. But she and I both knew
why, though we weren't ready to talk about it. Not just
yet. We purposely avoided talking about that October
day after boot camp.

"The scene after boot camp didn't go too well," I reminded her, treading gently.

I said that I'd probably just blocked her out. The truth
is, I never could have called Emily in those days. If she
had pretended not to know me or didn't want to re-

member, I never would have made it through the next
day. I would have felt that much more alone. I wanted
to tell her how my fingers went to dial her number a
million times that October night but I was afraid she
wouldn't care. I felt vulnerable. Thinking about that October day brought me back to when old friends didn't
know me anymore. It brought me far away from Clancy
and even further from Mary and it made me wonder if
the two of them could see right through me.

Then I lied to Emily. I told her about Mike Long and
the wine store but not the entire truth. You see, Long's
is really a wine department in this big old place kind
of like a farmer's market. It's one of those big discount
stores where they sell tires and chicken cordon bleu
and live lobsters all under the same roof. They made
me wear this red shirt at Long's where LONG'S is
printed in bold white letters across the front and on the
back and then I had this plastic name tag with my
name on it saying HELLO, MY NAME IS JIM. HAVE A NICE
DAY. I spent most of the day lifting wooden crates of
wine off the trucks and ripping open cartons until my
hands were dry and cracked. Then I stacked the bottles
up on shelves in the stockroom and brought some out
to the floor. My back ached so bad at the end of the day
I could barely stand up straight. Since Nam, I take as-
pirin like it's candy anyway. I figured that Emily pictured me working in a place like Sherry-Lehman on
Madison Avenue.

I went to Sherry-Lehman with my dad a few times.
The salesmen wore shirts and ties and the wines were
stacked in wrought-iron bins with prices scripted in
gold ink. And the salesmen said, May I help you, Mr.
Moran? Ah, one of our finest burgundies.

At Long's, there are big signs scrawled in black

Magic Marker and most of the people who come in buy bottles with screw caps. But the true part is, I was trying to get Mike Long to make the place different. I know that Asti Spumante isn't really champagne. Mike thinks all of us who work in his shop are just a bunch of redneck boys.

I wanted Clancy to think her daddy was really something. I didn't want Clancy to know that I wore a red shirt at work with my name on a plastic tag. In the mornings when I left, I always wore a white man-tailored shirt with the sleeves rolled up to the elbows. I kept the red shirt with LONG'S on the back in my car. I mean, Clancy thought I owned the wine store. Mary knew the truth. But Mary didn't expect anything from me but the paychecks.

Part of me wanted to leave everything with Emily as just a memory. Sometimes I run away from people before they can get to know me. But Emily made me feel so good. Just like the days when the guys called her Jimmy's girl. When being with her was like being in a secret place where I could just be myself and have her love me for what I was and what I wasn't. Talking to her again felt so familiar and comfortable. It was all coming back to me. Until now, I could only picture the day when I left her at the train station. But now I could remember the four months before. Suddenly I felt like the kid walking down the sidewalks in Manhattan with my girl. And there was no one else in the world but us.

She told me she was so in love with me as though she was reminding me. As though I had forgotten. And then I think she got self-conscious.

"You probably had a lot of weekend liberties that summer at boot camp, didn't you? Lots of girls, I bet," she said, like she was one of the guys.

"We didn't have any liberties at boot camp, Emmie," I said. I felt embarrassed that I was bold enough to call her Emmie. "This was the Marine Corps. The Marines are not like the other branches of the military. Nothing's loose and easy in the Marines." For a moment I felt a little puffed up.

"I guess there's an awful lot you could tell me," she said.

"What I want to tell you, Emily," I said, with the emphasis on her name, "are things that I can say only if I'm looking at you." Things like that October day, I thought.

I wanted to tell her everything. I didn't want to get off the phone and we had already been on for hours. I even told her how after she and I went our separate ways, I started writing letters to my grandmother. I never told anyone that before. The guys in Nam thought I was writing to my girl, the hog in the yellow bikini who'd been on the pinup board. I didn't tell her that I still had the picture. I didn't tell her about the hog board.

It's funny, she asked all about me and I had told her about Mary and Clancy but I hadn't asked if she was married. Then she just told me about Peter and her children as if I had asked. Four kids. Emily Hudson had four kids. And a husband.

"I always wanted to be a father," I said. "It killed me when Mary didn't get pregnant. But you know, I don't think I ever knocked anybody up in my entire life. I'm a father now, though. Just like my own father was when he adopted me. But better." And it sounded like I was defending myself.

And then Emily told me she had each of those four kids almost every year and I said, "You must get pregnant if someone spits on you."

that I wanted to take her in my arms as though I'd just come home. It was hard to hang up the phone. But saying I would speak to her tomorrow made it easier.

Mary was less than thrilled when I told her that Emily called me. I didn't tell her until the next evening. I thought maybe by then I wouldn't look so happy. In all the years I've been with Mary, Emily's name had never come up, well, just one time but just in passing so it barely mattered. It's not like you talk to your wife about some girl who was the first girl you ever loved. Mary is not the jealous type but I think she knows that after all these years, when I have so few old friends, and not too many new ones, well, I think she's smart enough to know how much this might mean to me. Who was she? Mary asked. And I thought it was odd that she used the past tense. And then I thought it was odd that I told her to begin with. But I told her to make it all seem meaningless. Nothing to hide.

Just as I was about to come up with an explanation for the reappearance of Emily, Molly came walking in through the kitchen door. It was perfect timing. I had just started to say that Emily Hudson was a girl I knew in high school. She was a girl who went to one of those private girl's schools, I said. You know, we had socials with them. Acting flip like none of it mattered. Using Emily's last name so she sounded less familiar. Trying not to puff my shoulders up too high. Trying not to look like I felt seventeen again.

I really tried to play down the whole Emily thing with Mary. But Mary wanted to know how come Emily suddenly called me. I told her how Emily ran into a mutual old friend, Chris. He had my number from ages ago, I said.

"But the number's been changed at least ten times," Mary said.

"I guess she looked it up," I said, trying not to sound impatient or annoyed.

She's an artist, I explained. She's working on a series of paintings about Vietnam. Mary cocked her head to the side and asked why she called me of all people. And because I didn't want to get her too riled up, I just shrugged. Mary had heard Chris's name before. I didn't tell her that Emily had run into him sixteen years ago. She said she thought the whole thing sounded rather odd. "Fishy" was the word she used. But she didn't push for more answers. Mary has watched me slip away these last few years. Clancy brought us together as a family but as I said before, this is no love affair. But why did Mary have to say "you, of all people"?

But with Emily, it was a love affair. Even though I barely more than kissed her and slipped my hand underneath her blouse. There was more to it than that. She was my girl, hanging on my arm, talking to me in the moonlight the night before I left for boot camp. I could see Emily's misty eyes at the train station. Molly was standing there the whole time I was talking to Mary. It was strange to look at Molly and think she was just the age that Emily was when I fell so hard in love.

"You're starin' at me, Mr. Moran," Molly said. And I was staring at her, but it wasn't Molly I was seeing.

A few days later I got a bunch of postcards with Emily's drawings on them and some stories written on the sides. There was also a large sheet called a triptych and I didn't know what the hell that was except it was in three pieces and folded but I never really looked at any of it. Something about the Holocaust. I flipped through the postcards and left them on the kitchen table. Mary didn't look at them. She moved them to the counter when we sat down to eat and then back to the table when we were done.

"You keepin' this stuff, Jimmy?" Mary asked me one night, leafing through it the way she does with junk mail, about to toss it in the trash, her foot poised on the trash-can pedal. I took the postcards from her hands and shoved everything back in the envelope, hiding it under the shirts in my bureau drawer.

I called Emily the next morning.

"So you want me to be your guinea pig, right? Paintings and poetry about some old love for inspiration?" I said. I was angry.

"I want to hear everything about the last thirty years," she said. "I want to hear about your family and where you were and what happened to you when you went to Vietnam. I want every detail. I don't need inspiration."

Her voice sounded annoyed, hot under the collar as my dad used to say, as she slurred the word *inspiration*, emphasizing it as though it was distasteful.

"I could get myself another guinea pig, if what I really wanted was a guinea pig, Jimmy Moran. You didn't even look at my postcards or my writing, did you?" she asked as though she was making a statement.

How did she know that I didn't look at them? I had no patience to look at them. Then she softened.

"If nothing else," she said. "It would be nice to see you again. Unless, of course, you don't want to remember."

For the life of me, I couldn't figure out why anyone,

especially someone like Emily Hudson, successful husband, big house in Connecticut, talented, educated, would have the slightest interest in me. Like Mary said, me "of all people."

"We could meet in Washington, D.C.," Emily said as though she were trying to talk me into it. "We could go to the Vietnam Memorial. That's a start."

I told her I'd never gone to the Memorial. Made an attempt last year but didn't have the nerve to look. Mary walked the wall with Clancy while I waited on the hill. But Emily had it all figured out.

"Pick a date," she said. "I'll pick you up at National Airport."

When I hung up the phone, I started taking socks out of my sock drawer and tossing the ones with holes in the heels into the garbage can across the room. I looked at myself sideways in the full-length mirror. A gut. I had a gut. No more skinny kid. No more Marine. Just a soft southern boy. She'll take one look at me and call the game, I thought. She wasn't just some old girlfriend. This was Emily. Jimmy's girl.

"Don't mess with Jimmy's girl," the guys used to say.

Just knowing I was going to see her made me feel alive at the same time that it scared me to death. I had made my peace with the South. I was long gone from New York City and the bright lights and fast talk. I had my dark red El Camino and my kid and my house by the stream. And a wife. I'd left the rest behind a long time ago and until Emily called, I tried not to think about it.

# 7

For some reason that I am not sure of, I started to call him "Jim" instead of "Jimmy" sometime during that first conversation. It might have been right after he called me Emmie the way he had when we were younger. He corrected himself after that and called me Emily. Perhaps it was because he had a wife and child and somehow the familiarity of Emmie seemed presumptuous and out of place. As for Jimmy, it was too diminutive a name for a man self-described with graying hair. Jimmy was a name you called a boy. The transition was difficult at first, defining time somewhat abruptly.

I had spoken with Jim a half-dozen times during those first few days. When the children hopped on the school bus, I dug into my chores with a desperation to complete them, placing me above suspicion if something was not done. I painted a bit in my studio before I called him, a slave to routine, fearful that I would let myself slide into that adolescent behavior where you are tied to the phone, waiting for "him" to call, waiting for "him" to answer. But I hadn't been back to the beach in what seemed like weeks.

For the first several days, Jim left Long's at two o'clock, telling them he needed some personal time. There were days that he called me and others where I waited anxiously for him to call. Annoyed at myself for sitting around. One day I didn't hear from him at all (it turned out he had to work an extra shift that day). I was angry with myself for not just picking up the phone and calling him. It seems the moment there is the slightest hint of romance there is that loss of abandon, the games men and women purposefully or inadvertently play. Who's on top? Who's on the bottom? Who has the upper hand?

Sometimes Jim would call me and after speaking for maybe five minutes he would ask me to call him right back. There was an urgency to his voice. "Listen, can you do me a favor and call me right back?" I never questioned the request. It occurred to me it might have been the cost and then I thought perhaps this way his wife wouldn't know. Neither reason really mattered.

Speaking with Jim Moran made me recall not just the memories of that summer but the geography of my life for the last thirty years. There were things I had forgotten about myself. Places I no longer ventured and others I had forgotten or perhaps denied. There were many memories that had been placed carefully in cottony fabric, folded and hidden away in imaginary drawers and some that were waiting perhaps to be taken out again and caressed.

I had taken books off the shelves. My name was scrawled inside the covers, decorated with hearts and flowers. I took out my old Rod McKuen books (I saw Jennie's name scratched out in *Listen to the Warm*, my name was written underneath) and the school year-book from 1967. I wished I'd kept Jimmy's letters. At least one photograph. Jennie's inscription in my yearbook (next to the picture of our eleventh grade class) was fashioned carefully although in pencil. It was a quote from The Doors song "The End," and then instructions to "Ride the Highway West. The West is the Best" and then she signed it, "Jimmy Loves You."

The pages of the Rod McKuen books were brittle and yellow with age. Some of them broke in my hand like little jaundiced chips of paint. I turned the pages of *Listen to the Warm* gingerly, hoping they would not only stay together in my hands but read as well as they did before. They read differently, though. But there was a passage in poem number 15 that was underlined:

*I have seen the march of beach birds and loved you.*
*I have lent myself to summer sun and loved you.*
*And seeing naked trees*
    *and raising my collar to the wind*
*and counting minutes till chartered hours were there*
*I have loved you.*

And next to that was, unmistakably, Jim's handwriting, the word "us" written with an exclamation point afterwards. I was relieved and excited to see something in his handwriting since all his letters were gone.

I saw the underlining on the pages and notes in the margins of textbooks. Notes I'd written on Jane Eyre's dilemma: "Receiving love without restrictions or demands," it said. The thoughts of a young girl that were so shameless, written boldly in red pen, dogmatically unraveling the meanings of texts and poetry with a wisdom not jaded by experience or ruined by reality.

And I found my old dance cards in a scrapbook,
ragged and faded at the edges, dates checked off when
I had attended class. I had forgotten how much I loved
to dance. When I first met Peter, I took classes every
night at a dance studio in Carnegie Hall. Jazz dance. To
my mother's dismay, I was never one for ballet. I felt
constrained by the classical music. I wanted to move
my hips and feel a beat. I went to the classes after work
every day. I'd take the subway to Carnegie Hall where
the second floor was filled with dance studios. There
are offices there now. But then, there were large rooms
with matte waxed oak floors, mirrored walls and bar-
res. I would stop at a coffee shop on West Fifty-seventh
Street where I sat alone with a paperback (I read *The
Harrad Experiment* there and *The Group*) and ordered a
hamburger and iced coffee, feeling with a free hand for
the dance bag at my feet holding my soft black jazz
shoes and leotards. I'd cross the street to the studios
and hand in my dance card where the aging ballerina,
relegated to a desk job, stamped it with hands that
were curled and arthritic. Her name was Melinda. She
wore a pink leotard and a long sweeping skirt. The
prima donna suspended in time. The dressing room
was sealed only by a purple velvet curtain. I changed
from my business suit into jazz pants and off-the-
shoulder top.

The other young women were professional dancers.
They didn't know I worked in the art department of a
publishing house. My body was as chiseled as theirs.
We stood outside the dressing room waiting for the
last class to end, leg warmers gathered around our ankles, arms straining to fasten our hair in a bun on top
of our heads. We made small talk: Who has on the
musk cologne? Someone let me borrow their hair

spray. Who talked to the guy who said he was a director last night after class? The men were mostly gay and nonthreatening, standing together in groups, backs straight, poised for the dance, eyes outlandishly fringed with dark mascara. They'd ask things like, Where did you *get* that sweater? Said things like, It's *mar*velous. You look gorgeous. Two drummers played (usually "Swing Time" or "In the Mood") in the back of the studio and for ninety minutes I felt as though I was on stage. Front row, center. I was twenty-one.

Peter used to pick me up after class. Sometimes he stood outside the studio and I could see him watching from the corner of my eye. He always kissed me as I walked out of the classroom. I would be perspired and red-faced and he acted like he'd never seen anything the likes of me before. I showered and changed and we walked to what would become our apartment but was his at the time. It didn't matter how hot or cold the night air was. We walked with arms laced around each other's waist, unable to get close enough. We talked and talked and stopped to kiss on street corners. I think that's what I miss the most now. That sense of abandon as though the world had to deal with us, like it or not. That's what I miss the most about Peter. About Jim.

A few years later, Peter and I got married and decided to move to Connecticut and start a family. The dance classes stopped then. A lot of things stopped. We stopped taking long walks and we stopped having conversations. Babies came one after the other and suddenly the stereo in the bedroom was replaced with an infant monitor and we awakened at night to the cries of an infant instead of cries for one another. It seems like it happened overnight.

Peter would leave home early in the morning, before
the sun came up, before the kids and I were even
awake. He came home late at night and he was weary.
He came home and I was equally as spent. When we
first moved to Connecticut, I found a dance class in a
small studio called just that, Dancin' Studio. The babies came with me. I dragged a double stroller for Sam
and Charlie and a Snugli for Julie and toted Jack by the
hand. I left the children in the baby-sitting room, while
Julie, still nursing, sat in a car seat in the corner of the
dance studio, her head dropped to the side nestled
against a pink gingham pillow.

The classes weren't really dance classes, though.
They were dancercize and aerobics. Rooms filled
with women whose bodies were less than chiseled,
whose waistlines were thickened by recent pregnan-
cies, who wore sweat pants and sweat shirts to dis-
guise their tummies instead of leotards. They carried
diaper bags laden with jars of baby fruit and formula
(instead of leotards and cigarettes) stuffed in the side
pockets. They were women who went from the
dance class to their mothers' group and spent the
next hour complaining about their lives and their
husbands.

I went to one of those mothers' groups once. The
women swapped stories about their husbands as
though they were a species. They were women who
once felt like the belle of the ball and now felt like the
old ball and chain. They'd forgotten their husbands
were once their lovers. Or maybe it was the husbands
that forgot. Who knows? Who even remembers?

You know what *mine* did today? they'd say, sitting
in the circle of the group. Comparing notes as though
each was married to the same man, same checkbook,

an excuse for a husband. Lives of quiet desperation. It was the first and last group I attended.

I cannot say it is Peter's fault that somewhere along the line we got lost. For certain, I got lost. There was never any adamancy on his part that I relinquish my career or give up dancing, but there was never any awareness either that if maybe he had been home just a little more often or listened to me when I bemoaned the things I missed, things could have been different. Instead, Peter became defensive and I became resentful. He proclaimed to be the one fighting the traffic to Manhattan to keep me in the style to which I was rapidly becoming accustomed. And I was the one feeling lonely and saying it was all hardly worth it. It seemed the more I prattled on and begged for conversation, insistent that I would rather have him home than have an addition on the house, the more I felt him withdraw from me. He stayed later at the office, scheduled meetings out of town, had business dinners I couldn't attend because it was either too early for me to leave the children with a sitter or too late to get an amenable sitter to stay.

One night, shortly after I'd spoken to Jim for the first time, Julie called me into her room. Julie is the one who, like Jack, feels what shows on my face. Unlike Jack, she is brave enough to ask why I look the way I do. Jack would prefer to make me laugh or pull me close to him. In some ways he is much like Peter, preferring not to address those things that rock the boat but simply putting down anchor, pretending the still waters do not run so deep. Lashing out for a moment and then pretending that nothing ever happened. Eventually Peter simply retreated, though. He stopped trying to pull me closer. Julie is the one who calls me on the carpet. Sit

down on my bed, Mom. We have to talk, she said. She
drew a determined breath. She asked why it seemed
that her father and I had little to say to one another. She
asked why sometimes I looked as though I was thinking so deep and so hard. When you're twelve, I said,
you can't wait to grow up but, in fact, growing up is
nothing more than a myth because, even at forty-six,
we keep growing up if we're lucky. Then Julie and I got
into those murky waters where she asked if Daddy and
I were still growing up. I knew from the stricken look
on her face that she was frightened. It took all her
courage to ask. Her face seemed to fall as she listened
to my words. She swallowed audibly and held on to
her lower lip with her teeth. She really was asking if her
father and I were growing apart.

And what do you say to a twelve-year-old? You in-
voke the power of your motherhood and tell neither
truth nor lie. You say people go through changes and
moods and phases only to wend their way back to
each other. For a moment you find yourself grateful
for the omnipotence of motherhood that quells the
fears of a child with a soothing tone and a hand placed
firmly on her shoulder. And you know the time is lim-
ited when you will no longer have this advantage.
And you wish you were able to believe your own
words as much as she believes them. At twelve, you
want to believe in forever.

# 8

The reality of boot camp set in with immediacy. On the bus, there was this great camaraderie. Until we pulled into Parris Island at two o'clock in the morning and the drill instructor was in our faces. Reality just hits you. Suddenly it's all too clear where you are. You realize that you've just given up every freedom you've ever known. There's no going back. This drill sergeant owns you. He's well-trained, well-experienced and he knows just how to get to you.

The first morning I went through the chow line and asked for tea. Tea was what I always drank as a kid when I felt sick. It was what my grandmother gave me when I went to visit at her house. Well, the drill instructor dragged me out of that line and into another room and kicked my ass. From that day on I drank coffee and I drank it black. The only time I touch tea to this day is when I have a sore throat.

They taught me how to spit shine my boots at Parris Island. It was the only time there when I can remember having moments to myself. I'd take those heavy,

Marine-issue black leather boots and sit on the edge of the cot and think. Mostly I thought about Emily. I'd close my eyes real tight and pretend that she was sitting next to me. If she had been there, maybe she would have been leaning her head on my shoulder, the way she did at the beach that summer before I left. She'd have her head on my shoulder and her hand reaching across my lap, resting on my thigh. Sometimes I thought about the guys from school and I wondered if they'd gotten someone else to sing with the band. And sometimes I'd lay back on the cot for just a few seconds and close my eyes, pretending I was back in my parents' house in Greenwich Village.

My mother always had pink and white geraniums in those black wooden boxes sitting outside the windows. In the winter, she put ivy in the boxes and wrapped white lights around the window frames. I loved our street with the experimental theater on one end and the greasy hamburger joint on the other. I went back to the hamburger joint a dozen years ago when I flew up with my dad's ashes. It's a gay bar now. I told the owner I always used to go there with my dad (which wasn't quite true since he only took me there a couple of times) and the owner looked at me and swept his hand, palm up, toward the center of the room, pointing to a group of men with bald heads, gold hoop earrings and black leather jackets, their arms around each other as they drank beers at the bar.

Things don't stay the same, pal, the owner said.

I couldn't wait to get out of there. His words throbbed in my head all day long: Things don't stay the same, pal.

The drill sergeant didn't say anything when I sat on the edge of my cot shining those boots back and forth

with the chamois cloth. I was doing what I was supposed to do, spitting and wiping until those boots
shined so bright that I could see my face in them. He'd
probably seen hundreds of kids like me, scrawny
teenagers who were so homesick they looked like deer
caught in headlights. All I wanted was to be back
home. Even my father, drunk in his armchair, was
looking good to me back then. I wanted to be back in
those gray flannel slacks and navy blue blazer. I
wished I had paid more attention in my classes and
not messed around in assemblies. I wished I was like
Steve and Chris, going on to graduate the next year,
and then going off to some college in New England
where the buildings were made of stone and covered
with ivy and you tossed a football around in the quad
and bought pitchers of beer at the campus hangout. I
couldn't believe I ended up in Parris Island at seventeen. I felt like I had it all and let it slip through my fingers. Like my father's ashes did that day in the harbor.

After boot camp, they bussed us to Camp LeJeune
for about a month. They said it was for infantry train-
ing regimen but really all you did was shoot off a lot of
guns and master all the weapons you'd be using in
combat and throw grenades. I did well on the aca-
demic testing in the Marines. Pretty funny, since I
would have flunked out of high school if I'd stayed at
home. Maybe I did well because I finally had those
glasses. I was sure I'd get some kind of occupational
specialty so I wouldn't be sent to Nam. A base commander actually told me I would get to work on
ground crew at home. Then I messed up just like always.

After LeJeune, we had a thirty-day pass before we
flew over to Memphis for six months and waited for

orders for Camp Pendleton, which was our last stop before Vietnam. It was during that thirty-day pass in between Memphis and Pendleton when I came home to see Emily. My mother picked me up at Kennedy Airport the night I came home. She pulled up in a black Lincoln Continental that she rented (we didn't own a car except my father's Jaguar that didn't have trunk space. I was glad to see her but I was disappointed that my father wasn't with her. "Where's Dad?" I asked. And without looking me in the eye, she said simply that he was busy, and I think both of us knew that was a lie. It was late at night and he was probably slumped down in that chair, so drunk she couldn't rouse him, so she just came alone.

"Where's Daphne?" I asked about my sister.

"Sleeping, of course," my mother said but part of me wondered why Daphne couldn't have weathered the late night. Daphne wasn't adopted. It was the typical story. Mom got pregnant with Daphne when I was just over a year old. Tall and red-haired, she looks a lot like my mom. The funny thing is, Daphne and my mom look a lot like Clancy.

Sometimes I try to remember what my mother said to me as we drove home that night and I can't. She let me drive the car.

We were silent and then she said, "I turned down your bed at home, Jim. I put on that big quilt you used to like."

Why did I feel she was talking about me in the past tense? She placed her hand on my knee and then took it away. She turned her head and looked out the car window the rest of the way home.

I couldn't wait to see Emily. It was too late to call her apartment that night and I was afraid to call early in the morning. The next day, I slept until almost noon anyway and I remember thinking how odd it was to shower in a bathroom where the door shut tight and there weren't six naked guys standing right next to me.

I couldn't find my work boots and jeans. The jeans wouldn't have fit anyway since my thighs were so pumped up. My mother had taken the clothing out of my closet and hung all her woolens in there with mothballs. She put my clothes in the basement of the town house but I didn't want to go down there and start rummaging through cartons. Why the hell my mother had to move my stuff was beyond me. I guess maybe she figured I wasn't coming back, or if I was, it wouldn't be for long anyway. I took a pair of my dad's black lace-up shoes and spit shined them. My dad's feet were bigger than mine and I felt like I had clown shoes on. I bought a pair of greenish pants at the army navy store down the block (they called them fatigues and part of me thought it was a riot that I was buying military clothes) and then I went to a regular men's store and bought a navy blue shirt with a collar. I didn't feel right in bell bottom jeans anymore with my nearly shaved head. I didn't know if I'd ever feel right anymore about anything.

I took the subway uptown from Astor Place to Sixty-eighth Street and walked across Lexington Avenue to Fifth Avenue. I knew exactly what time Emily walked home from school. Jesus, I walked her home enough times. When she turned the corner in front of her building, I was waiting. My head was down. I was looking down at my shoes trying to see a reflection, thinking about all those days I sat on my bunk thinking about her. See, I really liked Emily. I thought she was pretty and I thought she had a great figure, but mostly, I really liked her as much as I loved her. There were so many days in the service, after I left boot camp, when I would go on liberty and wake up in the morning next to someone I barely knew and didn't want to know. Those were the times I ached inside. I just wanted to wake up next to Emily.

When she came walking down the street, I swear I could smell her lemon cologne and I knew her footsteps. Her hair had gotten really long. She kept shoving a wisp of it back with her hand while she juggled all her schoolbooks. She didn't see me at first. She was looking right at me but I guess she didn't recognize me. I was standing real rigidlike. I was scared to see her. Maybe I was more scared for her to see me. I ran my hand through my hair that wasn't there and I was sweating even though it was October and there was a breeze that sent the leaves and the trash sailing over the sidewalk.

Emily stopped dead in her tracks when she saw me. I walked over to her. I went to put my arms around her and kiss her, slowly, real slowly like I dreamed about doing all summer. But when she leaned against me, I knew right away that things didn't feel the same. I took the books out of her hands and laid them down on the sidewalk. I took her hands in mine.

"God, Jimmy, you look so different," she said and she wasn't smiling the way I thought she would be. She looked almost puzzled, like she was searching my face, hoping I'd take off the mask and surprise her.

"It's me, though, Emily. It's me," I said, shaking her hands like I wanted to wake her up. I might as well have walked away right then because Emily looked at me as though I was a stranger. She looked as though she'd seen a ghost. And then the way that people hunt for words when they have nothing to say and don't really remember who you are, she asked me if I'd been in town long. I told her I hadn't gotten back until late last night and then I said, "In town long? Christ, Emily. What am I? Some tourist passing through?"

I could feel myself getting anxious and frustrated and I backed down. I told her how they flew me up the night before and my mom picked me up at the airport around midnight and the first thing I wanted to do was see her. And then she asked how long I'd be "in town," using that expression again and I knew for sure that something was wrong. It was as though she didn't know what to say and latched on to some lame expression like she was a broken record. This was our town and she acted as though it wasn't mine anymore. I mean, I was home for Christ sakes. Nothing went the way I planned. Nothing went the way I'd dreamed about all summer long.

I looked at her and thought of all those nights when I sat writing those letters. Emily had always believed in me. Some of what the girls in Emily's class said about me was true. It was true that I went to Finn's Pub after I'd drop her off at home for her curfew. It was true that I dropped acid in the men's room there and I smoked pot when Emily wasn't looking or wasn't around. But I didn't do any of that when Emily was around me. And why was it that Steve and Chris did that stuff, too, but no one seemed to talk about them the way they talked about me? Maybe because Steve and Chris weren't flunking out of school. Maybe because their parents weren't drowning themselves in glass after glass of gin. With Emily I could be myself. I was afraid to show everyone else certain sides of me so it was easier with them to just get high. No one but

Emily knew how embarrassed I was that I was failing in school. They believed me when I laughed it off. It was as though Emily peeled off a veneer that covered me, took me right down to the wood and loved me bare. I remember what she said to me one day when I was being flip with Chris about my failing grades. "I love you for what you are and what you're not," she said. "Don't act like a such wise guy. You're neither a wise guy nor a failure." And at the time I laughed and told her she was the only person I knew that could use *neither* and *nor* in a sentence.

That October day when I saw her for what I thought would be that last time, she was wearing these tin earrings with peace signs on them and she had eye makeup on and some kind of sticky white stuff on her lips. She said it was pink but it wasn't. I remembered her lips always looking so full and so red and glossy and they looked real pale and the eye makeup was hard.

"Why do you have that crap on your eyes?" I asked her. When I went to wipe it off, she pushed my hand away. She told me it wasn't crap and who was I anyway to call it that. And then she looked real self-conscious or maybe she looked worried and I felt almost sorry for her for a moment.

"Take a walk with me," I said. Just like that day in March by the fountain in Central Park. The day I'd met her for the first time and asked, "Want to take a walk with me, Emily Hudson?"

I picked up her books from the sidewalk and held them under my arm. I slung my free arm over her shoulder. She was thin, Emily, and she had never felt delicate to me before. I was a skinny kid when I left for boot camp and I knew I was so much broader now. I'd gained twenty pounds of solid muscle and Emily seemed so fragile. We sat down on a bench on Fifth Avenue right by Central Park and she just stared straight ahead of her. She asked me if I'd gotten her letters and I asked if she got mine (which was pretty stupid if you think about it since we wrote to one another all summer) and then I told her that I was leaving at the end of the week. It was the first lie I ever told her unless you count the one about being a Cherokee. I was leaving in a month but I didn't think at that point that Emily would give me a month. I told her how they were shipping me to Memphis and then to California and from there I'd go to Vietnam even though, at that point, I wasn't quite certain. I turned her earrings between my fingers when I told her and she looked at my face like she expected to see something telling on it and then she asked me why I had to leave again. She said I ought to ask my dad to write to someone and say the whole thing was a big mistake. He knows a lot of influential people, she said. He must have connections. She told me to go back to school and how next year she'd graduate and then we could be somewhere together. Then she put her hand on the back of my neck and dropped her chin down to her chest and began to cry. She said they had no business cutting off my hair and why did my skin look so rough and red now?

And then I told her that I loved her. Just like I told her all summer long in every letter I wrote to her. I didn't tell her that they hung her picture up on the hog board, though. And I didn't tell her that I was scared shitless of California and where I'd go after that. I told her that I wanted her before I left. I said if nothing else, send me off with a bang, Emily, and I guess that was probably not the greatest choice of words and certainly one I would never use now. I was fucked up, man. I really was. Send me off with a bang? I don't know where that came from other than maybe I was just so self-conscious at that point I didn't know what to do or say. And Emily stood up and asked me why I wasn't being tender the way I used to be.

I think it was that expression "used to be" that triggered something deep inside me since I knew I'd never be again what I was before the summer. I tried to hold her really tight against me but she was pulling away. I said she should trust me and come home with me and let me just make love to her (changing the expression right then and there, not to force her but because I meant it). But when I held her, she wasn't holding me back. Emily kept saying that she couldn't sleep with me and the more she said it, the more I kept demanding why and why and why, not realizing she was really just a baby, not quite seventeen. And so instead of letting it go, I told her she was being a bitch. Imagine that, I called Emily Hudson a bitch, and then I called her a cock teaser and I could feel everything getting out of hand as though it wasn't me that was saying all those things to her. I felt as though the world was floating around me and I was there but not there at all. I never would have used expressions like that in front of her before. If anyone had ever sworn in front of her, they'd get an earful from me if not a fistful. Emily let me protect her and here I was acting like a, well, like a Marine. I could feel myself losing control.

Emily stood up and took a step away from me. She was facing me as I sat on the bench. There's someone else, she said. She wouldn't tell me his name but she said he went to my old school. *Old* school. She said he was her boyfriend now and she'd lost her virginity over the summer and guessed I just didn't get home in time. And I wondered how she could have written me all those letters.

When she sat there telling me that, I knew if I stayed a moment longer I'd either slug her or break down crying and I didn't want to do either one, so I just got up and walked away. I thought I heard her call my name but I just kept walking and never looked back. I didn't care about California or Vietnam and I didn't care where they would send me and I didn't care if I lived or died.

I turned the corner and walked uptown, not toward my home. I walked across Eighty-sixth Street and some guy by the subway sold me a joint and I jammed it in my pocket. When I got home, I sat on the stoop outside my house and smoked it down. That night, as I lay on the bed in my room, staring up at the ceiling the way I did when I was a kid, I kept putting my hand on the telephone to call her. I wanted her to tell me the guy's name and for her to know he wasn't the right one for her. For all I knew, he'd been a friend of mine. He was probably some prep school twerp I'd gone to school with and the thought of him crawling all over Emily Hudson made me want to puke my guts out. But I never called her. And I wanted to so bad. I wanted to get right back on the subway and head up to her house and wipe that shit off her eyes and tell her she was mine. But I never called her. And I thought that was probably a good thing because she never called me either and there was a time when I swore she would.

That was when it all went downhill. For the next three weeks if I wasn't lying on my bed staring up at the ceiling I was buying dope on St. Mark's Place. I was smoking pot, popping reds, doing acid. I was wrecked. My parents never even noticed. By the time I was called to ship down to Memphis, I didn't know who I was anymore. But worse, I didn't care. I'd gotten my orders in the mail. I didn't care because Emily was gone and more because once you know or even think you're going to Nam, you go numb. That's the only way to cope. Emily had been my last hope. Once I thought she loved me for who I was and who I wasn't. But I didn't know who I was anymore. Maybe she didn't know either. Maybe it was just too hard to love a ghost.

# 9

When Jennie and I packed up our room in the Connecticut house that summer of 1967, I put Jimmy's letters in a shoe box covered with wrapping paper. Jennie took the record albums and stacked them in two grocery store cartons (one marked with her initials and the other with mine) and made a big production out of placing Kahlil Gibran's *Prophet* in a felt Crown Royal bag between the clothing in her duffel. We climbed into the back of my mother's Oldsmobile wearing voluminous paper ponchos with sunflowers painted on them (a local artist thought the idea of disposable clothing would catch on) and dangling peace-sign earrings that we bought at a head shop stand on one of our Saturday runs to the flea market. The last thing I saw when we turned down the windy beach road was the mailbox. Flag down. The blue shutters on the house were latched over the windows. My father had hooked the heavy metal chain across the driveway. The house had the trappings of finality except for an obvious sign stuck into the front lawn announcing that the summer was over.

Jennie climbed out of the car at her apartment building on Beekman Place. The doorman, in a braided navy jacket and captain's hat, lifted her arm under her elbow like she was a princess and helped her step over the duffel bags that sat at our feet. He lifted the carton of records marked JB (Jennifer Braddock) from the back of the station wagon and set them down on the sidewalk. Jennie, with her purple granny glasses falling down to the tip of her nose, said she'd call me later, held up two fingers in a V and disappeared into her building. The doorman trailed behind her, juggling the carton of records, the duffel bag still on the sidewalk.

It was very unsettling to be back in my apartment bedroom. My family's apartment was on the seventh floor of an old prewar building on Fifth Avenue. The windows in my bedroom were leaded casements that looked across one side street where an old church stood tranquil, taking up the entire block. The radiator beneath my bedroom window was covered with a ventilated metal casing, the top dotted with drops of colored wax from a night the winter before when Jennie and I left candles there for too long and they melted from the heat. That night, I took the pillow from my bed and laid it flat across the radiator. Not quite the window seat like the one in the Old Greenwich house but it would have to do. The room smelled musty, neglected all summer long. Chalky white dust coated the furniture; a thin layer of soot powdered the windowsill. My clothing sat untouched in my suitcase. The record albums remained in the carton. I looked down at the stained glass windows of the church and longed for the rustling of leaves in the country. Though the stained glass was appropriately Gothic. The beach seemed so far away. I tried to picture Jimmy's face. I took the photograph of us on the beach from the plastic casing in my wallet. I missed him. I missed Jennie. Missing Jimmy was more palatable when Jennie was there with me. I wasn't sure whether Jimmy was still in boot camp. There had been no letters for a few days now. The last one had come three days before we left Old Greenwich.

Jennie and I went back to school the next week. Our school uniforms were pressed and our blazers were dry-cleaned and to look at us, at least from a distance, we seemed like all the other girls standing at the Manhattan bus stop: new red bus passes in clear plastic sleeves, textbooks tied with elastic straps, our hair (longer and sunbleached) pinned back with white grosgrain ribbons, knee socks even on both legs leading down to navy shoes with twisted blue and white laces. But if you looked just a little closer, there was a very thin strip of eyeliner beneath our eyes and a pale, almost white, frosted lipstick covering our mouths. We loosened our hair from the ribbons when school let out, shaking our heads furiously, throwing our heads over and back again. We hid tubes of Yardley Surf Slicker in our pockets, along with buttons that said MAKE LOVE, NOT WAR and books of matches.

Jennie and I started meeting for coffee at The Pilgrim Café on Madison Avenue before school began in the mornings. Over the summer we cultivated a taste for bitter caffeine by drinking cups of Postum, sweetened with four teaspoons of sugar. That September we bought our first pack of cigarettes. Jennie was actually the one who bought them from the machine next to the men's room at Pilgrim's. Tareytons. She said she liked them because the man in the advertisement had a black eye. She said they had a charcoal filter and she acted as though she knew an awful lot about smoking. We lit the first one (with a stainless steel Zippo she swiped from her father's desk) in the vestibule of the church next door to the coffee shop (I think the city has a church on every corner). We choked and spat and giggled and then ran from the ruddy-faced priest who flew down the church aisle, his robes waving behind him. One hand waving away the clouds of blue smoke as he shook the finger on his other hand in the air. It was an outrage, he said. Smoking cigarettes in a house of God.

It was a Friday, about a month after school started, that I came home from school and there was a letter from Jimmy on the Chippendale desk in the hall. It sat beneath the floral Tiffany lamp next to the pile of mail my mother opened for my father with the jade-handled letter opener. My father's mail was in a perfect pile and Jimmy's letter sat off to the side as if perhaps it had been cast there haphazardly. As I opened it, I heard my mother's heels click on the marble floor.

"Is that boy still writing to you? I don't think you should be having much to do with a soldier, Emily. He's a man now, you know," my mother said, nodding her head. "Best to put this all behind you."

My mother. Standing there with her dark hair pulled back from her forehead in a severe bun. Her makeup was so pale and perfect. It hardly looked like she wore makeup at all except for the petal pink color called Posy that outlined her lips. Her nails were perfectly manicured in Revlon's Frosted Blush. Her light tan patent shoes matched the small patent clutch bag she held under her arm. I paid no attention to her. I kept reading the letter, holding it further and further to the side, away from her eyes that strained over my shoulder. What did she know about love? What did she know about men? She and my father slept in separate rooms.

The letter said Jimmy graduated from boot camp. He included a picture, wallet-sized, from the yearbook issue at Parris Island. His hair was cropped close to his head and it looked the way the plastic sculpted hair sat on the head of my old Ken doll. His eyes looked angry and too close together. His military shirt was buttoned up high on his neck and he scrawled "To Emily, I Love You, Jim" on the bottom across the right-hand corner the way you might have gotten an autographed picture from a movie star. It looked like the kind of picture that came with a wallet. Signed Jim, not Jimmy, I noticed. The letter was brief. It didn't say when he'd be home. I looked at the picture and thought, "They have him now." I knew right then and there: He was Corporal James Robert Moran just the way it said underneath the picture and he was gone.

I didn't want to show the picture to anyone, not even to Jennie. I searched the photo for a hint of how he used to look, but there was nothing even remotely familiar behind the eyes that mirrored any sign of former life. He was a soldier. It made me angry to think there was any truth in my mother's words. He was no longer like the boys Jennie and I talked to on the street corners or at the coffee shop. The ones with long hair and desert boots who slumped a little when they talked to us and wore pukka beads around their necks. Jimmy looked angry in his picture. No more tender boy.

"Oh, my," my mother said looking over my shoulder at the photograph. "He certainly does look like a Marine now, doesn't he? I can't tell you what to do. You never listen to me anyway. Be careful, Emily. I warn you, Emily." And as she tapped my shoulder I felt the jab of one of her long frosted fingernails. "Are you listening to me, Emily?"

I nodded my head but I wasn't really paying attention to her. Don't you remember what a sweet boy he is? I thought but didn't say. Don't you remember how he was so bow-legged in those swim jams at the beach last summer? And all I could remember was how he kissed me under her window when she ripped that shade up just as I felt myself melting into his arms.

"He's not really a Marine," I said. "His father made him go."

"Oh, Emily, come off it," my mother said. "He most certainly is. For goodness' sake, just *look* at him."

After the picture came, there were no more letters. I wrote three times to Parris Island and each of my letters came back unopened. "Return to Sender" stamped at least three times on the back and front of the envelope. How could he have just forgotten me?

Then, one day in the middle of October I saw him. He was standing, leaning really, against my apartment building. He wore greenish pants and a dark button-down shirt under a brown leather jacket. I barely recognized him at first. He was smoking a Lucky Strike and standing with his back really straight and his head down.

"Emily!" he said as I stopped in front of him. He took my arms just around the elbows (I was carrying my schoolbooks) and leaned down to kiss me. I turned my head because I wasn't sure what was happening. It wasn't supposed to happen this way. It wasn't supposed to be like this. I stared at him. But for a second I saw that look in his eye, the look where his eyes seemed to light up as if he was going to start to laugh or break out into a smile, and then his eyes just clouded over.

"What's wrong?" he said, his face deadpan as though someone had just given him bad news. His mouth was frozen.

I didn't answer him right away. I just stood there and looked at him. He didn't look at all like the boy who left me in July at the train station. His skin was rough and tanned and his neck was so broad and reddened at the nape. His hands were flat and wide and he wore black shoes with lace ties. He said I looked like I had seen a ghost.

I wondered what happened to the boy with the silky long black hair who sang "My Girl" with the band, strutting like Jagger and pointing his finger at me standing in the front row. The boy who wore jeans and a T-shirt.

"Jimmy! Oh, God," I said. "Well, look at you."

And he said that wasn't quite the reaction he expected. He took my books and placed them on the ground next to us. He put his arm around my waist and drew me next to him.

I brushed my hand over the top of his head, a sudden urge to feel the spiked hair, and he pulled away from me. He reached over and tugged at my peace sign earrings.

"You pierced your ears," he said and then with a sudden change in mood, "And now you've got this garbage hanging in them."

Garbage? I thought but said nothing. My mother's words haunted me. It wasn't that he was a man so much as he was a soldier. How could the boy I waited

for all summer long come home and look like this? Act
like this? What did they do to him? I thought.

He told me they sent him from Parris Island to
Camp LeJeune in North Carolina. He wrote the last letters to the house in Old Greenwich. I didn't realize
you'd already gone back to Manhattan, he said. I'm
sorry that you never got them. He told me he was
shipping out in two weeks. They were sending him to
Camp Pendleton in California, he said, and then a few
months later they would ship him overseas. Da Nang,
he said. Something like that. And then he said the only
thing he wanted to do before he left was make love to
me. I shook my head back and forth.

"I can't," I said. "I'm not ready for that."

But that was a lie. I was plenty ready for that but not
with someone who was a soldier like Jimmy Moran. I
had thought about making love to Jimmy all summer.
How his slender body would feel next to mine. How
his long black hair would fall over his face when he
strained on top of me. I started to talk to Jennie about it
one night but she got very clinical. Jennie told me she
saw a boy buying rubbers once in Pearl's Pharmacy
and then she said how it was really important to hold
them up to the light to make sure there were no little
pinholes or else you could get pregnant. I told her I
didn't want to talk about it anymore. It seemed too personal to me since I was really in love with Jimmy. For
Jennie, it was just another threshold. Promise me if you
do it first, you'll call me right away, she said, giggling.

But how could I make love with somebody who
called my earrings garbage and stood so straight with
his back against a wall? Suddenly his letters seemed
like forgeries. I thought of all the soldiers in those war
movies who went on liberties and danced with south-

ern girls in little redneck towns and towns in Italy. For the first time, I wondered if, maybe, when he was in South Carolina there had been a girl in a bar somewhere that he had taken to bed. And so being sixteen and not knowing how to just explain, I told him there was someone else. This is what girls did back then. There always had to be someone else. Break up with one because your heart was taken by another. As if that wouldn't hurt his feelings. In my sixteen-year-old mind I thought he could handle it better if I said there was someone else, rather than tell him it was because he wasn't the boy I used to know. Maybe it was my mother's words that rang in my ears. I could picture her face, her Posy-lips mouthing in slow motion, "Be careful, Emily."

So I told him that while he was away I ran into a boy from his school and lost my virginity and only wrote those letters to him because I wanted to get him through boot camp. And I saw my mother smile, pictured her head slowly nod up and down in approval.

Jimmy got pale, gray-green, as though the blood left his face. I remember thinking that he looked the way my grandmother looked once right before she fainted. Then his face reddened and he lit another Lucky Strike, cupping his shaking hands so closely around the match I was surprised it didn't burn his palm. He tossed the match down on the sidewalk and jammed the pack of Lucky's back into his jacket pocket. He threw his head against the building so hard (I think he forgot where he was standing) I wondered why it wasn't bleeding. I raised my hand to his head and he pushed it away. He asked me how I could have done that and I just shrugged, turned my head away from him, and told him he'd been away for an awfully long time.

"This isn't like you, Emily," he said. "Why is it that part of me doesn't believe you?"

"I have to go now," I said. "I have homework and my boyfriend's going to call."

"I don't get it, Emily," he said. "I can't believe you're doing this. What's gotten into you, Emily? Who is he?"

He held my arm above the wrist, so tightly that my fingers were throbbing. He told me again that he was leaving soon and didn't know if he'd ever come back. He said they were going to teach him about maintaining airplanes and helicopters he called Hueys and that he was a corporal. He said he got his high school diploma and that it was really important to fight for his country and then something about getting the gooks. Then he dropped his hand from my wrist, realizing perhaps that his grip was too tight, and fingered the peace signs on my ears again. And I was so afraid he'd yank them off.

I said that he should call his parents and have them call the Marine Corps and tell them it was all a big mistake.

"Your dad has clout," I said, almost pleading. "He has connections. Come back to school. Go to college. We can still be friends."

Jimmy just shook his head. He dropped his hand from my earrings and clasped it across his other arm. He looked into my eyes and all the while he was shaking his head slowly back and forth and then he laughed. Not a real laugh as if something was funny but one that caught in his throat and never quite came out. He took my face in his hands and then he ran the back of one hand down the side of my cheek the way he had that summer. His hands felt rough against my skin.

"Hudson, you just don't get it, do you?" he said. And as I started to say something—and I'm not sure to this day what it might have been—he just walked away. I wanted to go after him and tell him that none of it was true. There was nobody else. I wanted to tell him how there wasn't a moment that summer that I didn't wonder how he was and what he was doing.

I wanted to tell him it was only that he scared me a little now and maybe even tell him what my mother had said and have him tell me she was wrong. I wanted to tell him how he was still the first thing I thought of in the morning and the last thing at night. I wanted to tell him how his letters were tied with a red ribbon in a shoe box covered with wrapping paper under my bed and how all summer long I wanted him to gather me up in his arms and promise me forever. But I didn't. I watched him walk down the street and I stood frozen. I watched him turn the corner, his back straight. He never glanced back, not even for a moment. And he was gone.

I called Jennie when I got upstairs and I was crying. Jennie didn't have much to say. She really didn't comfort me at all. She said I did the right thing because Jimmy probably had some venereal disease and how people change and all that. Jennie said he probably had been brainwashed by the government and that once he got to Vietnam he'd be shooting up villages with women and children and that I really had to just forget him. And though I really wanted to believe that there was an ounce of truth to what she told me, all I could see was Jimmy walking down the street by himself.

Jennie didn't understand at all. How could she turn on him so quickly? But then, how could I? I couldn't get the image out of my mind. The way he shook his head at me and called me "Hudson" instead of Emmie, the way they probably had called him Moran for the last four months and how no one ever called him Jimmy or knew that he could sing like Elvis Presley or strut like Mick Jagger.

I sat by the phone all night that night but he never called. There were several times I began to dial the number at his parents' house and then just before I got to the seventh number, I'd hang up because I didn't know what I wanted to say. I only knew I was still in love with him. Soldier and all.

I took the shoe box out from under the bed and untied the ribbon. And I remember as though it was yesterday how one tear fell in a puddle, washing away the ink on an envelope. I took the ring he gave me with JRM initialed in gold and peeled off the Band-Aid on the back that made it fit my finger. I slipped it on and saw that his hands were probably always as big as they looked to me a few hours earlier. I looked at the photographs. Then I put the box and the pictures and the ring away (funny that he never asked to have it back) and decided I should no longer think about Corporal James Moran.

But I never did stop. Whenever they showed pictures on the news of the killing fields and the helicopters landing in the black-and-white jungles, I searched the television screen hoping I might see his face camouflaged under one of the helmets. When they showed the planes unloading the coffins draped over with flags, I wondered how I could have let him go without telling him the truth.

The morning after Jimmy walked away, my mother brought in my white blouse with the Peter Pan collar hanging on a wire hanger and my navy blazer with a

new school crest sewn on the pocket. The blouse was
starched and the buttons looked like pearls and I remember thinking it looked so prissy and there I was
just another spoiled little private school girl. I hesitated
when I put the black liner under my eyes. That crap on
your eyes, I kept hearing him say. All I could see was
Jimmy and the way he held my face between his hands.
I could still feel the back of his hand against my cheek.

I hardly ate breakfast that morning. My mother
asked, watching me pick at my toast, if I'd heard from
"that Moran boy." To this day, I think the doorman
squealed on me. I said it was doubtful I would hear
from him again. She let go a little smile on her lips and
said something about it being for the best.

I went to brush my hair. She followed me to my
room. She stood and watched me, talking to my image
in the mirror. She went on and on again about how it
wasn't good for girls like me to be involved with men
in the military and how it was best for me not to asso-
ciate with his kind.

"What kind is that?" I asked provocatively and
slammed my hairbrush down on the dresser.

"Behave yourself, Emily," my mother said sternly.
And then she said (again) that Jimmy was a man and I
was a girl and it was all over again the same old story
she said the day before. My mother said that boys like
Jimmy Moran would probably tell you that they loved
you and not mean it and wanted one thing and one
thing only. And then she said something about getting
milk for free and buying the cow and her voice was
just a drone in the background.

The last letter Jimmy wrote came a few days later. It
said he would be home soon and wouldn't I be a sight
for his sore eyes. And then he quoted a line from the

song "My Girl," saying I was his sunshine on a cloudy day. I never showed the letter to Jennie. I just put it in the shoe box with the others. I kept all of Jimmy's letters and the photographs until I married Peter. Then I threw them away. I guess I figured life was beginning again. But I kept the ring. It still sits on the bottom of my jewelry box, wrapped in tissue, still sticky from the adhesive where I took off the Band-Aid.

I don't like to think about that October day. I prefer to remember, instead, his letters from the summer and the months before the train station. Every day for a month or so after that October day I looked over my shoulder as I walked down Madison Avenue to school. No one was there.

# 10

There is an old black trunk in our attic with three brass clasps hanging across the front. It once had a key, a long time ago. But for the last decade or so, it has sat unlocked though untouched. Mary read Clancy a book once about kids who go through Grandma's trunk in the attic and pull out old clothes and flowered straw hats. Clancy always wants to look through the trunk with her friends but I've told her no, so sternly that she stopped asking. She flinched when I was so uncharacteristically severe with her so I explained that this was not that kind of trunk. It's filled with papers, I told her. Nothing that would be any fun for you at all.

The trunk is left over from my first summer at sleep-away camp. I was eight years old. Daphne was home that summer. And even though I went off like a big shot with sleeping bag, new slicker, flashlight, Hostess Twinkies and a Brownie camera, all I wanted was to stay with Daphne in the Mamaroneck house. I wet my bed almost every night that summer. Lucky for me, the counselor was a real cool guy and never told the other kids in the bunk. Seems to me, from the time I can remember, my folks were sending me away. My father was always making a man out of me.

When I got back from Vietnam in the spring of 1970, I put all the memories I had in the trunk. There are old photographs and old letters though none of the letters from Emily. I didn't tell her, but I threw her letters away as well the day I came back from Vietnam. A few days after Emily and I spoke, I went through the trunk. I saw my release papers, old photographs with my dad, one with Emily on the beach, Emily in the yellow bikini, blue ribbons earned at summer camp for tennis, a picture of Daphne and me on a first day at school. The stuff that at one time dreams were made of.

Remembering those months with Emily unraveled cords of history tangled up in knots inside me. I had avoided looking back for, God, so many years. Emily's reappearance in my life forced a journey that made me feel alternately amazed that I was still here and profoundly aware of the fact that my life did not turn out the way my parents thought it would the day they picked me up at St. Vincent's Hospital, the infant son of a teenage girl whose family did not want a bastard child.

There were nights when I lay awake, Mary beside me and, some nights, Clancy between us, when I felt a pounding in my head. I had resisted the urge to think about Vietnam for so many years. Even Mary, Mary knew very little about me in Vietnam. But Mary thought I was a hero. Still does. Mary never asked to see any medals or ribbons, which is really a good thing, since I don't have any. But Mary thinks my wounds, although they're not of the flesh, are still there. Still, she never asked a question. She's seen my face grow white and my neck break out in a sweat when the tornado sirens go off in the middle of the summer nights down here in Mobile. I've always hated that sound. It penetrates me. I feel it in my stomach the way I did when I watched the St. Patrick's Day parade as a kid. I'd stand behind the police barricades on Fifth Avenue with my grandma. When the drum majorettes marched by I could feel the drums thumping so deep in my gut that I'd place my hand over my stomach to stop the vibration. But the sirens here in Mobile put fear into my soul. Their whirring and screaming remind me of the air raids in Nam when someone would cry out, "Incoming." The sirens here in Mobile make me wonder how much fear I managed to mask when I was in Vietnam.

When I first got to Chou Lai and we'd hear the sirens, we'd run into our foxholes, helmets on our heads, ducking down the way the stewardess tells you when she gives that little speech on the plane. But after a while we stopped running for cover over there. We were too stoned to care and too accustomed to the raids. And even when Mary saw me pale and sweaty and heard me breathe real hard, she never asked a question. She never said anything like, Why are you looking like that, Jimmy? You know it's only tornadoes. Or, Here let me fix you a drink and we'll sit together down in the cellar with Clancy. I think at one time, in the very beginning, she must have said things like that. I'm not sure if she stopped or if I stopped her. Maybe it was because there came a time when she would place her arm around me for comfort and I simply didn't want her to be there. I'd get up and push her away. A therapist once asked me why it bothered me

when people got too close to me. I never answered her.
I canceled my next appointment and never went back.

But there was Emily on the phone asking me a million questions like she really cared. Like the answers
really mattered. Or maybe she didn't care. Maybe I
was right when I said I was just her guinea pig.
Though she was careful never to delve into Vietnam
even when I told her about the tornado sirens. I wasn't
sure about anything. My moods became so labile.
There were more gray areas than usual. I longed to feel
a sense of complacency and comfort in the gray. I shut-
tled between the past and the present. I was so uncertain.

I knew Mary would come home that first night after
Emily called and fling her parka on the couch and run
over and scoop Clancy up in her arms. Then she'd
walk over to the stove and lift the cover off the pot of
risotto and take a big sniff and tell me, "It smells real
fine, Jimmy," in that small southern accent of hers that
I used to love so much and suddenly every time I hear
it, my skin crawls. I knew she'd walk over to say hello
to me and I'd hold her at arm's length and kiss her on
the cheek. I'd see that look on her face. The way her
dry lips kind of shut real tight and her eyes blink and
I know she wants an answer but I just can't give her
one. I couldn't give her one because I didn't have any
answers. My life has become grotesquely predictable.
The odd thing was, there was a time in Chou Lai when
I prayed that tomorrow would be the same as today,
praying I would simply get through, come out alive.

When Emily asked me to describe my wife I said she
was beautiful. Mary was beautiful once. I remember
when I met her. She worked as a waitress at the drive-
in. I used to go there for a burger after work just so I

could see her. I couldn't get enough of her in that short checkered skirt and that tight white T-shirt. She looked like a cheerleader. Her thick dark hair. Blue eyes. Moist lips. She was nineteen. I don't know when I stopped feeling the way I was supposed to feel. One day I looked at her and then I looked at myself. We weren't where we were supposed to be anymore.

I look at Mary sometimes and I don't know how we ended up together, let alone in Mobile. I don't know how life got to be the way it is. I don't know when Mary stopped being the way she was. I'll be outside in the yard, washing down the deck and firing up the barbecue, and Mary will come outside in these khaki Bermuda shorts she wears on the weekend and that burnished orange tee with the Tilex stains all over it and those big old brown shoes with the backs flattened down and broken. Sometimes she has these little rough-looking cuts on the back of her ankles and for some reason, I don't know why, it makes me sick to the pit in my stomach. Maybe it's because she doesn't look like my mom used to look all done up in sheer stockings and a straight narrow skirt that zipped up the side. Or maybe it was, since I'd spoken to Emily, that Mary didn't look the way I pictured Emily. I pictured Emily fresh-faced and elegant, puttering in the garden of her big old house in New England. I thought for sure she didn't have any scrapes on her ankles from some gnarly razor that was sitting too long on the tub in the bathroom. Suddenly I was angry that I ended up in a little cedar house in Mobile. Maybe it wasn't even Mary. Maybe it was me I couldn't stand looking at anymore.

I thought my memory was more blurred than it apparently was. But I remembered seeing Emily so clearly that last time. I remembered that day when I walked away and then the next thing I knew I went to Memphis, Millington Naval Base or something like that. I went to Memphis, all right, but all I did once I was there was get stoned. I guess it all started that day when I walked away from Emily and bought that joint by the subway. Oh, I had smoked pot before but it was different. And I never smoked pot around Emily. I never drank around Emily. When she wasn't around I sat with the guys in my class in someone's apartment and we'd pass around a joint. The Doors or Hendrix were always playing in the background. It was unbelievable what we did back then. There we were, sons of the upper middle class. Apartments on Park and Fifth and town houses in Greenwich Village. Boys sitting around in faded bell-bottom jeans while our folks were at their place in the Hamptons or Europe. Our dads were flying around the country on the company jet with our mothers or their second wives or their girlfriends and we were drinking Tango wine and hoping the maid wouldn't rat us out on Monday morning.

Buying the joint when I walked away from Emily was different. This was me buying a joint from a Puerto Rican guy who pulled it out of his pocket and shifted his eyes back and forth while he handed it to me. And I was all alone.

I didn't leave for Memphis right away. I stayed in the city for the next three weeks or so. One day, I went back to my old school. When I left for boot camp I weighed about one hundred and fifty pounds and when I came back I was one hundred and seventy. All muscle. I went to my school and asked the football coach if I could work out with the varsity team. One of the guys was out that day so the coach gave me his uniform and said, "Go suit up, Jimmy" and I felt so good that he didn't call me Moran. Or Weasel. I changed in the locker room and the guys came over and slapped me on the back and said things like "You're looking good, Jimmy" but I remember thinking that they looked at me like I was a freak. They peeled off their desert boots and their sneakers and I untied those big leather shoes that I'd taken from my dad. I felt like a loser. Looking good, Jimmy. That was a lot of crap. But I got out on that field and I kicked butt. I mean, I left that school like a scrawny little kid and I came back a Marine. I was vicious, man. I tackled real hard.

Not one of them asked me about Emily Hudson. I looked at their faces and wondered which one of them was sleeping with her and I thought about that every time one of them tackled me while we were playing football. They were the cream-of-the-crop New York boys and there I was the one out of all of them who was a total fuck-up and ended up in the Marines at the height of a conflict. They were all trying to get out of Vietnam and there I was going into it. The strange thing was, even to me, it didn't seem like a real war. And to them, it was only a black armband or a button they wore on the lapel of their blazer.

I had no idea of what I was getting myself into being in the Marine Corps. I don't think anyone ever realizes how competitive and physical and mental boot camp is. You don't know until you're there and then you get so damn lonely. And the worst thing is, even though you miss everyone like crazy, you never have time to be yourself and let yourself feel how much you miss them. I hardened so fast. And I got so cold. That's how they want you. They want you cold and hard and mean so a bullet doesn't faze you. When I saw Emily that last time I wasn't myself. It was like I felt I deserved everything and anything from her that day because tomorrow I could die.

I lived on the base in Memphis with thousands of guys for about six months. I was there when Martin Luther King was killed. We were put on alert for a few weeks after his assassination but they called the National Guard in instead. Still, I remember feeling like everyone around me was dying and maybe I was the next to go. But my most powerful memory of Memphis was this freak snowstorm we had down there in March. A couple of days before the snow hit, I had flown up to New York City to get some opiated weed that a friend of my buddy Potter's was holding for us. I met a "contact" in a rooming hotel near Port Authority and headed back to the airport and flew home. I didn't even go to see my folks. You know, the service gave you weekends off and my parents sent me money from time to time. But really all I had to do was put on my blues and walk up to the ticket counter at the airport. Military. I was military and I practically flew for free. What did they call it? Free birds. I was a free bird.

I made it back to Memphis right before the storm. It was a Sunday morning in Memphis when the storm hit hard. Potter and I sat in this cluster of magnolia trees a few hundred feet from the barracks and smoked that weed. It was so weird to see those big, green-leaved magnolia trees and watch the giant snowflakes falling around them. We felt so isolated. I mean, we were only a few hundred feet from the barracks but we felt like we were hundreds of miles away. I felt like we were the only people in the world who knew anything about anything. Potter asked me about Emily and I said something about that "hog" and Potter and I threw our heads back and laughed real hard. I remember thinking I was glad the snow was falling so fast in my eyes because if Potter had looked closely enough he would have seen that my eyes were welled up with tears.

Six months later, a bunch of us were shipped out to California. Some of the guys flew, but I drove out there with a guy named Quinn from Tupelo, Mississippi, Potter and the guy who owned the car whose name I can't remember. He was from somewhere in Arkansas. We stopped in a Las Vegas whorehouse on the way out to California. It all seemed so surreal. Barely a year before, I would have been with Emily at St. Bart's. I would have gone to her apartment to pick her up and she'd smell like lemons and sweet egg shampoo and be wearing a real short skirt and a poor-boy top. Her dad would shake my hand and look me up and down and then Emily would come out of her room and we'd head for the door before her dad could say anything that might embarrass her (Run out of material for that skirt, Emily? Where's the rest of it?) and her mother would be shaking her head (Emily, dear, don't forget curfew). And then, when we'd get outside the building, I'd kiss her as soon as the doorman shut the door behind us. We'd walk down Fifth Avenue holding hands until we saw a bus rolling in and then we'd run for the bus and I'd put two tokens in the till like I was a real big spender and Emily would flop down in the green plastic seat, fish her lip gloss out of her slouch bag and sneak a peak at her face in the mirror. One time I stuck my face in the mirror next to hers. Every time you ever look at you, Emily Hudson, you're going to see me, I said. And then I kissed the gloss right off her lips. Everyone on the bus was staring.

So there I was in this Vegas whorehouse with these women wearing black net stockings and garters and lipstick that was outlined in red and painted on so thick it looked like you could peel it right off. Ten dollars and I got laid for an hour and I was such a geek that all I could think about was Emily and that guy whose name she wouldn't tell me. Quinn couldn't get into the whorehouse. Quinn was a black guy. They didn't allow blacks in the whorehouse. He was good enough for Vietnam but not good enough for the whores in Vegas.

It was like that all the time when I was a Marine: one-night stands with strangers and I usually had to pay for it. We had about two weeks in California at Camp Pendleton before they shipped us to Vietnam. On the nights we had liberty, a few guys would take a motel room in town and buy a few six-packs of beer. Sometimes a few whores came in but mostly we'd sit in that room until it was dawn talking about women and what we would do with them if we had them. We rarely made it out of the room. We just stayed in the room all night talking about it. Come morning, when I felt like my stomach was ripped out of my body and the room smelled like vomit and urine and sweat, I looked at those guys around me from the woods. Except for Potter (he was from Boston) they were mostly from small towns in the South and Southwest. And I wondered how the hell a city kid like me from New York, whose friends were still wearing flannel pants and navy blazers or were in some college up in Connecticut or Boston, ended up in that sleazy hotel room in California waiting to ship out to Vietnam and get his fucking legs blown off.

From the moment I got to boot camp, I had wanted

to go home but, now, on my way to Vietnam I felt even more desperate. Antiwar demonstrators had marched on the Pentagon. It was a joke. They were carrying signs: HELL NO, WE WON'T GO, and I was about to get my ass blown away. And Emily was probably peeling off some guy's gray flannel slacks, hiking up that plaid skirt.

After the whorehouse in Vegas, we got back in that car headed to California and flipped on the radio. And like I was in some fucking movie there was that song, "Nowhere to Run." And all I wanted was to be back at those dances with Emily where we danced so close and so still that we were hardly moving at all. When the music would stop we'd still be standing there feeling like the room was moving in a circle. But instead, I was on my way to the last stop before Vietnam. And there I was sitting in a rusty old car that belonged to some guy that I hadn't laid eyes on until a month ago cruising to California. And it seemed to me, as we drove to the coast, that I was driving farther and farther away from life as I knew it. And I knew I would never know life that way again.

# 11

It wasn't long after that day in October when I saw Jimmy for the last time that there were antiwar demonstrations all over the country. Suddenly the black armband under my jacket seemed far more stereotypical. Fifty thousand people had stormed the Pentagon and riots broke out in Chicago and Philadelphia and Los Angeles. Cassius Clay changed his name to Muhammed Ali and refused to enter the military. The border between New York and Canada was tighter than a drum. New words entered my vocabulary. Conscientious objector. Hawk. Dove. Draft dodger. Flower child. Hippie.

That October, Jennie and I would take the subway down to Columbus Circle where a guy with a pushcart sold us bouquets of pink carnations. We'd hand them out to people who looked "over thirty" and wore suits. We said the word "peace" and grinned these bright smiles, holding up two fingers in a peace sign like we were lost souls from Haight-Ashbury instead of schoolgirls from Manhattan. Every so often an older

woman or a man in a business suit would hold two
fingers up as well, say peace, and we would laugh and
feel as though we gained another convert to our cause.

In the spring, we met our friends at Bethesda Fountain in Central Park. Jennie and I carried rough burlap
slouch bags, embroidered in coarse purple and red
yarns, over our shoulders. Into the bags, along with
the requisite cake of Maybelline mascara, a stick of
cover-up and yellow boxes of Chiclets, went our Dr.
Scholl's sandals, which we removed from our feet
when we hit the perimeter of the fountain. My mother
would tell us that we'd get a disease (a name that even
she pronounced with difficulty, saying she wasn't sure
if that's what it was called but it was dreadful) from pi-
geon droppings and to put our shoes back on. How
she knew we took off our sandals was beyond me, but
she knew. She also said we'd look like dirty hippies,
"dirty" an adjective that always preceded the word
hippie but was better than my father's sobriquet.
"This is my daughter, Emily," he would say, apologet-
ically, as he introduced me at a dinner party. "She
thinks she's a beatnik."

The air was sweetened around the fountain with
heavy smoke from handheld pipes, bongs (for the
more courageous) and joints. There was always an am-
bulance rolling in to pick up someone who was either
too high or so strung out on acid that they ended up
convulsing on the ground. Sometimes you could hear
the quick deep pounding of a bongo. Someone always
played an acoustic guitar, the case opened, asking for
donations. You could always hear the jingle of a tam-
bourine. Jennie and I would sit under a tree, now past
the days of origami fortunes and, instead, braided
each other's hair and strung bead necklaces. At the

end of the day, Jennie and I would rinse our filthy feet
in the fountain and put our sandals back on and head
to our homes for dinner. We led a double life. Hippies
by day. Dinner served with cloth napkins and full table
settings at night.

It was around this time that my cousin Mike was a
freshman at Columbia University. His roommate,
Barry, was a big lopey guy from Brooklyn, the son of a
Jewish dentist who loved to wax on about his affilia-
tion with the Communist Party and the scourge of Mc-
Carthyism. Barry, with his father's full sanction, was
an active member of the Students for a Democratic So-
ciety and had nothing but contempt for any guy who
went willingly to Vietnam. I went out with Barry
though, at the insistence of my cousin. He was big and
hulking and when he threw his arm around my shoulders the way Jimmy used to, it felt like a lead weight
on my back.

Barry and I went to The West End Café up by Columbia and The Band was playing on the jukebox.
Barry ordered a bottle of Mateus. I'd never been with
anyone who ordered a bottle of wine before. He took a
pack of Winstons out of his pocket and turned the pack
toward me. I took one and lit the filter and got all flustered when he laughed as the cigarette flamed up in
my face. Jimmy wouldn't have laughed at me. And if
he had laughed, it wouldn't have been a mean, sarcastic laugh like Barry's. I didn't like Barry. He told me
about his friends who beat the draft by going to
Canada and he went on and on about the guys who
were in Vietnam shooting up villages. And when I told
him I used to know a boy who might have gone to
Vietnam, Barry shook his head and asked how anyone
in their right mind could agree to go there. It wasn't

possible to explain about Jimmy and his father and how it all came about and how he looked so lost that day at the train station. I just looked at Barry and let him ramble on and on. I didn't see Barry again after that. There were so many guys like Barry. Holier than Jimmy. Maybe they were also just afraid.

Jennie met a guy named Shade by Bethesda Fountain. He came over to us while we sat under the tree stringing beads and Jennie handed him a necklace. Love beads for you, she said with her most winning smile. Shade wore black bell-bottomed jeans and a silky black shirt edged with embroidery. His hair was stringy and greasy and hung down around his face. He wore a peace sign around his neck on a worn leather braid. He was a lot older than we were. Twenty, maybe, and he said he had his own apartment in the Bronx. He said he worked in the record business and knew Laura Nyro and Janis Joplin. I thought he was a liar and I told Jennie so. But Jennie left me one day at the subway at Columbus Circle and went to the Grand Concourse with Shade. That was the end of Jennie. Well, it wasn't the end in the sense that Jennie never came back. She came back and told me how she spent the day in Shade's bed wrapped in nothing but a shiny velveteen shawl with long black fringes that Shade draped over her shoulders after she got naked. Jennie finally crossed the threshold, delighted that she had lost her virginity before I did. She told me how Shade burned little cone-shaped pieces of incense on the nightstand and they passed a pipe between them in his bed.

According to Jennie, Shade's mother came home in the middle of everything. Apparently he didn't really live alone. His mother opened Shade's bedroom door, just a crack, peeked her silver-haired head through the door and asked them if they wanted some soup. Honest, Jennie said, that really happened. Shade's mother was a tiny little woman with frizzy gray hair, Jennie said, wearing a red pinafore with pockets in the front. She'd asked them if they wanted some minestrone.

Jennie and I were sitting on the floor in my bedroom when she told me this story. Actually I was sitting crossed-legged on the floor and she was lying on the bed with her elbow propping herself up on one side. Our hair had gotten so long it was hanging below our waists. Lying there like that I remember thinking Jennie looked like Lady Godiva. While Jennie was talking, I was filing a nail, back and forth nervously until it was practically worn down. I couldn't look her in the eye. Jennie was saying things about Nirvana and suddenly sat up in a lotus position with her thumb and index finger lightly touched together on each hand. She told me how Shade taught her to breathe om. She inhaled deeply, pressing her lips together in an "O" that made her look like a Kewpie doll. She breathed in the vowel until she was breathless. Then Jennie pulled a crushed joint out of her slouch bag. Jefferson Airplane played "White Rabbit" in the background. A poster hung over my bed: Two hands grasping a bouquet of pastel flowers, scrawled with crayonlike printing, MAKE LOVE, NOT WAR.

"Put the joint away, Jennie. My mom's home," I said.

She slid it back into her wallet. "Do you ever hear from Moran the Marine?" she asked, picking up my photo album from the shelf and stopping at the page where the picture showed the two of us on the rocks at Tod's Point.

"Not since that day in October," I said, purposely avoiding the photograph. "Come on, Jennie. Put the album away. I don't want to look at that now."

"He's probably toting his rifle right now. An M16," she said knowingly, placing the album back on the shelf. "Shooting the innocents. Moran the Moron."

"That's really a rotten thing to say, Jennie," I said, swallowing hard, resisting the urge to tell her that maybe it was time she went home. All I could think was how Jimmy was the innocent and guys like Shade who lived with their mothers who brought them soup while they were in bed with a strange girl, any girl for that matter, well, that was just about the sickest thing I'd ever heard.

"What's Shade's real name?" I asked Jennie.

She threw her head back and squealed, "George Terrakis. But he's about to have it legally changed to Shade."

Jimmy had walked away and now Jennie was slipping away from me as well. When I asked if she wanted her Rod McKuen book back, she laughed and said she was more into Ginsberg and Ferlinghetti and told me to keep it.

"McKuen's a little sophomoric, don't you think?" Jennie said, hesitating before she used the word sophomoric.

I felt like I'd lost my two best friends. I wondered who would come with me to the fountain, the Pilgrim's in the mornings, the dances at St. Bart's. Jennie didn't like the dances at St. Bart's anymore. She said they were queer.

Jimmy and I used to go to Bethesda Fountain the spring before he left for boot camp. Actually, that was where we met. I was walking past the fountain one day with Jennie and some other friends and he shot a paper clip at my rear end. That's Jimmy Moran, the other girls said knowingly. Just keep walking. But I didn't. He's going to Vietnam, they said, slurring the word *Vietnam* in a whisper as though it was obscene.

I picked the paper clip off the ground. "I'm Emily Hudson. Does this belong to you, Jimmy Moran?" I said, walking over and placing the clip in his hand. "By the way, it hurt."

"Want to take a walk with me, Emily Hudson?" he said.

And to the shock of my friends (except for Jennie) and the amazement of his, we walked away together and sat on the edge of the fountain and talked until it was well after six o'clock. Past dinnertime. He walked me home and held my hand and from that day on he met me after school every day and carried my books just like in those Sandra Dee movies. He never mentioned the Marines until one day when we sat at the fountain, he told me. I pretended that I hadn't known. I didn't want him to know that people talked behind his back. I asked him if he thought he'd go to Vietnam. He said he didn't want to think about it. He said he didn't know. Let's not talk about that, he said, his eyes looking straight ahead.

It didn't strike me until recently that Jimmy didn't spend the last few days before boot camp with his parents. It occurred to me that Jimmy never took me to his house. I never met his parents or Daphne. I'd heard from people that his sister was pretty, red-haired and slinky, and that his dad looked like a movie star and his mother reminded people of Ava Gardner. I never asked him why I couldn't meet them though. There was a sense I had that Jimmy thought maybe they'd dissuade me from loving him or that somehow they'd embarrass him. It was only just the other day that he confessed: He never knew whether or not his parents would be drunk. He was ashamed to take me home.

I knew that Jimmy smoked pot when we went to the fountain. Sometimes he'd go behind the boathouse with Chris and Steve and he'd come back with his eyes a little red-rimmed. And he knew I knew. He just didn't want me to do anything I didn't want to do. Whenever anyone teased me and said I should just take one toke he'd tell them to leave me alone and they backed off quickly, murmuring how they were just joking. No one knew quite what to make of Jimmy and I knew that. He intimidated even the boys like Chris and Steve who professed to be his friends.

There were so many stories about Jimmy. Mostly I heard that he was a big drinker. Some girls said that after he'd leave me off at my parents' door at midnight he'd be out at Finn's slugging back drink after drink. Finn's. They served kids who were underage since the owner's father was a judge and no one was going to bother him. They said Jimmy got into fights at Finn's and dropped acid in the men's room. The same girls who told me the stories (they said they'd heard them from the older boys on the football team) all looked at me sideways when Jimmy met me after school. I never saw the bad side of Jimmy. I loved the way he looked. He was tall and lean. His cheekbones swallowed up his eyes. When he smiled at me his eyes got this funny look to them, almost as though he was puzzled by what he saw and couldn't believe what he was seeing. And his eyes almost disappeared. Sometimes he'd take his hand and brush the back of it down the side of my cheek very slowly and push my hair behind my

ear. And then he'd breathe in deeply and just stare
straight ahead of him and then he would say, "I love
you very much, Emily Hudson" and I would tell him
that I loved him, too, and then he'd kiss me and kiss
me again and we'd stay wherever we were for hours.

Sometimes we'd talk about when he came home
from boot camp but both of us knew he'd be going
away again after that so we didn't speak of it too
often. Even at the time, I thought it was unfair to be
so young and yet to feel so uncertain about the future when everyone else was at least so sure that
their futures would exist. It was an odd thing to realize the possibility of death when the other kids felt
so immortal.

It was as though there was no one else in the world
when I was with Jimmy. It was probably the first and
last time that I felt completely safe, though we were
plagued by demons of a war that until that point we'd
only watched on television. It was, I had hoped, not
prescient that one time we walked by the East River,
on a footpath that was lined with yellow globe lights.

The moon was hanging like a giant copper penny in
the sky strangely juxtaposed to the neon Pepsi sign di-
agonally across the river. I heard footsteps behind me.
Jimmy's hand was on my shoulder at the time, slipping down to my waist when the footsteps came. He
was, I think, just about to kiss me again when I turned
around and saw the tall, thin man. He wore a dark ski
cap even though the night was hot. He grabbed me by
both arms. Two other stocky fellows came behind the
man in the cap and one held Jimmy, twisting his arms
behind his back the way police cuff a criminal, while
the other propelled his fist into Jimmy's groin. The one
who held Jimmy's arms let go and grabbed Jimmy's

long black hair instead, pulling his head back so his face looked almost grotesque. Then he grabbed his arms again, tighter this time, while the other continued to punch him from his stomach up to his nose until his nose was bleeding and his mouth spat blood that dripped onto his shirt. Jimmy's voice descended into what came out as grunts until I thought he lost consciousness. His voice became guttural and gagging as he whispered, "Run, Emmie."

I couldn't run because I was being held. Not that I would have left him. Let me go. Take my wallet. It's in my purse. Let me get it. I screamed. Please, please stop kicking him. And for some reason, I think because the muggers heard footsteps (a couple walked by a few moments later, arm in arm), they just ran off with my wallet. When the couple, our unwitting saviors, came by and saw Jimmy lying on the ground, they ran. Fear colored their faces. They ignored my pleas for help.

Jimmy and I managed to get ourselves off that river path. By then my jacket was bloody from Jimmy's nose and mouth since he was leaning on my shoulder. We walked over to Finn's and the bartender handed me a pile of cocktail napkins and some ice cubes in a rag and told me to get him out of there. I guess Finn's didn't want any more trouble than they already had. Jimmy waited for me, sitting on the curb. I put the wad of paper napkins and ice on Jimmy's mouth and he winced. Jimmy and I walked to my parents' apartment. He was leaning on my shoulder, sinking every now and then. We'd stop so he could right himself. People crossed the streets when they saw us coming and then turned back to look at us, quickening their pace, hands cupped over their mouths, whispering. The doorman at my parents' building wouldn't even let us upstairs until he announced our arrival on the house phone.

I washed Jimmy's face in my parents' kitchen and put fresh ice wrapped in a cloth dish towel on his nose and his mouth. He fell asleep that night for a while in the living room. I sat on the floor, leaning on the arm of the chair where he sat, holding his hand that dangled down almost lifeless. My mother wanted to call his parents but he protested so adamantly, she just went back to her bed, not without muttering that the whole thing with Jimmy and his parents was awfully peculiar.

Around three in the morning, Jimmy got up and said he was going to head home but he went back to the East River. Chris told me that a few days later. Jimmy told Chris he wanted to find the guys that did that to me. To me. They didn't do anything to me but in Jimmy's mind, they did. His friends told me he went back every night for a week until I finally convinced him not to. I know where you're going, Jimmy, I said to him one night when he dropped me off for curfew. When I felt he was ready to listen.

Chris and Steve told me. Please don't go anymore.

And with that he put the back of his hand on my cheek and stroking down gently he said he wouldn't go anymore.

Promise me, I said.

Promise you, he said.

Jimmy leaned in to kiss me. His mouth was still sore. Swollen.

Who ever would have thought it would hurt to kiss you? He tried to smile, but the swelling on his lips stopped him.

There were people who didn't believe that we got mugged. They thought Jimmy just got himself in trouble with someone. There were rumors about him buying drugs from a dealer on St. Mark's Place who pistol whipped him when he said he didn't have the money. A girl at school who'd dated Jimmy once came up to me in the coatroom. You'll get yourself in trouble with someone like Jimmy Moran. You'll see, she said, brandishing a wire hanger in my face. But no one knew him the way I did. He didn't let anyone know him the way I knew him.

I can honestly say that even on my wedding day I thought of Jimmy. Peter and I were married at a country club on the water in Old Greenwich. Yet another summer when my parents rented yet another country house. When we stood outside to take our vows, I was looking out over the Sound (by then I realized it was, in fact, only the Long Island Sound and not the ocean the way I thought it was when I sat on the rocks with Jimmy) and thinking of that summer when I was sixteen. But at the time I had just about convinced myself that all young girls have thoughts like that on their wedding day. They remember their first loves and think that they will never feel the same way with anyone else. The way they felt when that boy kissed them.

Peter's mother and his Aunt Bernie started putting in what they called "dibs" for Thanksgiving and Easter as soon as we said "I do." There were all those men (friends of my father-in-law whom I didn't know) holding crabmeat hors d'oeuvres on little napkins with "Peter and Emily" and the date etched in gold on the corners. The men, with oily hands, little dots of cocktail sauce hanging off the corners of their mouths, were slapping Peter on the back. All these women (whom I didn't know either), wearing crooked coral lipstick and strong perfume, kissed me on the cheek and said they were old friends of my in-laws and welcome to the family. I was sorry that Peter and I had gotten married. It seemed so much more private when we lived together.

"Get that look off your face, Emily," my mother whispered in my ear with a smile to everyone else as though she was really saying something endearing. "Be careful, Emily," I remembered her saying the day the last letter came from Jim.

And so, as yet another person went through the reception line, commenting that I was quite the blushing bride, I stood in my grandmother's wedding gown of Alençon lace and remembered Jimmy. The beach. The way the wind blew around the trees that summer. That last day in October. Jennie and Shade. Reading McKuen and carrying sandals in our slouch bags. I looked around and there were all those men, gathered around that table lathered high with cheese platters and shrimp boats, gripping Peter on the shoulder as if to say "Tonight's the night" and I was thinking of the night I lost my virginity, almost longing to recount the tale for the backslappers and shoulder grabbers.

It was probably a good year after that last day with Jimmy that I started dating his friend Steve. The other guys would say things like "Steve's dating Jimmy's girl" and I wondered if they knew how much I still wanted to be Jimmy's girl. The old Jimmy, though.

Steve was nice enough. His parents were divorced and his dad had an apartment in the East Village. One night we took the subway and went downtown. Steve bought a bottle of Boone's Farm Apple Wine and we walked to his father's apartment. It was a drab, stone building with a heavy glass door, metal bars around it. You opened the door with a key and then inside there were five brass mailboxes with names and apartments on them and a slot where the postman put the mail. Steve opened the heavy door and we hiked three flights up to his dad's place. His father's bedroom was mahogany. The bed had a big headboard with scrolls on the top and the sheets were white and pulled tight over the mattress under a soft blue blanket. I'm not sure how it happened. Maybe it was the wine and maybe it was the fact that Steve was Jimmy's friend. Steve put on a Joni Mitchell album. His hand must have been shaking because the needle scratched across the vinyl. Before I knew it the sheets were splattered with my blood and Steve was bringing in pots of soapy water from the kitchen and I was trying to scrub out the stains.

"Jesus, Emily. You better get that clean before my dad gets home," Steve said, nervous and flushed.

And I felt so embarrassed and so angry that it was so easy for him on his first time and so awful for me. I kept seeing Jimmy's face and knew he never would have given me a pot of water and a scrub brush and had me wash it by myself. He would have made sure I felt okay and taken his father aside and told him not to make me feel self-conscious. Like the time at the river when he told Steve and Chris he was going to find the guys who did that to vindicate me. That was the last time I went out with Steve. I saw him around and there were no hard feelings after that. But all I could think of was if Jimmy ever knew what happened that night he would have been so hurt and he never would have understood. I didn't understand, how could he?

# 12

Emily was the first thing I thought of when I opened my eyes in the morning. I felt disoriented when I awakened, the way I felt when I was in boot camp. Not exactly sure what day it was. Where I was. How I got there altogether. I wanted to close my eyes and dream: of the past. Of the future. Denying what had become my present.

At night, I lulled myself to sleep with memories. And then my body would twitch on the precipice of sleep and I'd remember that I was forty-eight years old, not seventeen and in love.

In the morning, I would hear Clancy and Mary clanging pots and pans in the kitchen and I'd just lie in bed with my eyes shut tight. The breakfast smell of sausage and pancakes wafted up the stairs. I could hear the tea kettle whistle. I knew that Clancy was sitting at the table, her Princess Jasmine cup on top of her plastic place mat, a map of the United States with each state a different color. I knew that Clancy was waiting for me to come downstairs and show her all the places on the mat that she and I would go one day but, instead, I was lying in bed, trying to remember and trying to forget all at the same time.

I kept remembering times I thought I had forgotten. Times that happened after Emily left me that day on that New York City street corner. Like when I met this guy named Ward at Pendleton Beach right before they shipped me off to Nam. Well, Ward was a bold guy and a mean son of a bitch. One day, he just walked right into the base commander's office and dropped a nickel bag of pot on his desk and told the guy he wasn't going to Vietnam and to go screw himself. And then Ward just took off.

So, Ward and Lainie, Ward's girlfriend, holed up in a motel off-base over in Huntington Beach. I went over there from time to time when I got liberty but then one day I never went back to the base. Ward turned me on to belladonna. Ward and I did it and went to a pool hall and I don't think we left that pool hall for a day and a night. Ward kept peeling off ten dollar bills and we shot pool and did shots of Tequila. And then a few days later we drove to Tijuana and got some more shit and stayed up again for days at another pool hall that was just over the Mexican border. We did acid every day and then we'd take massive amounts of vitamin C because Ward said someone told him it got the pollutants out of your system. We were insane.

It was Ward's idea to hot-wire this little green Volkswagen bug that sat in a parking lot behind a supermarket. That's when Ward and Lainie and I just took off. We drove from Southern California to San Francisco. We stole credit cards and stayed at Holiday Inns. One time we went to Ward's daddy's house north of San Francisco in a town called Woodland. Ward and his daddy got into a fistfight and I felt so sick to my stomach watching them swinging at each other, ducking low and coming up for punches. Ward was bigger than his father but his father had eyes even meaner than Ward's. And Ward's mother looked like she was a hundred years old. She was probably not more than the age I am now. And then Ward went inside and stole a pile of cash from his mother's underwear drawer and we got back in the car and left. It was unbelievable to me that a guy like Ward (he was big, six foot four and maybe two-fifty) could fight his own father.

After the fight, we drove up to Reedsport, Oregon, and that's where we robbed the all-night dairy mart that was attached to an Esso station. It was pretty simple, really. It was late one night, just after midnight, and there were maybe two customers inside. Ward always had some kind of scheme. He'd cased the dairy mart out for days, gone in to get change and, one time, even asked which was the better motor oil and did anyone know where he could get a good used car. But then that night, Ward went into the market with a gun while I waited in the car. Lainie was at a motel about five miles back. I knew what he was going to do. Ward fired one shot into the air and the cashier gave him a paper bag of money filled with about a grand. "One large" as Ward said. And then Ward walked out the door, got into the Volkswagen where I sat behind the wheel, and we took off.

When we got back to the motel, we ditched the car and stole another one from the motel parking lot. Lainie never asked a question. I think she loved Ward so much she didn't even want to know. I think even if he had killed someone Lainie would have justified it somehow. For me, well, I felt like if someone would just have held a gun to my head and pulled the trigger, I would have been grateful.

It was as though Ward was some kind of Svengali for me. I was taken in by his charisma. His madness. His ability to scorn and pull me around with him the way he did Lainie. It was this almost blind allegiance I had. I was scared to death of him and awed by him all at the same time. In an odd way, Ward nurtured me as he fed me belladonna and then the vitamin C to cleanse my system. I had such a longing to be somewhere that I belonged and for that month with Ward, he held the answers.

I remember those nights sleeping in the same room as Lainie and Ward. In the middle of the night when they thought I was sleeping, they'd be going at it. And I'd lay really still. It wasn't what they were doing so much that was bothering me. It was that I wanted someone to be with, too. But I wanted to be with someone in the right way, not the way Ward was with Lainie, banging her in some motel room when he was practically wasted. And somehow hearing Ward and Lainie going at it made me feel so uneasy. As if Ward was almost showing off for me. I felt threatened by Ward's sexuality as well as my own. My God, I was barely eighteen. My life was filled with so many uncertainties and Ward was adding to the heap. I didn't know who I was.

I turned up at Camp Pendleton a week after the Esso robbery. Just walked right into the camp, bona fide AWOL. But I'd had enough. After the Esso robbery, I had a sense that if I stayed with Ward I would be imprisoned like I think Lainie was. I needed Camp Pendleton in a strange way. I needed structure. Safety.

Boundaries. Ward was anarchy. He was the extreme. I was an outsider no matter where I turned, but I knew if I stayed with Ward I would self-destruct. To continue on with Ward would be living life on the ledge. I needed someone to stop me. The image of the butt of a gun to my chin was becoming too appealing.

They threw me in the brig when I got back to Camp Pendleton. It wasn't for long, though. A few days later, they shipped me off to Nam. The brig is a picnic, the guards said. Nam would sober me up.

It was just about two weeks after Emily called that my wedding anniversary came around for the twentieth time. Mary had made a reservation at a place called Carl's where folks around here go when they celebrate something. The front room is laid out in tables with glass tops over white tablecloths. Waitresses switch the soiled paper mats on top of the glass for clean ones. As soon as people finish their meal, the waitresses in their black dresses and white aprons spray the tables with a frothy pink liquid and wipe the glass down with a damp cloth. The tables have dusty little silk rosettes in bud vases and floating candles in small glass bowls. Hanging from the ceiling are silk flowers, covering the beige acoustic tiles.

Mary had her hair done the day of our anniversary and wore a full flowered skirt and a sapphire blue silk shirt scooped out at the neck. She wore a string of yellowed pearls that used to be my grandmother's. She sat across from me at the table and I toasted her with a joking "Here's looking at you, kid" and she smiled at me wanly. It was clear my heart wasn't in this celebration. Mary used to ask me why I didn't make love to her anymore. I always had a million excuses. Too tired.

A little depressed. Not enough money in the bank. And then one day, just like with everything else, she stopped asking.

Mary got a little tipsy that night at Carl's. We drank a bottle of champagne but I think it was the crème de menthe that Mary ordered with her coffee that sent her over the edge. That was when she started lecturing me (or at least I felt that she was lecturing me) about how I really could be making more money and maybe she could stop working and wouldn't it be better if she was the one at home with Clancy instead of me. Mary wanted to be the one to work part-time instead of me. Now, it wasn't so much what she was saying. What she was saying actually made sense. It was how she said it. How she seemed to talk to me like you talk to someone who speaks a foreign language, loud and halting. Her southern accent seemed to squeak and her voice got higher with each exclamation. She rode my nerves with each, "Are you listenin', Jimmy? Ah can't tell 'less you answer me. Jimmy? Jimmy?" Until I took my fist and hit the table so hard that the little bud vase holding the rosettes shook until it toppled into the jar holding the candle, the water from the vase dousing the flame with a slow sizzle. Mary sat way back in her chair, pursed her lips together and crossed her arms over her chest. "I hope you're proud of yourself now, Jimmy Moran," she said. I didn't give her the fake pearl earrings I'd bought her until the next day.

When Emily and I started to speak seriously about meeting in Washington, D.C. (not just that impulsive invitation Emily mentioned on the second phone call), I started working out like a madman. I mean, the last time Emily saw me I was a suntanned Marine and thirty years younger. My body looked soft now. I hated the scratches and cuts on my hands from hefting the boxes at Long's. I hated the fact that I was hairless on my chest and legs. I hated that rash on my forearms that is red and blotchy some days and other days it just fades down to a yellowish tinge.

I looked in the mirror and pushed my hair back from my forehead. I hated the gray that lined my temples and the lines that ran so deep across my forehead. I turned my face sideways and stroked my jaw. For sure the skin around my jaw was looser. Mary would laugh at me as I pumped miles on that dinky exercise bike she bought at the Kmart and did a hundred sit-ups with Clancy sitting on my feet. But she didn't say anything until I stopped slugging down the beers at night.

"You doin' all that for your old girl?" Mary said. "Well, at least someone got you to take care of yourself, Jimmy."

It was like she was my mother for Christ sakes. But she was so right and it killed me.

The day I bought the plane tickets for Washington I went out and bought a half dozen pairs of Jockeys (in black and navy blue) and two pairs of jeans and some new shoes. I took my blazer out of the back of the closet and had it dry cleaned. Crappy blazer. It must have been twenty years old. The buttons were falling off and the brass coating was peeling off them anyway because they weren't real brass. The blazer used to belong to my brother-in-law Dennis, Daphne's husband, the investment banker. He left it here what was probably five years ago and when I offered to ship it, he said I might as well keep it since he had a closet full of them. Daphne and Dennis live outside of Boston. Dennis buys his clothes on Newbury Street. The blazer was too small on me anyway. The sleeves were too short. I bet Emily's husband has a closet full of navy blazers, I thought. I bet Emily's husband never wore any secondhand jacket. I would have laid money down that he was the kind of guy who had a tan for all seasons and wore Burberry suits to work with trousers that had a perfect crease held up by a smooth black leather belt with a shiny gold buckle. He probably wore turtlenecks on the weekend and Topsiders. He probably wore pajamas to bed.

So I went out and bought a brown tweed blazer (on sale because the manufacturer forgot to make the pockets deep enough if that isn't the biggest irony) and Mary ragged my ass every day for a week about spending eighty dollars on a jacket. All I could think was that Emily's husband probably spent more than eighty bucks on a tie. Eighty bucks. My dad carried more than that around in his wallet thirty years ago.

I sat in the sun and sprayed myself with cocoa butter and when Mary wasn't looking I covered a piece of cardboard with tin foil and held it under my chin. One time though Mary caught me sunning. I saw her peering out at me from behind the kitchen door that leads out to the deck. For maybe a moment I felt like I was being a louse. I mean, I guess I wasn't what Mary bargained for either.

Mary and I were married in Myrtle Beach. Mary's family is from a little town near there called Conway. There were about seventy-five people at our wedding. Mostly Mary's side. Except for my mother and Daphne, I have no one. I was thinking of tracking down Steve and Chris. I was afraid they might not remember me. I was afraid to find Potter or Quinn. I was afraid of what might have happened to them.

Mary's brothers and sisters were there and, southern-style, her brothers got into a fight with some of their cousins in front of the cash bar and I remember looking at Mary's mother and I saw my whole life flash in front of my eyes. My dad's aunt was a sculptor. His brother was a neurosurgeon at Columbia-Presbyterian. My mom's sister was a big-time interior decorator. My mom is still gorgeous. Her hair is dyed dark red now and her eyes are green and she wore a tailored green silk suit to our wedding. Dennis and Daphne looked liked they stepped right out of the pages of *Town & Country*. Mary's mother is way overweight and wore a bright red dress with a clashing pink taffeta rose on the shoulder. During the ceremony, she kept blowing her nose in a big white hanky, her shoulders heaving up and down. I wondered whether it was sentiment that her baby girl was getting married or fear that her daughter was marrying someone the likes of me. Mary's oldest brother drives a tow truck. The other brother does roofing. Her two older sisters never married and live at home with my mother-in-law. The last Mary saw of her father, she was five years old. He was a long-distance trucker and one day he just went the distance. They found the truck on the side of a highway. Parked just fine. Keys on the seat. The bank account had been emptied and all Mary's mother was left with were five kids and a whopping bill from the IRS. Maybe that's why Mary's mother was crying at our wedding. Maybe she just kept thinking about Mary's father taking off like that.

So I got drunk at my wedding. I was so drunk that

at one point the room was spinning. I didn't want to
embarrass anyone so I went and sat outside the hotel.
The hotel was on the beach and I sat with my head in
my hands. I was thinking how maybe I married Mary
because it was time. I owed it to her. It wasn't like I
got down on one knee and pulled a ring out of a blue
velvet box. It was Mary who just told me one day that
she wanted to have a baby and either we get married
or she's leaving. So I went to a jeweler where I got her
a diamond the size of a pinhead and asked her to
marry me.

Mary and I moved into our house fifteen years
ago. We were unloading boxes of old photographs
when I found the one of Emily in the bikini. It was
tied with a red elastic band to the one of Emily and
me that her friend Jennie took by the water in Connecticut. Mary asked who was the girl in the picture
and I said she was just a friend of Daphne's from
school. I didn't want to tell her about Emily. I didn't
want to tell anyone about Emily. Maybe I'll send the
picture to Daphne, I said. But when Mary wasn't
looking, I put the photographs back in the bottom of
the box.

I never told Mary about Ward and Lainie. I never
told her how much I hated Long's or how I felt wearing a secondhand blazer. But I told Emily the story
about Reedsport on the phone.

"You must have been so sad," she said. "So scared."

"I robbed a place, Emily," I said. "For Christ sakes."

"You were about the same age as Jack," she said.

"It's no excuse," I said.

"Did the police ever look for you?" she asked.

I said that the store had no camera. And then all she
said was that it was a long time ago.

"That wasn't you back then with Ward, Jimmy," Emily said. "You didn't know who you were."

I wondered what it was that Emily saw in me thirty years ago. I wondered what part of me I allowed her to see. And why I am afraid to trust Mary to see that part of me at all.

# 13

Peter was fine with the idea that I was going to meet Jim in Washington. As a matter of fact, that was precisely what he said. "Fine, Emily. Sounds like a good idea. Just fine."

I made the announcement about Washington one night after dinner as I stood at the sink washing the dinner dishes. Peter was uncharacteristically sitting at the kitchen table. It took me a while to rehearse the studied effort in nonchalance. To pick the perfect moment when it was almost a casual remark.

"It's not like you to sit here while I do the dishes, Peter," I said. "Everything okay?"

Peter laughed. "See how unpredictable I can be?" he said. "Actually, Julie thought it would be nice if I sat with you. She said she was at Amanda's house and Amanda's father was helping to clear the table while her mother loaded the dishwasher."

"Ah, so this is the enlightened Peter Walters sitting with me," I smiled.

"You have a great smile, Em," Peter said.

"Now I am very suspicious," I laughed.

I drew in a deep breath. "I want to meet Jim Moran in Washington," I said. "I want him to help me with the series of paintings on the Vietnam era." I took a Brillo pad and scrubbed the burned-on grease from the side of a frying pan. The grease had really been there for months. "Do you think that would be all right with you?" I was scrubbing furiously, looking up but seeming preoccupied. I had told Peter about the next series. Mentioned an old friend who was a veteran of the Vietnam War. He never paid much attention to any of it.

If I picture how Peter's face looked when he nodded up and down after I asked him, I think he stared at me too directly as though he was looking through me in the way that people do when they are trying to be sincere. The way children stare you directly in the eyes without a smile crossing their faces or even blinking when they're outright lying to you. As for my eyes, they most definitely avoided his as I continued to battle the now imaginary grease stain, remarking that it would be a shame to mar the brand new pots and pans his mother sent us last Christmas. Trying to change the subject as if the Le Creuset frying pan carried far more importance than the trip to Washington.

"I want him to come with me to the Memorial," I said, after Peter already said that it was fine. I was trying to answer questions he hadn't asked. Simple questions like "Why Washington?" or "How well do you know this man?" Was he reluctant to probe or did he simply not care? As I told Peter my plan, I wiped another imaginary smudge off the countertop with a barely damp sponge.

"We can just sit on those stone benches by the

Memorial and, oh, I must not forget my tape recorder—remind me will you?—where I can interview him and sketch him and go over his photographs," I said.

It was one-sided conversation. The way I spoke to my grandfather after he had the stroke that left him aphasic and I would second-guess what he might have wanted to say. My words came out in one breath, convincing, pleading. I breathed the way I would when I asked my father if I could go to the late movie with my friends. I'd give him a string of reasons why I must be given permission or else I would be the only one who stayed home. All in one breath. Give the reasons all at once before he could say no. Await the verdict. All Peter said was to take extra tapes. He was sure this man would have a lot to say.

"He's a vet," he said. "They like to talk, you know. Old war stories. It's fine, Em. Sounds fine."

Then Peter asked where the morning paper was and went into the den.

My brother, Robbie, came over the next day, a Saturday, when we thought it might be fun to open up the Weber kettle for the spring. Robbie's eyebrows shot up in the air and stayed there when I told him that I was going to Washington and why. I didn't tell my sisters. For sure, Sara and Catherine would have disapproved. They remembered Jim from that summer. Robbie didn't. All Robbie remembers from that summer is leaving his turtle so long in the sun that the water in the shallow bowl dried up and the turtle turned into an immediate fossil that we buried in the garden with a plaque above: IN MEMORY OF SHELLEY. REST IN PEACE.

Sara and Catherine have always been known as the twins, as opposed to me who is the third child and

Robbie, The Baby. The twins are three years older than I am. The summer I sat and waited for Jim's letters by the mailbox, Sara and Catherine were already in colleges and had summer jobs. Sara worked as a gift-wrapper at a shop that sold Limoges china and Lladro figurines. Catherine worked in Woolworth's cosmetics department, giving what she called expert help in makeup application. "Lessons" in the art of eyelash curling and lip lining.

At night, my sisters went into town, dressed in jeans so tight they had to lie down on the bed and pull them on with a wire hanger hooked into the zipper. They'd meet their boyfriends at Friendly's. At least that's what they told my mother when she'd ask where they were going. Friendly's for a soda. Maybe catch a late movie, they'd say. And my mother would smile approvingly. They really went to a bar called The Rusty Nail and sat in the backs of cars on Lover's Lane. I know this because I overheard them talking one night in their room, whispering and giggling about the cop that shone his flashlight in the backseat of Billy Richardson's Corvair and told them to move on. They taunted me relentlessly that summer while Jennie and I sat home writing in our diaries by threads of moonlight on the porch.

"Emily's waiting for her soldier boy," Catherine would say with a smile that could easily be confused with a smirk so it was hard to discern whether she was being as mean as I thought she was. And then Sara would chime in with a chorus of "Please, Mr. Postman" or "Return to Sender." My sisters were wicked that summer. They smelled of Ambush and wore frosted lipsticks. They teased their hair and plucked their eyebrows almost bare and wore cheap gold hoop earrings that I think Catherine probably swiped from Woolworth's jewelry department. Their dressers were cluttered with worn brown compacts of Cover Girl makeup and their bathrooms smelled like camphor and gardenia. Now they wear Ferragamo flats and beige trousers with expensive cashmere sweater sets. They drive Mercedes and play tennis in the mornings at the country club. They are loath to remember that summer whenever I've brought it up to them.

That summer of 1967 I found Catherine's diaphragm in a black patent leather clutch bag in the back of her closet. I was looking for an empty shoe box to hold Jimmy's letters when I discovered it. I opened the round baby blue plastic case, thinking it was just another compact, and saw the rubber device sitting under a dusting of talcum powder. At first I wasn't sure what it was but then I remembered that a girl in my class, Lauren Tyler, had shown me the one in her pocketbook and told me she was sleeping with a senior boy named Brian Sweet from Loyola. Lauren was Catholic and I remember being aghast at the pious way she crossed herself after Lord's Prayer each morning, clutching her pocketbook with the contraband birth control inside. I rolled Catherine's diaphragm around and around in my hands, wondering how it was used, how it fit, careful not to puncture the rubber. Remembering what Jennie had said about the condoms. I couldn't imagine why Catherine needed a diaphragm. I couldn't envision her in the throes of passion. Not someone like Catherine who dressed so meticulously even in her blue jeans and wrapped her hair in pink foam rollers before she went to bed at night.

A few years ago I told Catherine that I'd found the

diaphragm in her closet that summer. She looked at me blankly. She said I had no business going through her things.

"Who was he that summer?" I asked. "Was it Billy Richardson from down the road? Did you do it in the back of his Corvair?"

Catherine said she didn't remember his name and turned her head away from me. Maybe she had loved him, I thought. I mean maybe she had really been in love with him. Maybe that's why she kept plucking her eyebrows and setting her hair all summer. Maybe she had loved him so much that was why she couldn't bear to talk to me about him now. But somehow I felt that her refusal to engage in this memory was more likely because she couldn't intertwine her life now with what was then. That summer, there was far too much abandon for Catherine; her memories juxtapose too violently with the conservative beige life she leads now. Sometimes the past is best left alone.

Peter was firing up the kettle as Robbie and I sat on the porch swing.

"I'm meeting with a man I knew thirty years ago," I said to Robbie. We were watching his two-year-old daughter, Tara, play horseshoes in the front yard. "He's a Vietnam vet and I'm going to do a series of paintings about him. You were just a baby, Robbie, when I knew him. It was the summer Mom and Dad rented the yellow house in Old Greenwich. The summer your turtle fried."

Why did I feel I had to convince even Robbie? I'd done a series a few years before where I'd traveled around and talked to the daughters of Holocaust survivors. Of course, Peter and the children came with me. Some of the women were in Philadelphia and

Providence and then there were a few in California and Miami. We worked it all out around family vacations and weekend ski trips. The paintings were of mothers and daughters and each one's story was written along the side. How the mother remembered the concentration camps. How it was to be the daughter of a woman who was such a survivor. The paintings were watercolor on collage. Layer upon layer like the lives of the women. I sold seven of them and they got a good review in the local weekly newspaper. They even had a brief run in a Soho gallery on Prince Street.

"How does Peter feel about this, Emily?" Robbie asked, still looking at Tara.

"He says it's fine," I said.

"You can't sit there and tell me, Emily, that Peter doesn't mind you meeting some old beau. Why don't you just go down to the VFW and find some vets down there? Why don't you interview Tommy Rourke down the street from Mom and Dad? He was in Nam. You're basically full of it, Emily," Robbie said a lot more venomously than I thought he ever could.

"For goodness' sakes, Robbie. I was sixteen," I said.

"Did you sleep with him that summer?" Robbie asked so directly that he startled me.

"No, I never slept with him. Not ever," I said trying not to be too defensive and then, "What would it matter, anyway? This is business."

"Monkey business," said Robbie as he got up from the porch swing to toss an errant horseshoe back to Tara. When he got up, the swing lurched and pitched forward.

I don't know whether I was angrier because I was so transparent to Robbie or because I wasn't transparent to Peter at all. Or angry because men can take business trips for days and spend their evenings at strip clubs and no one ever questions their motives.

I cannot say that Peter's cavalier attitude didn't bother me. If he had tried to stop me I would have kicked and screamed and told him I was going anyway. But he could have tried or at least asked more penetrating questions. Robbie said he would never "let" his wife Corinne do something like that. Then Robbie and I had a discussion and then an argument about the notion of husbands and wives "letting" one another do things. But if I had really been completely honest, I would have confessed to Robbie that a part of me wished Peter took that stance with me. I wished that Peter wasn't always so "enlightened" as he called it. Every once in a while I wished he'd taken a caveman approach and uttered some anachronism like "No wife of mine is running off to Washington to meet some guy she knew thirty years ago." And I wasn't sure if Peter's approach was merely resignation because he knew I would do as I pleased anyway. I wondered if perhaps Peter thought that my behavior would always be above reproach because infidelity was simply not in my lexicon. I must have asked Peter a million times if he was sure about my leaving.

"Are you sure you don't mind?" I asked Peter over and over again in the days before I left. "I don't have to go if you're not comfortable with me being away."

But Peter was unfazed.

"It's fine. Have a good time, Emily," Peter said. "Try to relax. You deserve it. Don't worry about us."

Fine. Fine. Fine. A word so muddy, so insipid, it barely has a definition. Don't worry about us. Us. I wondered for a second what "us" he was talking about and then I realized it was he and the children. So then I wondered why it was that suddenly I was so deserving of a solo trip away to Washington yet all the nights he walked in the door when I was standing over a sink full of dinner dishes or mopping up Hawaiian Punch from beige carpet there was little appreciation. Why was it that I always had the fantasy that maybe Peter would come in one night and see me with the mop in my hand, wipe a stray hair away from my perspired forehead with the tips of his fingers and tell me to run upstairs and get dressed. Then we'd go out to dinner at some little bistro with red checkered tablecloths that had a wine bottle in a basket dripped with candlewax in the middle of the table. But instead, he'd lift up the cover on the pots still on the stove, take a deep sniff (though appreciative) and ask me if I'd eaten yet. And then he'd stand to the side while I finished mopping the floor, self-consciously, offering a *tsk* now and then, and we'd sit at the kitchen table and have a dinner that wasn't so much silent as it was prosaic. I keep a lipstick in the kitchen drawer. I wondered if Peter knew that to this day I slid it across my lips whenever I heard his car turn into the driveway whether the mop was in my hand or not.

I packed a suitcase and a box of pencils and a sketchbook. I put Jim's ring in tissue with my cosmetics. *Listen to the Warm* between my nightgown and robe. The day before I left I bought new jeans, three new tank tops, had my nails done, my toes done and my hair highlighted.

"You look different, Emily," Peter said as we drove to the train station early the following Friday morning. And then, "Your hair looks different, too. You look good, Emily. Did you have your toes done for Moran?"

Was there just the slightest tinge of jealousy? Did I hear just the thinnest bit of angst in his voice? Was there a subtle hostility when he called him "Moran"? I told Peter that I often have my toes done and I guessed he just hadn't noticed before because I usually wear sneakers not sandals. But Peter just kept driving. He looked straight ahead. He didn't say a word. For a moment I thought he was going to place his arm over my shoulder and pull me toward him but he was only stretching his arm. His tennis elbow was flaring up again, he said.

When we pulled up to the Stamford train station, Peter took some cash out of his pocket.

"You should have cash on you, Emily," he said, peeling off twenty dollar bills and placing them into my hand the way my grandmother used to with one dollar bills when I was small. "You never carry enough cash."

"I have my credit cards," I said. "Just take care of you and the kids."

"The kids will be fine. We'll go to the movies. Just try to relax."

Fine. Relax. All the wrong words. For just a second I wanted to shake him and ask why he was letting me go so easily. It was all I could do not to ask if he had any doubts at all about this trip. He took my suitcase out of the trunk. I kissed him on the cheek. I yanked the handle out of my suitcase so I could pull it down the platform. I watched Peter drive away as I waited for the train and I wished more than anything that I knew what he was thinking. Did he pull out of the parking lot rather quickly as if perhaps he was feeling temperamental? I wasn't sure. Was he thinking anything at all about me? About us? I concluded that he wasn't and if he was thinking anything at all, he was probably thinking all the wrong things. It made it easier to leave.

Union Station in Washington was not as I'd remembered it. It looked more like a museum or a mall than a train station. I was nervous on the train ride. I couldn't sketch. I couldn't read. I couldn't sleep. At Union Station, I went into The Body Shop and bought a bottle of Satsuma Bath Gel. I stopped by the window at Victoria's Secret and then felt myself blush as a woman with a baby in a stroller smiled at me as I looked at the little nightie that hung in the window. Like a slip with spaghetti straps, it was black and sheer, covered strategically with red roses. It's funny how women, even when they're strangers, talk to one another.

"Not exactly great for nursing," she said and laughed a short little laugh. "My husband would faint if I ever showed up in something like that. He wouldn't know what to do."

And I wondered if she figured that I had children and a husband, too. Despite the tight jeans and the skimpy tank top, I guess I still looked like a Mom. Peter never bought me anything from Victoria's Secret. Before we were married, he went into a shop on Madison Avenue and bought me a red and black gingham skirt with a black peasant blouse. After Jack was born, Peter bought me a flannel nightgown with nursing pockets in the front. He hasn't bought me anything since except for earrings that are so conservative I only wear them to Peter's business dinners. He's never bought me anything remotely sexy. Maybe it was because I became a mother so soon and there wasn't time or place for sheer lingerie. But I wasn't *his* mother.

The hotel was only two blocks from the train station. The day was hot and hazy, a change from the cool New England spring. I decided to walk even though the suitcase pulled heavy behind me. I checked my watch. In two hours I had to be at National Airport. It was one o'clock and Jim's plane got in at three. Just enough time to check in and take a hot bath, call Peter and the kids, grab a taxi.

The front desk gave me my room key. I was relieved that I didn't need a bellman. I felt self-conscious checking into the hotel by myself. I wanted to state a disclaimer: "I'm here on business. It's not what you think it is despite what Robbie might think." I was so used to being with Peter and the kids. Peter would sign the register. The bellman would load up the umpteen suitcases onto the gold cart that looked like a massive crown and the kids would scurry ahead, dragging their Walkmans, their pillows. We always took connecting rooms. Peter and I always took the one with the king-size bed. In younger days, one kid or another always ended up between us at night.

We hadn't been away alone in years, Peter and I. Both his parents and mine moved to Florida shortly after Jack was born and somehow we never managed to find anyone who was willing to stay with four children born in stair steps. As the children got older, I worried that leaving teenagers in a house alone for the weekend was a bad idea.

Once when Jack was about five and Julie was still an infant, Peter and I spent a night in Manhattan and my parents stayed over. But I was so nervous about the kids. I kept thinking that my father wouldn't put his pipe out properly and would burn the house down. Or my mother would forget to turn the jets off the gas stove since she was accustomed to electric. Or Sam would get another ear infection. Or Julie would awaken in the middle of the night and long for me. The night was just a waste of time and money. Peter was angry that I couldn't relax. I was angry that he could. We ended up watching a pay-per-view film and falling asleep before it was even finished.

I slid the thin card key into the hotel room door and there was a huge king-size bed and suddenly I felt so uneasy. What exactly was I doing? I ran a bath and poured the orange bath gel under the water. I slipped off my clothes and stepped into the tub. I think I was only in there for about five minutes when I got out again. I wasn't used to languishing in hot bubble baths. I was used to staying long enough in the shower just to get clean and then pulling my clothes over still-damp skin so I could be downstairs in the kitchen in time to make breakfast for four hungry faces that lined the counter. This wasn't me.

The phone rang and jarred me as I stared at my face in the mirror, deep in thought. It was Peter. I was so distracted I had forgotten to call.

"Emily? It's me," he said. "I just wanted to know if you got there all right."

It wasn't until months later that Robbie told me he and Corinne were back at the house on the Saturday morning after I left. He said that Peter greeted them at the door and his face looked grave. That's what Robbie said. He looked grave. He said that he sat down with Robbie and poured them each a beer at noon and put his face in his hands. But Robbie said when he asked Peter if something was wrong, he just laughed and said not to tell me he was drinking beer at noon. I guess this is freedom, Peter had said sourly.

I told Peter that I was fine (tempted to use a superlative such as "wonderful" and then decided to fling back "fine" at him and see how he liked it) and the room was "nice." Peter told me he missed me and I thought that was not only odd but unfair.

"I've only been gone a few hours," I said.

Peter asked why it bothered me to hear that he missed me. I had no answer. But this was not the time to miss me. This was not the time to tell me. He should have told me things like that before I left. Peter's face became distorted in my mind. I pushed away thoughts that wouldn't let me justify this journey I was taking. Thoughts that made me feel guilty and question how much of the wrong in our marriage was my doing as well as Peter's. Thoughts that made me understand why Peter let me go so easily: perhaps because I'd left a long time ago.

I looked at the pale blue tank top spread out on the bed next to the black jeans with the price tags still attached. My mind shifted to the plane that was going to land in another hour. I took my place again before the mirror. And as I ran the brush through my hair, I flashed back to the day I stood at the dresser in my bedroom as a girl.

My mother's voice was very distinct, "Be careful, Emily. He's a man now, you know."

# 14

Mary didn't go to work the Friday morning that I left for Washington. Clancy had a runny nose so she was home from school. They sat on the bed as I packed my bag. I rolled up my shirts and my sweaters, packed the new Jockeys still in their cellophane packages. Mary was surprised that I packed a tie but I explained that Washington was a city where some of the restaurants might ask you to wear one. Then Clancy said she was hungry and Mary took her down to the kitchen for breakfast while I finished packing.

Mary was standing in the hallway by the front door when I came walking down the stairs with my suitcase. I had sprinkled Brut on my neck before I went downstairs. At the last minute, I shoved the bottle into the carry-on's side zipper. Mary was holding Clancy in her arms. Clancy's long legs dangled down to Mary's knees. Mary was standing under the light of this gold-colored chandelier we have. Well, it's not really a chandelier. It's just a hanging fixture with a single bulb, tinted etched glass covering the sides. But when the light from the bulb shone on Mary's face, shaded by the smoked glass, for just a moment she looked the way she did when I first met her. Something came over me and I thought of leaning over to kiss her. Really kiss her. I don't know what stopped me and I don't know why I wanted to. It might have been guilt. Or maybe it was just that she would have thought it too strange. She just looked so pretty that was all. And maybe she looked as lost as I was feeling at that moment. She stepped back after I kissed her cheek.

"You smell good, Jimmy," she said, forcing a smile.

Clancy was squirming around as she clung to Mary's neck. She looked so sweet still in her pajamas, her nose a little red from running. She wore the ones with the pink and yellow butterflies on them, telling me she wore them especially for me.

" 'Cause you're flying like the butterflies, Daddy," she said.

One of her pant legs was scrunched up above her bony white knee. Her shirt was pulled up over her pink belly as she squiggled down and came over to me, putting her arms around my thighs.

"Bye, Dad," she said. "Mama says you're going to a big city."

"Take care of Mama, honey, okay?" I said and kissed her on the top of her head. She smelled like strawberry shampoo.

"You're the princess, remember?" I said and Clancy lifted her head. Her face reddened when she smiled.

"And you're the king of the castle," she laughed, rubbing one eye with the back of her hand, knowing that expression was one that irked Mary no end when I jokingly used it. She looked at Mary sideways. Mary just laughed and shook her head.

I was all done up in my new jeans and my new brown tweed sport coat. Dressed too warmly for mid-May in Mobile. I wished I had one of those hanging suitcases that looked more elegant like I was a frequent traveler. The leather kind that come with those black folding hangers and zip up with plastic lined sides, wheels on the bottom and a strap for pulling. I accidentally left the new leather-framed identification bag tag in the wooden salad bowl that Mary put on my dresser for my loose change. I didn't want to go back upstairs and get it. I'd bought it the day before at a luggage store and filled it out in my finest handwriting. Mary always tells me that my penmanship looks like a chicken was walking across the paper so I really made an effort to print my name and address. Funny, when Emily said my handwriting looked like chicken scratch, it didn't bother me. When Mary said it, I got angry. When I filled out that tag I felt like Clancy does when she writes her name on those broad-lined sheets she uses for her homework. So fastidious. So careful. No matter, I figured how many people would be looking for an old brown leather suitcase? It had a tag, anyway. It was just worn and the ink was faded.

I drove my El Camino to the airport that Friday morning. The sun was hot. The air conditioning in the El Camino had died years ago. I kept hearing the sounds of airplanes overhead. There were probably always engine sounds in the sky but I'd never noticed them before. I thought how it was like when Mary and I were trying to have a baby and it seemed everyone in the world was having one except for us. Now all I heard was airplanes.

When I stopped at a red light I counted the cash in

my wallet. Seventy-five bucks. That's what I'd have in my pocket after I paid the eighty bucks it would cost to park the car at long-term parking. I had a Visa card with me for my hotel room and that was it. Seventy-five stinking bucks for a three-day trip.

Mary wasn't happy when I took the cash out of the jelly jar that she keeps behind all the jelly jars filled with the real thing in the kitchen cabinet. When I took the jar down, I thought of Ward and how he stole the money from his mother's underwear drawer and wondered if I was any better than he was.

"That's my mad money, Jimmy," Mary said as she watched me unscrew the lid of the jelly jar. "It's not right for you take my money to go see that woman."

It was interesting how Emily had suddenly become "that woman" in the days before I left. I told Mary that a man still needs to have cash on hand and she'd better not get too mad over her mad money because I was taking it anyway. Sometimes when I raise my voice just the slightest touch, Mary shrinks away from me and for the life of me I can't figure out why. I've never laid a hand on her and never would. She told me that one time she saw her father strike her mother clear across the face and she would never tolerate that from a man. Not that having her say that deterred me. I just would never think of hitting a woman.

"She's not some woman, Mary," I said, lowering my voice. Trying to be tender. "She's an old friend."

"Then how come you never mentioned her before?" she said.

"There wasn't much to say," I said. "It was so long ago. We were kids."

I promised Mary that she'd have her money back but she and I knew full well I never made good on too much of anything when it came to money. She seemed to have calmed down, though, by the time I left.

"Have a fine time, Jimmy," she said as I loaded my suitcase into my truck (pronouncing "fine" like she was saying "ah" before attaching the "F" to it, a way of speech that used to delight me) after she got over the jelly jar robbery and the notion of another woman. "Call us tonight so we know you got there all right." And then Mary and Clancy walked back toward the house. Clancy kept turning around and waving.

"I will. I'll call as soon as I get there," I said.

Mary had never asked me exactly what I was going to do in Washington. I gave her a very skeletal description of Emily's project and said how Emily wanted to talk to me so her paintings and the text would have just the right feel. I was really just talking in circles. I knew that Emily didn't need me so much for the text but for the sense of the past. I wondered if maybe our conversations were simply steeped in the past and once we were done reminiscing, there would be nothing left to say.

I parked the car at long-term parking and hopped the jitney over to Delta. My carry-on bag slung over my shoulder. New aviator-style Ray•Bans on my face. Anyone looking at me probably wouldn't think I was on a business trip. But then again, I sort of fantasized, maybe I did look like I was a businessman. I mean, I didn't have on a jacket and tie but I could have been doing business in jeans and tweed. And then my mind just took off and I started to believe that I really was someone important after all. I mean, I was the one that Emily wanted to call. Maybe Emily would end up having a show at one of those galleries in Soho where everyone comes in wearing black on black and pads around the room, stopping at the paintings, stepping back and forward, leaning in and rubbing their chins, sighing. Red dots on the corners of the paintings to indicate they've been sold like the ones in that Italian restaurant in town. Warhol and Monroe. Hudson and Moran.

"Are you the young Marine in the painting?" a young woman wearing sleek black pants and a high black turtleneck would fawn. And then Emily would walk over to me and straighten my tie (a gold color on a black denim shirt) and I would place my arm over her shoulder and say something like "This is the artist. And, yes, I am the Marine. Pleased to meet you." I shook myself. Too much fantasy.

The first leg of the flight from Mobile to Atlanta was about an hour and half and the plane was nearly empty. I sat alone and read a stack of magazines the flight attendant gave me but nothing held my interest. The plane from Atlanta to Washington was jam-packed. A young woman came and sat beside me. I was sitting on the aisle (because I like to know that I can get up and get out if I have to without crawling over people) so I stood up to let the woman into the window seat.

The pilot announced that we were coming into the Washington area and we should prepare for landing and fasten our seat belts. The plane bumped down on the runway and while everyone else immediately started to get up and unload their things from the overhead compartments, I just sat there. The woman by the window stepped over me again, missing my toes this time.

"Aren't you going to get off the plane?" she laughed.

And I told her I wasn't in a hurry, that it was better if the crowds went ahead of me. I wanted to say I'd already waited thirty years. I didn't tell her that all of a sudden I could feel my heart pounding. How my mouth was dry. How I was thinking that maybe the past is best left in the past. You would think that after two Stoli's I'd be a little loose, but I wasn't even close.

I finally got up and walked off the plane, down the long gray corridor to the gate. At first I didn't see her standing there. She was looking all around and searching the crowd. Her eyes were squinting a little. Her hair was still long, though only to her shoulders. More stylish. The blond was streaked but darker, no longer sun-bleached. But except for that, Emily didn't look much different than the girl I'd left that day at the train station. I stopped right in front of her and stood still.

"Don't you grow older?" I asked her, pressing my face next to hers. "Let's go get my bag."

It was that easy. That simple. And I felt myself smiling. And I swear, it felt like the first time I had smiled like this since Clancy was placed in my arms.

"You look wonderful, Jimmy," Emily said. "I knew you right away."

And just like it was yesterday, when I put her books down on the sidewalk, I slung the carry-on over my shoulder and slipped my arm around her waist. It felt like my arm had always been there. But unlike the last time it was there, this time Emily didn't pull away. She leaned into me. I would have sworn we were kids again. I wished we were.

# 15

It took me longer to get to National Airport than expected. I forgot about rush hour in D.C. It was nearly impossible to get a cab. The drive to National Airport seemed to take forever. Every light was red. Every intersection was tied up and gridlocked. Horns were honking. Irate drivers were yelling out car windows. It had started to drizzle. I kept checking my watch, leaning over the front seat of the cab as if that would make the traffic go faster.

. The cab finally pulled up in front of Delta. Just as I was running in the door of the terminal, my cell phone rang.

"Mommy? It's Julie. I just wanted to say hello because I miss you. Where are you? I'm on the porch swing with the cordless phone."

My heart sank. Why now? Why is she calling now? But I stopped and stood over to the side. I had never been away from her before that she could remember. That night she stayed with my parents she was just a baby, still in her crib. She didn't remember. Peter travels quite often. I don't recall there ever being a time when one of them asked for Peter's number just to say hello. I doubt they even know his cell-phone number.

Julie's voice was a dose of reality, stopping me in my tracks, making me forget that Jim might be waiting at the gate, looking around and wondering where I was. How could I be so far away when she wanted me to be there? What was I doing?

"I miss you, too, honey," I said. I felt guilty. Part of me longed to just turn around and go home where I felt I belonged. Another part of me felt resentful that Peter wasn't able to dispel Julie's sense of missing me. Didn't he see her take the phone and sit alone on the swing? I should have asked to speak with her when Peter called me earlier.

"Where's Daddy?" I asked, trying to be casual. Trying not to let the resentment in my voice bleed through where Julie thought I was angry that Peter wasn't there for her.

Julie said Peter was outside in the driveway shooting hoops with the boys.

"Daddy's taking us out to dinner," she said, brightening. "And he said we don't have to make our beds until you get home."

I rested easier when I heard her voice lilt and giggle when she told me that Peter said they didn't have to clean their rooms.

"Sounds like you're better off without the taskmaster there," I said. "Julie, I'll be home in two days. Day after tomorrow. Sounds like you're going to have a party without me though."

"Have you seen Mr. Moran, yet?" she asked.

I looked at my watch. "Not yet but he should be get-

ting off the plane any moment. I will call you later,
Julie. Be good."

"I love you, Mom" she said.

"I love you, too," I said, wishing I had been the first
to say it.

I hooked the cell phone back on the belt of my jeans,
feeling somewhat like a commando, readying for battle. The computerized boards in the airport were flashing with the flight that came in from Atlanta. I wasn't
certain at first if the flashing one was Jim's arrival or a
departure. I dug into my purse and pulled out my
glasses. I bet people thought I was picking up a child
at the airport that day. Mom on the cell phone. Mom
putting on her glasses. Mom looking apprehensive
and anticipating someone coming home. I ran to the
gate and waited in the soft gray carpeted corridor. Lots
of people were waiting for that plane. A couple of
women with kids in strollers (probably waiting for
Dad coming back from a business trip), sleek-looking
young women with perfectly styled hair and young
men in double-breasted suits carrying briefcases, uniformed drivers holding up signs with the last names of
passengers printed in bold Magic Marker.

It seemed to me that everyone waiting in the corridor for that plane had a reason to be there and suddenly I was very unsure of my own. Julie's phone call
had shaken me. I felt I was deceiving her. The boys.
Though I never felt I was betraying Peter.

I stood at the gate and watched the businessmen get
off the plane. They carried briefcases and bulky carry-
ons and wore suits with ties loosened around their
necks. Some had gray hair and some were balding.
Some were thin and others were paunchy. Young. Old.
Tall and short was the only way I could decide imme-

diately if one of them was Jim Moran. Jim was tall.
That I knew. For a moment I felt like I was meeting a
stranger.

My hair was pulled up halfway in a ponytail, ten-
drils down around my face, kind of like the way Julie
wears hers. It was, I guess, the way I styled it thirty
years ago when it wasn't hanging straight down. I
wore tight black jeans. I never wore jeans anymore. I
laughed at all the women who wore jeans with shoes
that looked like loafers. Jeans with creases down the
front because someone had ironed them or taken them
to the dry cleaner. Not me. I usually wore overalls over
leotards tops or T-shirts but never jeans.

"How come you bought all these jeans?" Peter had
asked while I packed. "You never wear jeans."

"I don't know. Just felt like it, I guess."

Peter never pushed the point.

As I stood there waiting for Jim to get off the plane,
I wondered if perhaps the jeans were not a mistake.
And the cowboy boots. They'd been sitting in my
closet for fifteen years. I dusted them off with Pledge
and they were slightly streaked. Oh God. Maybe I
should have stuck to the baggy overalls that worked
well after four children and went better with the station wagon. Maybe I should have worn the sandals. Or
sneakers. Maybe I looked like I was trying too hard.

All the passengers had disembarked and I was almost ready to walk away. Maybe Jim had come to his
senses. Considered that you don't hop on a plane to see
someone you haven't seen in a lifetime. Maybe Julie's
call had augured the weekend and I had no business
being here in Washington. I thought of how Robbie's
eyebrows shot up in the air. How when he left that day
he said, "Don't complicate your life, Emily."

And then I saw him. It was impossible not to recognize him. His jet black hair was sprinkled with silver. His face was broader. His jaw was squarer, edged with definition. This man was clearly no longer a boy but, oh, his eyes. His eyes let me know him right away. Deep-set and dark and piercing, buried in those high cheekbones that made me believe him years ago when he said he was a Cherokee. His eyes darted around the waiting area and I remembered the way they looked at me that day at the train station when he asked me never to forget him.

Voices in the airport terminal converged on my ears all at once as though I were in a dream. Announcements for arriving and departing flights boomed meaninglessly around me. I walked toward Jim. Without saying a word, we stopped. He placed the bag he carried over his shoulder on the floor beside him and looked at me.

"Emily." He said my name. He didn't ask. There was no question.

And then my mind raced, wondering if he was disappointed with what he saw. I wondered if every line around my eyes jumped out at him and screamed the time that had gone by.

He asked, "Don't you age?"

And then he did what I had wanted him to do for thirty years. He placed his arms around me and held his cheek next to mine. Pressed real hard. He stepped away from me and looked again as though he was checking to make sure I was there. He took the back of his hand and slid it down my cheek.

"It's good to see you, Emily," he said into my ear.

"I recognized you right away, Jimmy," I said.

And we stood there motionless while I felt the airport terminal swirl around me and suddenly everyone inside it disappeared.

When Jim Moran walked off that plane it was as though he finally had come home. We stood at the baggage claim. His arm held me next to him. My hip was wedged below his. His lips brushed against my hair when he spoke to me. Something as simple as "There's my bag," not letting go of my waist as he reached down to get it. I was sixteen again. I didn't want to spend the rest of my life missing him anymore. I didn't want to spend my life missing life anymore.

# 16

It was raining when Emily and I walked outside the Delta terminal. Emily held my carry-on bag in her left hand. I carried my suitcase, my left arm around her waist. I was surprised at how natural it felt to walk with her that way. There was nothing tentative about it although at every moment I was conscious that my arm was around her.

Neither of us said a word. We walked to the line of taxis waiting at arrivals. I stood back and took the bag from her hand. Opened the door to the cab. Took my arm from around her waist, ushered her into the backseat. Left her only long enough to place my bags in the trunk. Insignificant details yet I remember each one so well.

I was apprehensive when I walked off the plane. I think I was the last one off. There were crowds of people at the gate and there, off to the side, was Emily. I knew her right away. I knew it was Emily right away because as I approached her, I saw that smile. The one that met me after school thirty years ago. The one I longed for and didn't get when I got back from boot camp. To me, she still looked sixteen. She made me feel like a boy again. I hadn't felt that way for, God, so many years. The way I felt when I'd meet her after school and I couldn't wait to round the corner from the school's entrance and kiss her mouth, her neck, slide my hand down to her breasts inside the starched white uniform blouse. I pressed my cheek next to hers as we stood in the airport. I didn't know until then how much I'd missed her. How much I'd missed me.

Emily told the cab driver the name of the hotel. It all seemed so unreal. It seemed that I should hold her hand but then again it seemed that would have been too bold. The airport crowds were no longer there. It was just the two of us in the back of that cab.

"It's still early enough to go to the Memorial," she said, breaking what seemed a long silence.

"I want to get cleaned up," I said. "Unpack my bags, a quick shower."

"We could get a drink first," she said. "Call me when you're ready."

The cab pulled into the circular driveway of the Regency Hotel. Emily paid the cab driver before I could even make the gesture to reach for the wallet in the back of my jeans. The doorman was opening the door for us and the driver hopped out to pull my luggage out of the trunk. I took both bags and we walked into the hotel lobby, down the escalator to the reception desk.

"Mr. Moran is here to check in," Emily said. And then to me, "I got you nonsmoking. You gave up those Lucky Strikes, didn't you?"

I signed the register. The desk clerk handed me the card key. When I thanked him I wondered if my voice had a false air of aplomb. Did I sound like I was trying to act like I did this type of thing all the time? Mary and I hadn't stayed in a hotel since the five-day honeymoon we took in Myrtle Beach.

Our rooms were on the same floor, on opposite ends of the corridor. Emily walked me to my room. I felt as though my arm was noticeably absent from her waist. It seemed that her hands, hanging free by her sides, were so apparent. Like when you're a kid and sit in a movie with a girl and you're trying to muster up the courage to put your arm around her. You stretch and yawn and finally rest your arm there, sense her back straighten and wonder whether she wants your hand to drop down to her shoulder or stay where it is. I opened the door to my room. She stood outside.

"I'm in 612. When you're settled, come knock on the door," she said.

"I brought a bottle of champagne for you," I said. "It's probably warm, though. I'll put it in your minibar."

"You've come quite a way from Tango wine," she smiled.

"It's Perrier-Jouët," I said.

"Miles from Tango wine," she laughed.

She still had not stepped a foot into my room. I was thinking of saying, Would you like to come in? but it didn't seem the right thing to say. She craned her neck over my shoulder.

"Nice room," she said. "I think it's larger than mine. Have a good shower. See you later, okay?"

She turned and walked away. I closed the door and let the latch click softly, not wanting it to slam or shut too hard. I sat down in a stiff-backed leather chair by the window. I could see the Capitol in the distance, though it looked pale in the drizzle. The streets were a flurry of black umbrellas. I picked up the suitcase off the floor and threw it on top one of the double beds. I took my carry-on into the bathroom, placed it under the sink. Lined up my shaving cream and toothbrush and deodorant on the glass ledge. I took the Brut out of the side pocket. It had leaked a little and I wiped out the plastic liner with a washcloth. Part of me wanted to hurry, jump in the shower, knock on her door. Part of me wanted to take this slowly.

I sat on the edge of the bed and called Mary.

"I'm here," I said, instead of hello when she picked up the phone, trying to make my voice sound cheerful, guileless.

Mary said that Clancy was down by the stream with Parker, the boy who lived next door. She was reading *Cosmopolitan* and drinking a Vienna coffee, she said. How was the flight? Would I give her the number of the hotel? She and Clancy were going to the Fireman's Carnival in town that night. And then, "How does she look after all these years?" Mary asked, trying to be casual, as though it was an afterthought.

I said she looked the way you might expect someone to look after thirty years. I didn't say that to me she looked almost the same. I didn't say I thought she was even more beautiful than I'd remembered or hoped for. I didn't try to explain that it was a soft beauty, not the kind that Mary saw while flipping the pages of *Cosmopolitan*.

"She looks all right," I said, disinterested, striving to be nonchalant, uncaring. "Kiss Clancy for me."

When I got off the phone, I laid a fresh pair of jeans out on the bed, a black collared shirt, a pair of the new Jockeys in navy. I took off my clothes and walked naked to the shower, catching a glimpse of myself in the mirror on the way, turning my head quickly, trying not to look.

The shower poured down my face and the steam billowed around me. Soon I'd get dressed and walk down to her room. I pictured how I would knock on her door. Would it be a strong and firm rap or a gentle tapping? Would she ask me to come in or would I wait outside and then we'd go to the bar? Maybe she would say something like "Come in while I hunt for my key." I shut off the water and grabbed a towel, wrapping it around my waist. I wiped the steam off the mirror with my hand and stroked my beard. Time to shave again, I thought. This beard is too rough to place against her face. And while I was shaving, stroking the shave cream carefully from my cheeks and my neck and my jaw, I wondered if she wanted to kiss me as much as I wanted to kiss her.

I wondered what she would feel like lying beneath me, if she would fit with the curve of her belly the way she did when we lay under the Ping-Pong table in Connecticut. Would she be disappointed when she saw me, no longer the lean young boy with ripples across his stomach?

As gentle as I had been with the razor against my skin I felt the sting as I nicked my cheek next to my ear. The blood trickled down my face and I just stared at myself in the mirror. I splashed my face with cold water, placed a piece of tissue over the cut.

By the time I got dressed, the cut had stopped bleeding and was just dry and dark-looking. I slid the room key into my wallet, tucked the wallet into the back pocket of my jeans. At first I walked the wrong way down the corridor and then, realizing the room numbers were going the wrong way, I turned around, finally getting to her door. There was no thinking about how I knocked. No time to think before the door opened.

"You cut yourself shaving," Emily said and touched my cheek with two fingers. Then her hand withdrew as though she had just touched something hot. She said, "Just let me grab my purse."

The champagne was under my arm.

"Put this in your fridge," I said. "Take it home for you and Peter."

I tried to sound relaxed, familiar. Her urgency to leave, to grab her purse, had made me feel self-conscious. The champagne was never intended for Peter. It was for her. For us.

She was having a hard time opening the minibar. I walked over and helped her. We were on our knees, emptying out little bottles, cans of sodas, tins of peanuts, making room for the champagne. I said something like, There, all done. Extended my hand to pull her up. Her face flushed. A moment later we were in the elevator, headed for the rooftop bar.

The elevator door opened to a panorama of the city.

"Two for drinks?" the maître d' asked.

"That table in the corner," I said, pointing to a table by the window.

Emily walked ahead of me. And as I watched the sway of her hips I began thinking again what it would be like to hold her. To place my flesh next to hers in a room lit by a candle while the rain trickled down outside. There was something about the way she touched her fingers to the cut on my cheek. It was a way that was shy and withholding. The way that her fingertips almost stopped in midair until they rested so briefly on my skin. It was so quietly passionate.

Emily sat down, resting her elbows on the table, resting her chin on clasped hands. She turned her head to the window.

"It must look beautiful at night when it's clear skies," she said. "Too bad it's raining."

I had ordered a special bottle of wine, Morgan, even though I could feel a voice inside telling me that I couldn't afford the price tag. The waiter brought it over and showed me the label. I nodded my head, as if I did that sort of thing all the time, and sipped the wine from the small amount he poured in my glass and nodded again.

"Just leave it on the table," I said. "We'll pour it ourselves." And with a little bow, he left me there alone again with Emily.

I was staring at her and she asked what I was looking at. She reached into her purse and took out a small mirror. I remembered the days when she would take out her compact, the way she'd lift her chin and move the mirror around in a circle so she could see her face. It was the same gesture.

"You still do that," I said. "You still check the mirror."

She laughed. "You were looking at me so intensely. I thought maybe there was something wrong. Mascara under my eyes. Lipstick on my teeth."

"I'm looking at you because I can't believe we're sitting here together. Did you ever think thirty years ago that thirty years later we'd be in Washington?" I said. I didn't say "and married to other people."

She didn't answer me at first. She tilted the glass of chardonnay held in her hand, back and forth, as if she were thinking of what to say. And then she looked at me and smiled.

"There was a time, thirty years ago, when I thought we would always be together. That day I took you to the train station. That day I thought that life was unimaginable without you," she said.

It was just at that moment when I felt it come over me with the ease you feel when you know someone well. When you know every inch of their body and what they do when they first wake up in the morning. It is a feeling that is so simple: The way you might get someone's coffee without asking if they take milk or sugar because you know. The kind of feeling when a woman knows you well enough to straighten your tie or fasten a button that you missed. When a woman knows you well enough to touch a cut on your cheek.

Emily said the rooftop bar was certainly different from Finn's and even though I really hadn't thought about that place in years, I suddenly remembered it like it was yesterday. She said she'd had lunch there with her mother not long ago. It wasn't Finn's anymore, she said. It's a gourmet spot for ladies who lunch. And then we both remembered her mother that summer. How her mother disapproved of our romance.

"She said that kissing would lead to other things," Emily laughed.

"It never did for us, though, did it?"

Emily's eyes stopped looking at me then and faced down. I reached my hand across the table, taking the wineglass that she was tilting in her hand, back and forth. I set down the glass, off to the side, making a path straight through where nothing could be accidentally knocked over. You're going to spill that, I said. I wanted to simply take her hand but, instead, I reached out to her, my hand palm up. Offering. She put her hand in mine and I squeezed her fingers, then released them, holding her hand in mine. I turned my hand and clasped our fingers together in the center of the small table.

"I wanted to make love to you that October day," I said. "I know this sounds crazy but I wanted the moment to be exactly right. I wanted to have dinner by candlelight somewhere. I wanted to walk with you first, my arm around your waist. You think that's ridiculous, don't you? Too sentimental? Forward? Crazy?" And I began to laugh, partly out of self-consciousness, partly because she smiled and shook her head, laughing as I posed each question.

She lifted the hand not held by mine to her face. She took a finger and placed it on her lip, biting down on the nail. And then she said, almost in a whisper, "So did I." And it drove me crazy. I wanted to take her right there. Take her in that glass elevator right up to my room and lay her on the bed.

It was a far cry from that day thirty years ago when she said she wasn't ready for that. The day she told me there was someone else and she guessed that I was just too late. And I couldn't help but think that even now, as Emily's hand rested in mine in that familiar way that lovers have, fingers entwined the way bodies might be, that, once again, it was probably just too late.

# 17

It was hard to tell whether I felt a greater sense of disappointment or relief when Jim didn't invite me into his room. It was the same mixed feeling when we got into the cab at the airport. He had let go my waist as he ushered me into the backseat and slid in next to me, placing the carry-on bag between us. I longed for him to touch me again as my hand sat on top of the bag, so easy to hold, to cover with his own, and yet he didn't.

When we took the elevator up to the sixth floor of the hotel, people might have thought we were brother and sister except for the coloring of our hair. At least that's what I told myself. I felt uneasy. The elevator was glass. We stood a distance from one another, staring out, remarking how pretty it was to shoot through the atrium that way. Trying to guess whether the hanging plants were silk or plastic or real, and if real, how did they manage to water them? Small talk. And I wondered if he, like myself, felt as though we were in a fishbowl, people in the lobby pointing to us, perhaps remarking and wondering why we were there.

I asked him if he was hungry and he said he'd eaten only snacks on the plane. He didn't say he was hungry, didn't say he was not. And I wondered if his answer was noncommittal because he didn't know which answer was the one I wanted. Hungry, meaning that took precedence and we should go to a restaurant. Not hungry, meaning it was less important than doing something else but not sure what that would be. Maybe I sounded as though I was speaking to a child. Are you hungry? Are you cold? Are you tired? Did you pack your toothbrush? Have you done your book report? Do you need to use the bathroom? It struck me that I couldn't remember the last time I had asked Peter a question like that. If you're hungry, dinner's ready, I might have said but that was all. I pushed the thought out of my mind.

"I am hungry," he said. "It's not like the old days when the airlines gave you trays with silverware wrapped in cloth napkins. Now they throw some peanuts at you and that's it."

We laughed uncomfortably, filling in conversation that neither of us was ready to have just yet. The visceral affection at the airport was a homecoming. For a few moments, time had stopped.

I walked him to his room, down the corridor from mine and on the other side. I wondered if the desk clerk had done that intentionally, separated us knowingly, protecting us from the same maid who sees one bed falsely undone, the other rumpled. He fumbled for the card key in his pocket. The carry-on bag, slung over his shoulder, slid down his arm, jogging his hand as he tried to place the key. I said, "Here, let me take the bag." And as he slipped it off his arm, our hands touched briefly, both of us retracting. He placed the card key into the slot. Green light. Door open.

"I'll change," he said. "I could use a hot shower."

He hadn't stepped into the room yet when he said this. He was standing still in the doorway, leaning to hold the door open, facing me.

"Knock on my door when you're ready," I said. "Room 612."

"It's early," he said. "Not quite four o'clock."

"We could go to the Memorial," I said.

"Not yet," he said. "I'm not quite ready for that yet."

And then with an obvious ill-at-ease, I said I would see him later. I turned around, heading at first in the wrong direction down the corridor, coming back around and walking past his room again, the door shut this time.

I didn't know what to do with myself when I got back to my room. My instinct was to call Peter and then I thought better of that, concerned that uncharacteristic communication could be misconstrued. I changed from the tank top to a sleeveless white blouse. I picked up the book that I'd tried to read on the train and couldn't focus, reading the same sentence over and over, flipping pages backwards to see if I was in the right place. I turned on the stereo and, as luck would have it, there was the song "My Girl," one of Jim's repertoire from Siddhartha, and I wondered if it was some sort of sign, an omen. Was it good or evil? Warning or affirmation?

It wasn't long before he knocked on the door. I opened it wide, not asking who was there.

"You should always ask who it is," he said, as the door flung open.

"I knew it was you," I said.

"Could have been Jack the Ripper," he said.

He was carrying the bottle of champagne. His hair

was damp around the edges. He had a fresh shaving cut by his ear. I reached my hand up to his cheek, touched the abraded skin and then, abruptly, self-consciously, pulled my hand away. Too personal, I thought and yet it felt so natural to touch him.

"Yes, ouch. Missed with the razor for a change," he said. "Emily, are you going to ask me in or should we spend the evening in the doorway?" He laughed. "Put the champagne in the minibar. Bring it home and share it with Peter."

He might have seen my face visibly fall after he said that because then he said softly, "Of course, you could open it here if you like."

I took the champagne and walked to the minibar. Fumbling as he had with the room key. I couldn't get the door open and Jim walked over, knelt down next to me, took the key from my hand, again brushing against me, opened the bar, took out cans of 7UP and ginger ale and laid them on the floor, nestled the champagne bottle on a shelf.

"You and I are lousy with locks." He smiled.

"There's a bar on the roof," I said. "It looks over the city. We could go there. It's raining."

I jammed my tape recorder, notebook, pen into my purse. Jim fixed the tag on the back of my blouse. Lifted a few strands of stray hair caught beneath the collar. All this in silence, deliberate straining in the quiet of our movements. We walked to the elevator, my hand dangling self-consciously by my side.

The maître d' asked "Table for two?" And I thought how Jim and I had never been in a place like this before. Would never have envisioned a place like this when we were young. It wasn't like Finn's where you shimmied up to the bar or the coffee shops where we went before the movies. I wondered how often he and Mary had been places like this together. If he placed his hand on the small of her back as he did mine and led her to the table. Our table was in a corner, next to a window. In the distance you could see the Capitol, though it was gray and raining and the view was hardly dazzling as the brochure pictures showed.

"We've become our parents," he said, echoing my thoughts.

Jim asked the waiter for the wine list and ordered Morgan chardonnay, a wine I'd never heard of before and I don't know whether it was the wine or the fact that Jim ordered but it tasted like velvet.

"I can never smell the oak or taste the fruit in wines the way they say you should," I said. "But this is delicious."

And Jim's face beamed as though he had crushed the grapes himself. He had the waiter leave the bottle on the table.

"It's not true about chilling chardonnay," he said. "You really should leave it on the table. Drinking it ice cold takes away the flavor."

And I wondered if I looked as much the schoolgirl as I felt, hanging on his words as though he were preaching a homily to wine.

"It's a far cry from Tango wine," I said. "A far cry from Finn's."

"Finn's," he said, nodding his head, pressing his lips together. "I haven't thought about that place in years."

"Jerry Finn died of AIDS. I saw his obit," I said.

"Doesn't surprise me. Finn was promiscuous even for the sixties," he said.

"It's a gourmet deli, now," I said. "I had lunch there with my mother a few months ago. At first I hadn't realized where we were, but the ladies' room is in the same place."

"Ah, your mother. The impenetrable Mrs. Hudson. How is she?" he asked and then he grinned. "Remember the time she was peeping at us from her bedroom window? She let that shade roll so hard I thought she'd wake up the neighborhood."

"She told me the next day that kissing could lead to other things."

"But it never did," he said.

He looked me in the eye when he said that, his mouth still open when he finished the sentence, as though perhaps he would say something else, continue in some way, but he didn't. Was he thinking as I was about that day when he came back from boot camp? The day I told him there was someone else. I wanted to tell him right then and there that what happened that day was not the way I'd told him. I wanted to tell him the whole thing had been a lie. How there had never been anyone else. Not then.

"If you tip that glass any more, it's going to spill, Emmie," he said.

He took the glass from my hand, placed it on the table. He moved the bud vase and the candle to the side and reached his hand to the middle of the table. Palm up. I hesitated at first, not sure if I was to place my hand in his. But when my hand reached over, he clasped it tightly, looking at me so intently that I breathed in deeply, so audibly that he told me to relax, that it would all be okay.

He told me how he dreamed about me all summer long at boot camp. How he dreamed about coming

home and having me throw my arms around his neck
the way the girls did in all those old black-and-white
photos that *Life* magazine ran after the Second World
War. The way their dresses are sort of blowing up as
they reach for the neck of the sailor who tips them over
and kisses them the way they wanted to kiss them for
months. He said that when he got back to New York
City, he wanted to take me to dinner.

They had a little restaurant in Beaufort, the town
outside of Parris Island, he said. His mother took him
there after boot camp graduation. His father hadn't
gone to graduation. Jim wanted to take me to a place
like the one in Beaufort. He knew there were places
like that in New York City. In Little Italy. Where the tables were covered in red oilcloth and lit with candles
stuck in wax-coated wine bottles. After dinner, we
would have gone for a walk, he said. Maybe back to
the fountain or back to the river.

"No, probably not the river," he said, speaking as
though we were back there making plans. "I would
never take you to the river again."

He remembered that night by the river.

He didn't know where we could have gone after
dinner, he said. My house was out of the question. His
house was even more forbidding.

"I thought maybe about asking Steve if I could use
his dad's apartment. His dad was out of town a lot or
just out on the town," he said.

And I remembered that night with Steve and felt
guilty just thinking about it.

"I wanted the moment to be just right," he said. "I'd
thought about it all summer long. I'd planned it.
Dreamed it."

He said all this as he looked right into my eyes.

"And then something went so terribly wrong," he said. "What happened that day, Emily? What was it?"

"I wanted that, too," I said. "I should explain."

"What was it that day?" he asked me again.

"It's not the right time now," I said.

"I'm not even sure I want to know."

The waiter came back and we ordered a platter of cheese. We finished the wine. Jim offered to pay the bill, reaching for his wallet, but I signed my room.

"You didn't have to do that," he said, almost gruffly.

"It's a business expense," I said.

A look of uncertainty came over him. "You get the next one," I said.

We left the bar, took the elevator down to the lobby. The rain had stopped. The air was heavy, steam rising from the concrete, still misty.

"Let's walk," he said. "Head to the Memorial."

"Are you sure?"

He slipped his arm over my shoulders. I put my arm around his waist. We were back at the fountain. I could almost hear the tambourines.

# 18

There was something about the Washington side-walks after the rain that reminded me of New York City. The dun concrete, darkened by dampness. The acrid scent of city soot in the thick humid air. The stone buildings that lined the avenues. Or maybe it was just my arm over Emily's shoulder as we stepped into the street from the hotel lobby that made me feel a certain way again. It came over me as though someone had thrown a brick through a plate-glass window. A feeling so powerful of youth, of a fire burning inside me that I hadn't felt for years. There was a casualness to the gesture of my arm around her, of feeling the flesh of her shoulder under my hand, that was possessive, the way I felt when we were younger. I tried to forget she was another man's wife.

It was a long walk to the Vietnam Memorial. We stopped along the way and bought bottles of spring-water from a sidewalk vendor. We were going to sit on a bench but Emily pointed out that it probably was wet. Always the mom, I said, teasing her.

I was more afraid of seeing the Memorial than I had been of enlisting in the Marine Corps. It wasn't until that last day at the train station in Old Greenwich that I felt fearful and, as I look back, I'm not sure if I was fearful of the war as much as I was fearful of leaving behind the life I knew so well. The Marines were the devil I *didn't* know. Until that moment, I almost looked forward to being a hero. I dreamed of medals pinned to my chest, coming home to a parade. I'll show them all, I thought. Show them that I'm not a failure. And then after being in Chou Lai for a few weeks, I simply prayed that I wouldn't come home in one of those gray metal boxes I'd see lined up on the Tarmac. Part of me felt like a coward. I felt almost guilty as I walked the endless stretch of the Memorial wall and saw the names. Over fifty-eight thousand dead etched on stone.

Emily and I walked the wall in silence. She kept a step behind me. Giving me room. The space I needed to mourn. It took us nearly two hours because I read each one like they were elegies. There were three names I recognized: Jerrold Hale, Beau Roberts, Quinton McBride. Hale and Roberts were in my unit at Chou Lai. I knew about them. But Quinn McBride. Son of a bitch couldn't get into the whorehouse in Vegas but had himself blown apart in Nam. I'd often wondered what happened to Quinn but as with everything else, once it was over, it was over. I'd always been afraid to find out, to look back. I ran my finger over Quinn's name on the wall and I cried. Emily touched my arm but I withdrew from her touch. At first, she pulled her arm away. But then, unlike Mary, she was undaunted, refusing to be shut out. She touched my arm again, pressing firmly this time with a grasp on my forearm.

"Do you want to stop?" she asked. "Maybe this was a mistake. Please don't pull away from me."

But I told her I wanted to go on, taking her hand in mine, clasped finger around finger. This is the church. This is the steeple. Look inside. See all the people. Fifty-eight thousand dead people. I wanted her there. I was grateful she hadn't let me push her away. Quinn's name was, thankfully, the last one that I recognized.

When it was over, Emily and I walked to the top of the hill. We sat on a bench looking down on the wall. No longer caring that the wooden slats were damp. For what seemed like a very long time, I stared up at the sky before I was able to speak. I wanted to tell her so many things but felt I couldn't speak until the lump in my throat dissolved. It never did. My words came out choking and sputtering. I stopped many times to fight back tears that caught in my throat. I hadn't cried like that since the day at the harbor with my father's ashes. At one point, Emily took a wad of mashed yellow tissues out of her purse and handed them to me. People passed by and glanced at us. They shook their heads and nodded. Weak smiles. Understanding. They knew. They held thin sheets of paper, parts shaded. Names they'd rubbed off the wall, as though carrying the printed sculptures around with them would help in some small way. The way I held my father's ashes in my hands.

I spoke as easily and freely as I did that day in the harbor. But this time I knew someone was listening. The someone I had wanted to listen, to hear me, all along.

And so I told her. We got into Da Nang about four o'clock in the afternoon. The airplane cabin had been cool. It was May. Even California was cool when we left. The first thing I remember when I got off the plane in Da Nang was the heat. My only frame of reference was when I was ten years old and the experimental theater at the end of our street burned down. People emptied out in droves. I heard the fire engines clanging and smelled the smoke. There were thick billows of black choking up the night sky. I ran down the stairs into the street and stood in the crowd behind the police sawhorses, feeling the heat from the crush of people and the burning frame building. It was the same wall of heat in Vietnam when I stepped off that plane. The heat stopped you. We had flown to Anchorage from Camp Pendleton, refueled and gone on to Okinawa where we stayed for two days. They said that Okinawa would prepare us for the heat in Vietnam. It didn't. It wasn't the same. And then there was the aroma of Vietnam. It's indescribable, but I know that if I ever smelled it again I would recognize it immediately. It's different. A tang. A pungency that is foreign to the senses. But it almost grows on you. It's something different. I can't liken it to anything. Maybe it was sugarcane, cassava, rice fields, cattle, diesel, Napalm all rolled into one. I'm not sure what it was. I'm not sure if I ever want to smell it again.

The flight from Okinawa to Da Nang was only a couple of hours. I didn't want to be in my shoes. Da Nang was surrounded by the enemy and the enemy was so hard to detect. You could see a grandmother a few feet away from you and not know if she had a grenade in her hand under the rice satchel.

There were about three hundred of us on the plane. I slept through most of the flight. I needed to escape. I was on edge. Scared. It felt like my life was out of control. We flew there on a civilian jet with stewardesses and rolling food carts. I felt like the crew was looking at me in a way that meant they would never see me again. Of course, in all likelihood they never would see me again, but I felt they were looking at me like I was going to die. When I got up from my sleep the guy next to me said that Chou Lai had been hit the night before. Two hundred guys were killed, he said. His mouth was dry. His pupils were fixed. He was scared.

When we got off the plane, there were a bunch of guys walking toward us, heading for another gate. Going home. They were looking at me like they were saying, "Forget about it, man, you're dead. You think this is hot? You're walking into hell."

One guy actually spoke. "You're dyin', boy," he said. "Where you from boy?" And I'd barely uttered New York when he said, "You think New York was bad? Wait until you spend some time here." And he laughed a mucus-filled chortle.

They were all young men heading home. Maybe not a year older than I was but they looked haggard and worn and old. Cadaverous.

The silence in Da Nang's airport terminal was staggering. No loudspeakers. No small talk. No laughter. You heard the bombs in the distance and somehow that made the silence even more defined. It was like that all the time I was there, from the time I got off that plane until the time I left country. There were always those sounds in the background reminding me where I was. Rumbles like short bursts of thunder, but deeper, at quicker intervals and singular. Mortar fire.

Da Nang was just an airport but there was a lot of activity once we got outside the terminal. Supplies being hauled and diesel trucks carting things everywhere. A lot of loading and unloading. They grabbed all three hundred of us and sent us on buses downtown. In a strange way, war is like a business. There were military there who had desk jobs, nine-to-fivers, so coming in at four o'clock, there wasn't time to do the necessary processing to give us orders and destinations. The buses took us to a transit barracks downtown.

We sneaked out to dinner at a hotel. Potter and his cousin, Tony, were already in Da Nang. Potter had flown out ahead of me since I'd been delayed by the trouble I had with Ward. Anyway, Tony had been there for a while and he showed us the ropes. We paid an ARVN (Army of the Republic of Vietnam) guy with a jeep to take us. He put us in the back of the jeep and covered us with a tarp. The hotel was a nine-story brick building. What you might call a cheesy hotel stateside. The restaurant had the requisite ceiling fan, Formica tables and geckos. Little green lizards that climb the walls and run around the room eating all the bugs.

It amazed me how Americanized everything was. The waiters were smiling and happy, brought us bowls of rice and quart bottles of pale Vietnamese beer. The rice bowls were fine. We were hungry. They even gave us forks. I didn't recognize anything on the menu anyway. By the end of the evening, we were plastered. We were sitting there staring at the geckos. The quart bottles kept coming. The waiters smiled at us like we were just tourists.

The next morning, we got back on the buses and went to the base for processing: name, rank, serial number, name of your unit, next of kin. Next of kin. I put down my father's name. There were hundreds of us there but I felt so alone. We went to the section of the base where our units were lodged and waited for orders. It didn't take long for Potter and me to hear. Six hours later they divvied us up. Put us on the goony birds and sent us to our stations. Potter and I went to Chou Lai and Quinn, God rest his soul, was shipped to Khe Sanh. I kept thinking of the guy on the plane: Chou Lai was hit last night.

Potter and I were stationed in this remote area of Chou Lai near the sea. When the copter landed it was dark and they said, be prepared to get hit again. We went right to the bunker. A hole in the ground dug maybe six feet deep that fit ten of us side by side. We sat there upright, helmets on. M16s strapped to our shoulders. Buck knives wedged at our ankles in straps. Snakes and rats crawling around us. We had a dilemma: Do we shoot the snakes or just let the rats get them? We decided to get rid of the rats. Snakes were easier to decimate. With knives. With our boots. The rats and the snakes bothered us less than the bombs. We were glad it was dark.

The sirens warned us that night and then the rockets went off. And now that I live down in the South, when I hear the sirens before the tornadoes come, my heart pounds and I begin to sweat. The sirens are the same pitch, the same screeching, frenzied urgency like the ones I heard before the rockets flew over our heads in Nam. And I knew that very first night in the bunker that when the rockets came, the bunker wouldn't really do much good. You feel like there's a bullet out there with your name on it and you just have to believe and pray that somehow it won't get you.

After I'd been in-country for a while, the rockets stopped bothering me as much. I didn't give a damn anymore what happened to me. By then we were getting stoned. Marijuana and poppy fields were everywhere. Everything in Vietnam grew big except for the people. There were bugs as big as birds and rats as big as cats. Rock apes roamed on top of Monkey Mountain near Da Nang. You could look down from the top and see the South China Sea. It was a beautiful country ravaged by war.

Some of the guys would even be tripping, standing on top of their hooches and watching the rockets go over their heads, crying out war whoops as each one flew by. Like they were playing Cowboys and Indians. Everyone was doing something to make them forget, reminded only by the M16s at their sides and the rats.

The first few times we were shot at, I was scared. But then it became more frightening when there was no shooting. The enemy was in the dark. You couldn't see him. It was like walking through a haunted house at Halloween and not knowing when something was going to jump out at you, except this was real. When the shooting finally started, there was a strange sense of relief. You breathed easier. The anxiety and the fear left you. Because then you knew. Once the shooting starts you have answers. The only two questions that mattered were where and when. The only way you could beat the bullet was once you knew where it was coming from and when it would come. Once you knew, you were less afraid.

The bullets always missed me but guys next to me got shot. Got killed next to me. What do you do? You suck it up. It's so much easier to say that now. In the first few months, nine guys in my unit were dead. We called the medics. We tried to airvac them out. You do what you can. But after a while you get cold. You freeze the first time the guy next to you drops to the ground and the second time you try to do something that doesn't matter because they're dead anyway. The fifth time, you're just doing what you're there to do and you try not to get in the way. By the tenth time, you tell yourself that you'll cry later but by then, you can't even cry anymore.

At first I made friends because I was scared and I needed them. But after you start to lose them, you stop getting close. You don't want to be anybody's friend anymore. I don't think I ever quite got over that, not wanting to be anyone's friend anymore. Not even Potter's. You don't have time anymore for friends and you don't have time to be lonely. It's all right to be scared because that keeps you alive. Lonely was too dangerous a place to go. Friends could be too temporary.

It was a black-and-white world over there. The pendulum never swung in between. We're supposed to live our lives with gray and different shades but there was no gray over there. It was kill or be killed. Everything had to make sense. Everything had to be defined. Black and white was the only way to make that world work. Living in a black-and-white world can drive you mad. I still avoid the gray. I never quite got over it. Sometimes it drives me crazy.

But don't get me wrong. We had liberties. We had fun. When we were away from that war it was party time. See what I'm saying? It was black and white: You were either cold sober staring down the sight of an M16 or you were getting stoned or drunk and getting laid.

There were liberties in Bangkok. Sin City. Bangkok was heaven and hell rolled into one. I think I came closer to dying in Bangkok than anyplace else. The only words I knew in Thai were the dirty ones. I knew when people were swearing at me but otherwise I had a real hard time communicating with them. All I could do was swear back. It's a funny language, Thai. One word can mean several different things depending on how you accent it. You should never try to compliment a young lady when you've been drinking. I tried to tell a young lady once that she had a very pretty face. I'd been drinking and accented the wrong word and she pulled a knife on me. Apparently I said something rather derogatory.

G.I.s were big business in Thailand. It was whatever you want and whenever you want it. And it was cheap. Whatever. Booze, pot, acid, heroine, gambling, women. The girls were young. The younger, like fourteen, the more expensive. The girls all wore numbers. The dance clubs had names like The Manhattan Club and The Nevada Club. At one of them, The Cleveland Club, I remember this guy singing "Do You Know the Way to San José?" in broken English. The whole thing cracked me up. They served pizza and hot dogs at the clubs to make us feel at home. But the girls, standing around and posing, sitting on chairs with their legs crossed and skirts hitched up, reminded me of the Museum of Natural History. You know, how they have those fake gorillas sitting on the rocks inside those glass cages? All you had to do was walk in and sit down and the girls would come right over to you. Pick a number. Five dollars for a night. The only thing they wouldn't do was blow you. "Buddha says no good," one girl explained to me.

But otherwise, it was party time. I was drinking Scotch out of the bottle, shit-faced drunk, smoking joints and getting laid. And the girls gave you a bath every time you nailed them. I was the king of the hill. Twice, I got the clap. The numbers on the girls' backs were supposed to mean they were healthy. The girls were checked on a periodic basis but I guess I got one in between checkups after the girl had done forty or fifty guys. She probably gave forty guys the clap before they checked her again.

One time I met this guy, Mike Prescott. Prescott worked with AFRTS, Air Farts we called them: Armed Forces Radio and Television Service. He was pretty tight with the boys from Air America, the CIA company that ran the secret war out of Thailand into Laos. Anyway, Prescott had a membership at this place called The Yellow Bird. Prescott bought two bottles of Chivas at the base for two dollars and sixty cents each and anything at The Yellow Bird cost us eight baht. One baht was worth a nickel. It didn't matter whether we wanted our Chivas with ice or soda or water: It was eight baht. But the real beauty of The Yellow Bird was that the owners hired the best young hostesses they could find from Germany and France and England and Australia. Round-eyed girls. And round-eyed girls were very special even though they were really just whores who spoke English. They took special care of the guys at The Yellow Bird. No one caught the clap at The Yellow Bird. It was a damn good time.

The other wars were never brought home to the living room, though. They were fought quickly. Vietnam was a daily, nightly dose of entertainment for seven and a half years. There were no great victories. There were no valiant headlines. No Iwo Jima. No Normandy. No Hiroshima. Only My Lai and there were thousands of My Lais. Every day was a My Lai in Vietnam. One night they sent me out with a Huey squadron. Those guys were bad motherfuckers. They really thought they were hot. It was a reconnaissance mission. We were flying maybe two or three hundred feet over a friendly village and there in the middle of the village was Charlie. Charlie, surrounded by a throng of women and children who were clinging to their mothers' skirts. Charlie was shooting at us. Oh, but we couldn't shoot back because this was a "friendly" village. And we couldn't have a clean shot at Charlie because of all those kids and women. Charlie hit the copter a couple of times and then suddenly the gunner at the copter's door slapped out his M60 and just started rapid firing. It seemed like the bursts would never stop. He killed them all. I saw them all—the women, the children, Charlie—crumble to the ground. For a few minutes, no one said anything. I turned to the gunner, a kid not much older than I was.

"I thought you weren't allowed to do that," I said.

The gunner took a long drag on his cigarette and then he asked me if I knew how to fly a Huey. I told him that I didn't.

"Well, neither do I," he said.

See, the gunner wasn't going to risk the pilot being hit.

"It's legal over here," the gunner said.

And I knew he meant the killing. The murder. He wasn't going down because Charlie was surrounded by a village. Tell me that wasn't My Lai. Tell me there weren't a million My Lais. I'll never forget the look in that gunner's eyes. I had to turn away. I think that after a while you lose sight of the killing. Death doesn't matter.

But this was the hard part. We all grew up and lived in a world where there was right and wrong. You could bend the rules and twist the rules but you had to play the game fair. Lord knows, I had bent enough rules before I went to Vietnam. But breaking the rules, well, then you paid a price. See, you get to Vietnam and there are no more rules and no more laws. What was right was wrong and what was wrong was right. You're killing people. It was okay to burn houses and to set traps. It was okay to lie and cheat and drink and do drugs. It was okay to be with hookers. It was okay to blow up a village. Everything that was wrong was right. And then you get home and you try to undo it. And while you're trying to undo it, you offend and hurt and disappoint. And slowly, after a while, you begin to recover but you're never really whole again.

I was twenty when I got back from Vietnam. You change a lot between the ages of eighteen and twenty. My tour was up in 1970. I came home via California. The same route that brought me there, brought me back. It was one hundred and sixteen degrees when I left Chou Lai that February and twenty-six degrees when I flew into Kennedy. Johnson had begun to withdraw troops the summer before. The Paris peace talks had begun. It was good to be home but antiwar sentiment was everywhere in my face. I had been away for too long. I slept for days. Got up to eat something and then back to the bed. Over there, I went for days without sleeping. And sometimes I slept in the bunker and sometimes I slept leaning up against a tree. I really hadn't slept for years.

Don't get me wrong. I don't think we were any different than any other soldiers who fought anywhere else. World War II, say, or even Korea. We weren't special. It was the way we were treated that was special. We weren't heroes. I tried to call old friends but no one was home or seemed to remember me. I knew it was bullshit. I was the enemy.

It was a different sort of war but it was no better or worse than any other war. People died. Those poor slobs crawled on Omaha Beach while everyone around them was getting blown to bits. They tried not to die while the sea was running red. Those poor slobs must have looked down the barrels of their guns and seen someone wearing a different color uniform and pulled the trigger. That part remained the same in Vietnam. We also pulled the trigger if someone wore a different uniform. And we walked on back and put our bodies here and their bodies there. Dead bodies are dead bodies. Slant eyes or blue eyes. German or Asian. It doesn't matter.

I bummed around for a couple of years until I made it down to Mobile. I was a short-order cook, worked in some gas stations, sold television sets, worked as a waiter, booked movies in theaters. I was twenty-eight years old when I married Mary. It would be easy to say that I'm just an asshole and that's why our marriage is lousy but that's too easy. It's hard for me to get close to people. It's even harder for people to get close to me. I'm not sure if I was always this way. I don't want this to sound too pompous: Saying there was pre-Vietnam and post-Vietnam. But until Emily called, I didn't remember too much of the before Vietnam. I remembered more about the last thirty years than I did about the first seventeen.

I told Emily how when she called, I got so nostalgic. How I wanted to go back and back. I told her how I saw this television commercial for a phone service where you can dial a certain number for directory assistance and you don't even need the area code or the city. You just give them the name you're looking for. So I tried it. I wanted to find Potter. I hadn't seen him since 1970. Since he flew to Boston and I flew to New York. I don't think there were any memories we wanted to share. His mother's travel agency in Boston told me Potter was living in Rockport, Mass. I was always a little afraid of finding him after all those years. I was always afraid of what I'd find out. The only thing I knew was that he'd married this Vietnamese girl named Gina. Anyway, I finally got to him and we talked for hours. It turned out that Gina committed suicide and Potter raised the two kids they had on his own. The irony of it. How deathly afraid I was of having Gina tell me that Potter was dead and there was Gina, dead. They'd been having some problems, he said. She was very depressed after their second child was born. I said I was sorry. That it was too bad. But he remarried about five years ago. Someone he's very much in love with, he said. They have a two-year-old daughter. I told him about Clancy and Mary and he asked if the three of us could visit. Then he told me that one of the sons he had with Gina is married and has a baby boy. He's a grandfather now. Hard to believe. I wondered if Potter was over Vietnam. Over Gina. I doubted it.

So I cried that day at the Memorial. We all cry. There are fifty-eight thousand names on that wall. I only saw the three that I knew. The names don't even matter anymore. The names I knew. The names I didn't know.

The first thing people ask me, when they hear I was in Vietnam, is if I ever killed anyone. It's always the first question. I never answer them. I tell them I shot my gun a lot of times. I say I really don't know if I killed anyone. But I know. And I knew then. It's simply

no one's business. My family never asked me when I
came home. They didn't want to know. They asked me
what I wanted for dinner and I was too crippled inside
to even answer. The whole time I was over there we always talked about going home. We counted the days.
"Time's getting short. I'm short now," we'd say. "Only
eighty-six days to go." And you prayed that you'd
make it. But it was the biggest disappointment when
you finally got home because your family didn't know
who you were anymore. They didn't know how to
react to you, what to say. For me, I was a stranger before I left them but not nearly as much a stranger as I
was when I came home.

For years I slept with a knife under my pillow. The
scary part is that I am not afraid of dying. It doesn't
scare me one iota. I have looked death square in the
face and it's stared right back at me.

I'm not sure if the War created all these things in me:
The defenses. The pushing people away. For sure, it
heightened them. I allow myself to go so far with people and then the warning signals go off and I run.
Maybe it's just survival. I stopped getting close to people when it hurt to watch them die. I'm not even sure
whether it would have mattered had there been a parade when I came home. If we had been hailed as heroes
with ticker tape. Would it have made watching those
people die any easier? I don't think so. More than fifty-
eight thousand Americans died as a result of the war in
Vietnam. I don't think so.

I must have talked about all that for an hour. When
I stopped, I realized it was pouring. It was hard to tell
at first if Emily was crying. Her hair was wet and her
cheeks were wet from the rain. But we both were crying. For what was, what is, what couldn't be. And it

was then we fell into each other's arms, our heads resting on each other's shoulders. And despite the feeling of overwhelming pain, I don't think I had ever felt closer to anyone in my life. It had been a long time since I let anybody in.

# 19

We sat on the bench, up on the hill. The Memorial lay below us. It was quiet. Around eight o'clock when we finished walking the wall. Most of the visitors had gone home. It had started to rain.

Jim was staring at the sky as he told me the stories. What happened after that October day. When his life was never the same again. He took me from California to Vietnam and home again. My mouth was dry, parted open. I could taste the rain on my lips, the only thing that dampened them. I licked the drops away. Not wanting to move. To break his words with the slightest interruption of even a hand to my face. I wasn't even sure whether he was really speaking to me. It was like he had just opened up his veins and the blood poured out of him. And as he spoke, the rain kept coming down harder and harder. It soaked our hair and dripped down our faces. My blouse was saturated. Jim's shirt clung to his body. He seemed unaware that it was raining. It was hard to tell whether the dampness on his body was only from the rain. I could smell the sweat on him. But more, I could feel his pain. And I wished there had been some way I could have rescued him when he was seventeen.

I looked at him as he stared at the sky. The way I'd looked at him when he'd stared across the horizon at Tod's. I never took my eyes off him when he spoke even though he was staring only upwards. He was the boy I knew. He was the one who put the ring in my hand. The one with the tight white T-shirt who held me on the beach. The one who sang to me from the stage. And yet he was a man I felt I knew so well, so deeply, as though thirty years had never separated us. And as he spoke, so evenly, so quietly, as though it was a dream, I pictured the sea running red. The rats in the bunker. The skinny boy who was lovelessly fucking whores in Thailand. I could feel myself trembling.

How little had I known when I was sixteen. Jim was robbed of his youth while I was handing out carnations at Columbus Circle, running barefoot in Bethesda Fountain in my peace earrings and black armband, going home to full place settings and a maid that served us dinner. Jim was sitting in a bunker as I sat in my bedroom gazing at the stained glass of the church next door, reading McKuen, purposefully not looking at Jim's picture. For me, the war was a cause. Not as real as I thought it was. As Jim spoke to me, I found myself reviled at the thought of guys like Barry from Columbia who thought they knew. None of us knew. We didn't have a clue. We gave them no parade. No welcome home. Guys like Barry called them killers. None of us realized that even those who came back alive were dying.

There was nothing I could say when he finished. I never brought out the tape recorder that was in my purse. I didn't use the pen or the notebook. When he finished, the only thing to do was hold on to each other. And as the rain came down around us, and he breathed the end of the sentence that told me he was done, had enough for now, it was so easy to fall into each other's arms. There was nothing even remotely sexual about it. It was the embodiment of friendship. Like two children who were hiding in the darkness, finding salvation in each other, saving each other from the bumps in the night. Monsters, lightning, thunder . . . all the things that make children fearful and long for the warmth of a friend to comfort them. All the walls came down.

Until that moment I don't think I ever knew heartbreak. I felt as though I had reneged on a promise. Foolish young girl who said she would hold his heart in both her hands and never drop it. And I felt as though on that October day I had not only dropped it but tossed it on the ground, shattering the promise like splintered shards of glass.

We must have stayed in that embrace for minutes. Minutes that seemed to be over too soon when we let go.

"We're drowning," he laughed, pushing my hair behind my ears the way he used to. Wiping my face with the sleeve of his shirt. "Let's get you someplace where it's dry."

I took my hands and wiped the wetness off his face. "And you? Look at you," I said, raising my shoulders and breathing in deeply. "You're soaked to the bone."

It was dark by now. We had been at the Memorial for hours. The lights on the base of the Memorial were bright. The wall glowed eerily, shining on the statues of the veterans in a way that made them appear more ghostlike. Like apparitions, their bronzed clothing hung in folds that looked all too real. Their rifles appeared as though they could fire at any moment. Only three mourners stood at the wall. They placed a limp, rain-soaked wreath on the ground. One brushed the wall with a rose, then placed it on the pavement.

Jim and I walked to the street and hailed a cab. It was a short ride to the hotel, ten minutes maybe. And in the cab, I leaned my head on Jim's shoulder, our hands clasped in his lap, leaning on his thigh. We never said a word. You could hear each breath. There was the swishing of the road under the tires. The rhythmic clicking of the windshield wipers. Muted music from a Spanish radio station. And then Jim broke the silence.

"You used to smell like lemons," he said.

"You used to wear Canoe," I said.

He threw his head back and smiled. "How on earth did you remember?"

"How did you?" I said.

There was no conversation as we took the elevator up to the sixth floor. There was no question as to which direction we would take when we got off the elevator. The awkwardness was gone. The questions had been answered. We knew where and when. I slipped the card key out of my purse and handed it to Jim. His hand was noticeably steady while he slipped the card into the door. He opened the door and stepped to the side, his hand on my back. He looped the DO NOT DISTURB sign on the doorknob, closed the door behind him, locked it, slid on the chain. I watched him, saying nothing.

There was nothing unusual about the way he peeled the shirt over his head. It stuck to his flesh at first. He used the shirt to wipe his face and neck and hair. His shoulders were broad. He had a scar on his left side. He walked to the minibar and took out the bottle of champagne. He got two glasses from the bathroom and removed the ruffled paper tops.

"Do you mind if we drink this here?" he said. It wasn't really a question.

He turned on the radio. A golden oldies station. He popped the cork on the champagne, covering it with a washcloth, telling me to turn my face the other way. And then he sat, cross-legged on the floor and reached up for my hand, pulling me down. I sat facing him. He poured two glasses and handed one to me. And looking into my eyes, he clicked his glass against mine, holding it there.

"Here's to us," he said. "Here's to today."

And without taking our eyes away from each other we drank the champagne. Finishing the glasses too fast. Gulping them as though they were water.

It was so easy how it happened. Johnny Rivers was singing "Tracks of My Tears" and Jim stood up. Not without saying his knees were stiff from sitting that way. Laughing a little as he pressed his palm into the small of his back, leaning backwards, shaking his head and making a mock moaning sound. He reached his hand down to me and pulled me up.

"Come on," he said. "Dance with me. Dance with the creaky old guy."

"Don't pull too fast," I said. "I think I've been in this position for too long."

And we danced the way we danced when we were kids and barely moved. And as he pressed against me I could feel him, growing hard next to me. And I could feel myself pressing closer into him. His cheek touched mine. He clasped my hand low against his hip. I could feel the roughness of his damp blue jeans. His other arm was around me. It felt cool against my bare shoulder. The song ended. The deejay came on. "That hit number ten on the charts in July 1967," he said.

We stopped dancing and looked at each other, shaking our heads. Jim stroked my cheek with the back of his hand. And then he kissed me. First the curve of my neck and then my cheeks, my eyes, my nose and then my mouth. His tongue found its way inside, circling my lips, my teeth. And I remembered so well the way he kissed me. The way he smelled and tasted. It was all so easy. And for a moment I thought we'd hear that window shade fly up and ripple on the roller.

"Take off the wet clothes," he said. "Get into the bed."

And he smiled at me so gently. As though I was a girl. And I swear I saw a look in his eyes that was the same one I saw thirty years ago. And I knew all this was right. This was mine. This was ours.

The rain had dried on our bodies. We were gritty and sticky. Our hair was damp. The radio began to crackle and lose the station. In the static we heard "A Whiter Shade of Pale." It seemed that they were playing every song from 1967 but maybe those were the only ones we heard. None of it mattered. From the corner of my eye I saw the digits on the clock. Ten o'clock. For a moment it crossed my mind to call home. But nothing else mattered. When he slipped out of his jeans and got on top of me, I forgot it all: where I belonged, who I was now. I was where I was supposed to be. With whom I was supposed to be.

We finished the champagne that night. We ordered rock shrimp and smoked salmon and another bottle of champagne at two in the morning. And then with the ease of a lifetime of yesterdays, as though we were sitting on those rocks at the bluff, he said, "I never stopped loving you, Emmie."

And as though I were sixteen, I kissed him. Boldly. Brazenly. Almost defiantly.

"I loved you more, Jimmy," I said. "I never stopped."

"I never told anyone the things I told you today," Jim said.

"They're not secrets, though," I said. "Why? Not even Mary?" And I wondered if I should have mentioned her name but he seemed not to notice.

"But don't you see?" he said. "You were always the only one who could understand. You were the only one who ever did. The only one who really knew me. Why did you do it, Emmie? Why did you walk away?"

He rolled on top of me and at first I thought he was angry. I was almost afraid for a moment. His eyes searched my face. But then, as he began to love me again, the look softened. He said as he slipped inside me, "Tell me some other time. Not now. Not now."

# 20

I fell asleep easily that night. I held her in my arms.
There were times I awakened, still fitful in my sleeping. Certain things, no matter what, will probably
never change for me. But looking at her comforted me.
I touched her hair. I ran my finger down the side of her
face. She stirred and smiled at me.

"I love you, Emily Hudson," I whispered.

"I love you, too, Jim Moran," she said. And then she
put her face on my chest.

She was still lying on my chest when we awakened
the next morning. It was early. Too early. Maybe seven
o'clock. But I was glad we didn't sleep away the day. I
wanted every moment with her.

"Those of us with children have internal clocks," she
smiled, looking at the clock in the morning.

"There was a time I would have slept past noon," I
said.

And then, without a word, I loved her again. I wondered how I would let her go the next morning. Tomorrow was something we were both aware of.

Neither of us wanted to talk about it. It seemed we were always saying good-bye. Not knowing when we'd see each other again.

It was difficult to hear her calling home that morning. I was in the shower when she called Peter. The water was running when she made the call but when I shut it off I could hear her speaking. She was telling Peter about the Vietnam Memorial. I can only call him Peter. It's irrational, I know, but it pains me to call him her husband. She showed me his picture along with pictures of the children. The girl looked like Peter. The boys looked like her. See what I mean? It's always like that.

I didn't bring a picture of Mary. I brought several of Clancy though. Clancy on a pony. Clancy dressed for her birthday party. Clancy with me on the sofa. Emily said Clancy was beautiful.

I heard her tell Peter that I gave her "valuable information." She said I was "helpful." And for a moment I wondered if that was what all this had been about. Fodder for a text. A human still life for oil on canvas. She must have known that I heard her speaking. I was shaving, standing at the sink with a towel wrapped around my waist.

"You can lie by omission as well as commission," she said when she saw my face look up at her in the mirror.

"Don't ever lie to me by either," I said.

"You would probably see right through me," she said.

"I'd like to think I would," I said. "Once I think I did."

She didn't answer me. She put her arms around my waist. Leaned her head on my back.

We thought about renting a car. Driving somewhere

to a beach. Bethany wasn't far, she said. Rehoboth Beach in Delaware. Maybe just a few hours. Or Virginia Beach. But it seemed like precious time to waste. We had so little left. It felt like we were clinging to hours. Trying to slow down a clock that ticked away relentlessly in our heads.

She took a shower. I walked into the bathroom when she was standing at the sink, putting a lipstick to her lips. Her hair was combed straight back off her face. She wore a long white dressing gown. She was naked underneath. The robe was tied loosely, open in the front so I could see her breasts. I came up behind her, bent down and kissed her neck. Reached my hand under the robe.

"You don't smell like lemons anymore," I said.

"We could go buy lemon cologne," she laughed. "Do they still make Canoe?"

But the funny thing was the memories weren't as important anymore since we made new ones. The sad thing was that everything with us always seemed to be a memory or the making of one. A past that for one reason or another could never be continued. I wanted her to fall asleep in my arms every night. I wanted to wake up next to her every morning. When she painted, I wanted to bring her a cup of tea. I wanted to cook dinner for her while we drank wine and talked. I wanted her there when the tornado sirens went off at night. And then I'd think of Clancy and Mary and the next morning. Thinking about the next morning was unbearable.

"I don't think we need anything for old-time's sake anymore, do you?" I said.

We went to a coffee shop and took out breakfast. Stopping to buy Clancy a souvenir T-shirt from a pushcart. We sat on the steps of the Lincoln Memorial. It was beautiful, anchored by the Washington Monument. The Reflecting Pool separating the two. In the distance we could see the Vietnam Memorial. The sun was trying to come out through the clouds. Crowds of people lined the Memorial wall. I never want to go there again, I thought. Seeing it from the distance was enough.

She took my coffee out of the white paper bag. Made a tear in the lid and handed me the cup. Why did it touch me so that she gave me my coffee? Maybe it was that after only a day she knew I drank it black.

"Remember the night we went to St. Thomas Church and made out in the back pew?" she said. "It was freezing cold that night. We had nowhere else to go."

"We were always looking for places to go in the city," he said. "Places we could be alone."

"I think that's why we loved the beach at night. It was perfect," she said.

We. That's why *we* loved the beach at night, she said. There was such a sense of continuity with Emily. Of history. Childhood.

There was the day when we went to the beach and it was overcast. No one was there except for us. Signs were posted saying there was no swimming. The snack bar was closed; the metal casing rolled down. We heard thunder in the distance. It was all coming back to me now. Things I was no longer afraid to remember. I lay out on the rocks that day and she held my head in her lap. That was the day I gave her the ring.

"Remember the day I gave you the ring?" I said. "We were on the beach. It was about to storm."

"My father said to give it back to you," she said. "He

said it was inappropriate for me to wear it. He said I was too young."

"But you didn't," I said.

"No. I hid it," she said. "And then I'd put it on my finger when I was out of the house. I brought it with me."

"Let's go back to the room. Show me the ring," I said. "I brought the photographs."

We sat on the floor in the room like children playing with toys. I opened my suitcase (now in the corner of her room) and took out an envelope. Pulled out the photograph of her in the yellow bikini. It made her cringe.

"Jesus," she said. "I can't believe I sent that picture. I remember when Jennie took it. It was definitely a planned picture. I must have posed for hours. We took about twenty snapshots. We spent all day choosing the right one."

"They put it up on the wall in the barracks," I confessed. And then I told her about the hog board. She threw her head back and laughed as though she were sixteen again. Covered her face with her hands. And then I showed her the picture that Jennie had taken of us on the beach at Tod's.

"Look at the innocence," she said.

My hair was long and dark. I was standing with my arm around her shoulder. She had both arms around my neck. She was facing me, leaning into me sideways. Looking at my face while I looked straight ahead, smiling. We wore faded blue jeans. I wore a white T-shirt. She wore a peasant blouse. Our feet were bare.

"You always looked out at the Sound," she said. "Back then I thought it was the ocean."

"It made me feel so free," I said. "It seemed to go on and on."

She took out the ring. Unwrapped the tissue.

"I'm so glad I kept this," she said.

I slipped it on her finger.

"I never did get to give you a better one," I said. And then I pressed her hand to my lips.

She took the Rod McKuen book from her suitcase.

"Look here," she turned the pages. "Look what you wrote. 'Us.' "

When we turned the pages of the book, it seemed like every poem was written for us. There was this one.

*You won't believe this*
*but I'm going off to war*
*I know that's hard to understand.*
*To think of me knee-deep in mud*
*when I so love the sand.*

*When I so love the water*
*to run along the beach and play*
*it's hard to think of killing someone*
*on a beach today.*

"We have to talk, Emily," I said. "We have to talk about that October."

She put her fingers to my lips. Maybe to quiet me. She traced my lips with her fingers. I took her finger in my mouth.

"First, make love to me again," she said.

We didn't go to the bed. I pulled the bedspread down on the floor and pulled her on top of me. We made love on the floor strewn with old pictures and old poetry. And then when it was over and we lay back, she was staring at the ceiling. She turned to me, lying on her side, running her palm over my chest. Tracing the scar on my side.

"How did you get this?" she asked.

"A guy in my platoon was tripping. We tried to get him to calm down. When the sirens went off, he pulled out his buck knife and started flailing. I was in the way."

"I'm afraid to tell you about that October day," she said.

"There's nothing you could say that would change anything now," I said.

"I know," she said. "That's the sad part."

# 21

That first night in Washington, I slept so soundly in his arms. It was the first night in seventeen years that I slept naked. The sheets felt cool around me. My head rested on his chest. My leg was twisted around his thigh. I wasn't ashamed of my body. Before I saw him, I worried that maybe he was expecting a sixteen-year-old girl. I told him that as we lay in bed. He laughed. You'd be jailbait, he said.

I felt like I belonged with him. Like we belonged together. Like we had never been apart. But I knew that in another day I would start missing him again. I tried to focus on today. But I found myself thinking about all the tomorrows without him.

Jim stood at the sink after he showered. A towel wrapped around his waist. Shave cream on his face. I came up behind him. Slipped my arms around his waist. Our faces were in the same mirror. I remembered that time on the bus when I pulled out my compact. Whenever you see your face, you'll see mine, he had said.

He turned his head around as I held him around his

waist. He kissed me, getting shave cream on my cheek.
He laughed. I wiped it off with the back of my hand.
He kissed me again, first wiping the cream off his face
with a cloth.

"Now you have to start all over," I said.

"I wish I could start all over," he said.

I didn't answer him. The thought had been going
through my mind all night. All morning. Since he
walked off the plane. Part of me felt so guilty. I wanted
to stay with him always. I wished I had been with him
always. Did this mean I was forsaking my children?
But a part of me rationalized: They're my children, I
thought. I would have them anyway no matter what.
Somehow Peter didn't figure into the equation.

Jim and I didn't talk about Peter or Mary. There was
a silent understanding not to vilify them. It was almost
protective. We seemed not to notice each other's wedding band.

"I heard you talking on the phone," he said. "Have
you gotten all your information?" He was sarcastic. It
cut me to the quick.

I realized he'd heard me speaking to Peter. I had
tried to make my voice sound as natural as possible
yet I couldn't wait to get off the phone. Peter was taking me too close to reality. I didn't care whether or not
Jack or Sam was sleeping. It didn't matter that Julie
was going to her friend's house. I didn't want to hear
Peter's disapproval of Charlie's root beer breakfasts.
Didn't care that the gardener hadn't shown up for the
spring cleanup. How many times had Peter been away
and not been included in the details of everyday life?
It seemed so unfair that he had to give me a play-by-
play of life at home. I wanted to be away. I didn't want
to know.

"What did you want me to tell him, Jim?" I asked. I went and sat on the edge of the tub. "I lied by omission."

"We're avoiding an issue," he said, still facing the mirror, drawing the razor down his cheek.

"We'll talk about it later," I said.

"We're leaving tomorrow," he said. "What are we going to do?"

I didn't answer him. I had no answers.

"Will he know by the look on your face when you get home?" he asked.

"Will Mary? You sound like my mother, Jim," I said.

"Now that is just about the cruelest thing anyone's ever said to me," he laughed and tossed a towel at me.

Would it always have been like this? I wondered. Would the edges always have been smoothed over with a kiss? A tease?

I showered after he did. He came in while I stood at the sink putting on my lipstick. He kissed the curve of my neck. Slipped his hand inside my robe.

"If I wasn't going to faint from starvation I'd take you right back to bed," he said. "Get dressed. You take forever."

It was hot and humid when we left the hotel that morning. I thought of times in the summer when the humidity weighed on me. When the kids would cling to me. When I carried Julie in her Snugli, feeling as though I would wilt from the heat. And Peter walked coolly ahead of us. And yet despite the humidity of Washington in May, I wanted Jim next to me. Stuck to me.

We took our breakfast from a coffee shop near the Lincoln Memorial. I ordered our breakfast, waiting on the line while he went to the payphone and called Mary. He was speaking loudly over the din of the coffee shop. I heard him speak to Clancy. Or was it Mary? I wasn't sure.

"I'll be home tomorrow, baby," he said. "I can't wait to see you either."

And I wondered if he was lying the same way I lied to Peter.

"I was talking to Clancy," he said, answering a question I hadn't asked.

"How did you know I was wondering?" I asked.

"From the look on your face," he said. "See what I mean?"

We sat on the steps of the Lincoln Memorial while we ate. Coffee and cheese danish. I took out the paper cups of coffee. Poured cream into mine. Handed his to him black.

"Careful. It's hot," I said.

"Thanks, Mom," he said, "I like when you give me my coffee. How did you know I liked it black?"

"You told me," I said. "No more tea. Just black coffee."

"You listened," he said.

"The sergeant kicked your ass," I said.

We watched the line of people below us, to the left, walking along the wall of the Vietnam Memorial.

"I could never go there again," he said, looking down at the wall. "I suppose one day I should take Clancy."

"Peter and I took the children several years ago," I said. "I stood off to the side with Julie. She was still in a stroller. I couldn't bear to look."

"Did you think my name would be on the wall?" he asked.

"I didn't know," I said. "I was afraid of what I might see. I remember thinking that if I saw your name I wouldn't be able to control my grief."

"Poor Quinn," he said. "I knew about Khe Sahn. It was a massacre. I always wanted to think Quinn got out alive. Hardly anyone got out of there alive."

After he spoke of Quinn he placed his coffee beside him on the step.

"Come here," he said. He held me close to him. In the way that someone does when it's cold outside. "Let's go back to the room and look at the pictures."

The pictures were old. They even had those frilly white borders around them. He showed me the one Jennie took of us on the beach. We were so young. I thought of Jack and the girl, Kerri, he took to the prom. I never thought of Jack and Kerri as a couple. Jack took her to the movies and borrowed Peter's BMW on Saturday nights (Jack refused to drive the Volvo on dates). I wondered if Jack and Kerri were in love like Jim and I were. Somehow I thought not.

My hair was long, nearly to my waist and Jim's was jet black.

"No wonder I believed that line about the Cherokee," I said. "I like the gray, though. It's distinguished. See how lucky guys are? A little gray and they look elegant. A woman, well, that's a different story."

He laughed. "A woman feels extinguished."

And then he showed me the picture of the girl in the yellow bikini. He told me about the hog board.

"I always thought you'd sleep with it under your pillow. Nothing like cheering up the platoon," I said.

"That's what the sergeant said when he posted it on the wall," he said, laughing. " 'We'll cheer up the platoon, Moran.' "

I took the ring from my cosmetic bag. Unwrapped the tissue.

"Look, it's still sticky from the Band-Aid," I said. "I took the Band-Aid off that October day when I went upstairs. I wanted to see how big your hands were."

He pressed his palm next to mine. His hand was large and rough. He had calluses on his palm.

"Give me the ring," he said.

He slipped it on my finger. He took my right hand. My wedding band was on my left. Jim's ring flopped and turned on my finger.

"I remember just where we were sitting when I gave it to you. We were on those rocks at Tod's."

We took out the McKuen book. The copyright was 1967. And, strangely, the dedication was "To E." I'd never noticed any of that before. We turned the pages and I showed him where he had written "us."

"I didn't see the 'us' that summer when you were away," I said. "I didn't see that until a few weeks ago."

"Maybe if you'd seen it before I came back from boot camp things would have been different," he said. "I remember when I wrote it. You and Jennie were making lunch. Emily, what happened in October?"

I knew it was getting to the point where avoiding the issue was becoming impossible.

"Make love to me," I said.

"Don't distract me," he said. "You're changing the subject."

But he pulled the spread down from the bed and we made love. The book and the photographs lay next to us on the floor. His ring fell off my finger.

# 22

When Clancy said she missed me, it tore me apart. The Fireman's Carnival was great fun. Mommy won two goldfish, she said. But riding on the Ferris wheel was not the same without you there.

"Mommy got the pennies into the goldfish bowl. She won the bowl, too. Today we're going to buy blue stones for the bottom so it looks like a swimming pool. Mommy misses you, too, Daddy," Clancy said.

Why did Clancy say that Mary missed me? I wondered if children have a sixth sense. If Clancy was trying in some way to heal what was wrong.

"I miss you, too, baby," I said.

"Should I tell Mommy that you miss her, too?" she asked.

"Absolutely. I'll see you tomorrow, baby. I'll be home for dinner." And after I said it, I dreaded the thought. Not of seeing Clancy. Not even of seeing Mary. Of leaving Emily.

That night Emily and I went to dinner. Part of me wanted to order room service but I wanted to go some-

where special. I wore the tweed sport coat and I was
sweltering. I dressed in my own room, leaving her to
dress in hers.

"It's like a date," I said. "I'm waiting for your father
to open the door."

But it was only Emily who opened the door. Emily
wore a black dress, sleeveless with a high neck. She
had on high heels with slingbacks, sheer black stockings. Her hair was twisted up on top of her head. It
was the first time since I saw her that she looked so
much like a woman to me. A woman instead of a girl.

"You're stunning," I said.

"You look so handsome in a shirt and tie. Can you
believe I've never seen you wear one?" she said.

"I had to wear one to school, remember?" I said.

"You always had the tie off by the time I saw you,"
she said. "Rolled up in the pocket of your blazer."

The restaurant was called Calvin's, one of Washington's "finest" the concierge had said when I asked for
a recommendation.

"Shall I make a reservation for you and your wife?"
he asked me.

And though I started to explain at first, I let it go.
There was no explaining who she was. What she
meant to me. It is strange how words like husband
and wife define you somehow. State to the world that
even if you don't love her enough now to be with her,
there was a time that you did. State to the world that
the two of you are entrenched somehow, through love,
through kids, money, family. I thought how odd it was
not to be able to define this woman whom I loved so
dearly. Another man's wife loved by another woman's
husband.

When we walked through the lobby to dinner that

night he said, "Have a wonderful evening, Mr. and Mrs. Moran."

Neither Emily nor I said a word.

We sat on a banquette in the middle of the restaurant, looking down at the bar. I ordered a bottle of champagne. There were aquariums with exotic fish lining the wall of the bar. I thought of Clancy and the goldfish bowl with the blue stones.

"So tell me," I said. "Now's as good a time as ever. And it's a public place so there can't be any scenes."

"Tell you what?" she said.

"Tell me why you left me that day in October."

"You were the one who walked away," she said.

"You told me you were sleeping with someone else. What was I supposed to do?" I said. "Who was he?"

She had a hard time even beginning. She said that when they left the house that summer, everything felt like it was over. Her sisters had teased her all summer long. Talked about her "soldier boy." Taunted her by singing "Return to Sender." The day after I left for boot camp, she made her mother drive her to the jeweler.

"I had my ears pierced. It was something I was always afraid to do. I always wore those screw-on earrings. But I figured if you could go to the Marines I could get my ears pierced. It was good luck," she said.

"You're changing the subject," I said.

But she said it was all part of the story.

There wasn't a night that summer that she ever saw anyone else. There were two boys down the street who were up from the city for the summer as well. One went to Cornell and the other went to Case Western. College boys with a Pontiac GTO.

"Even they didn't tempt me," she said.

"So the guy who finally did must have been something," I said. She ignored me as though I hadn't said anything at all.

There were a few weeks after school started that she figured she would never hear from me again though she found it hard to believe even at the time. Letters hadn't come for weeks. She and Jennie went a little crazy. They started smoking cigarettes. Jennie started smoking pot and even she tried it herself. They wore black armbands under their blazers. Peace signs in their ears that they bought over the summer.

As Emily spoke to me, her hands were moving all around. I took them in mine.

"You're going to knock something over," I said. "Don't be so nervous."

"I am nervous, though." She took a deep breath and managed a smile. "I've wanted to explain all this for thirty years and I'm having such a hard time."

I held her hands. It seemed to calm her.

She had put my letters in a shoe box, hidden the ring from her father. That October day she went upstairs to the apartment and spent the night by the telephone waiting for me to call.

"I waited more than just that night. I looked over my shoulder every day when I walked home from school. You were never there," she said.

"But I called you as soon as I got back," I interrupted her.

"Shhh, wait," she said. "Let me finish. This is hard."

And I was almost afraid for her to go on because her eyes were filling up with tears. Part of me wanted to tell her that none of it mattered anymore. A greater part of me needed to know.

Her mother kept telling her I would no longer be a boy, she said. That I would be a man and, worse, a Marine and Emily should recognize the difference. Emily remembered how she argued. How she screamed at her mother that no one could change that much in three months. But her mother warned her that the service does strange things to people.

"Over the summer I had decided I would 'give myself' to you when you came home," she laughed. "That was the expression I used. I never spoke to Jennie about it. That's how personal it was. I grew up so much that summer when you were away. I never loved anyone the way I loved you that summer."

"So, what changed all that?" I asked, but by then I knew the answer. It was the same thing that happened when I called old friends after Vietnam. Jim Moran? Jim Who? No one wanted to remember.

She said it was the way I looked when I came back that day. It scared her. The way I called her peace-sign earrings garbage. There was no more long hair and blue jeans. You wore man's clothing, she said. Your hair was cropped. Your skin was rough and tanned. Your body was so much bigger.

And her mother's words haunted her.

"I couldn't tell you I was afraid of you, because I was so afraid," she tried to explain. "I didn't think you'd understand. It was easier to say there was someone else. To end it. It wasn't that I didn't love you."

"So, you mean there was no one else?" I asked.

"It was the way you spoke to me. 'Send me off with a bang, Emily,' you said. It wasn't you anymore," she said.

"You aren't answering the question," I said. "Was there someone else or was it just me?"

"Not then," she said. "There was no one else. I went upstairs after you walked away. I took out your letters.

All night long I wanted to call. You walked away so easily. I wasn't sure that I mattered to you anymore. I didn't know who you were anymore."

Neither of us said anything for a very long time. The waiter came over and poured another glass of champagne.

"Is everything all right?" he asked.

And I thought it was an odd question.

She rested her hand on my arm at one point. Part of me wanted to push it away. She took her hand and placed it over mine but only for a moment. She knew enough to withdraw.

"You're angry, aren't you?" she said. She irritated me. She sounded timid. I didn't want to feel sorry for her.

"How could you have done that to me?" I said.

"I was so young, Jimmy," she said. "I didn't know better."

"But you were the only one that was supposed to know better," I said.

Did she know how tortured I was, wondering for all those months who "he" was? Trying to guess who took her away from me. I knew I was rough that October day. I know I wasn't the same person who left in July. But when it came to her, I was the same. How could she not have seen that?

We ate the rest of our meal in silence. The waiter brought the check and I paid for dinner. I didn't care how I would explain the charge to Mary. I was drunk. And I was angry.

"How can you be so angry over something that happened thirty years ago?" she asked.

I didn't answer her. I could feel my teeth clench. My jaw tighten. We began to walk. The streets were empty. She lagged a few steps behind me. I was walking rapidly. I wished I could run from her.

"I can't keep up with you," she said.

That was when I stopped and turned around.

"You fucking bitch," I said. I was afraid of myself. I didn't know what was coming over me.

"How can you say that now?" Her eyes looked wide and fearful.

"If you know what's good for you, you'll leave me again," I said.

She walked away and hailed a cab. I watched her step inside. And just like that night when I went to dial her number a million times, I wanted to go after her. I stood and watched the cab pull away.

# 23

When the cab pulled up in front of the hotel, the doorman peered inside after I stepped out.

"Only me," I said.

He must have known that something was wrong. I was upset. Distraught.

"Everything all right, Miss?" he asked.

"It's fine, thank you," I said.

I went upstairs to the room. The message light on the phone was flashing. I was hoping it was Jim. But Peter had called. He took Sam and Julie to dinner and a movie. Jack was at Kerri's house. Charlie was sleeping at his friend Paul's. More details.

"Hope you're having a great time," Peter had said. "Call us in the morning."

It occurred to me that Peter was all too benign.

I washed my face, took the corners of the washcloth and wiped the mascara that streaked beneath my eyes. The cloth smelled like Jim's shave cream. I didn't feel like changing my clothes. I took off my shoes and stockings. Sat down on the chair. I toyed with the idea of reading the McKuen book but I didn't want to look at it. I flipped on the television. Flipped it off again. I dialed Jim's room. There was no answer. I walked down the corridor and knocked on his door. Maybe he was inside and not answering, I thought. I tried not to worry. He wasn't a child. I walked back to the room, realizing I was barefoot. I took out my sketch pad and my pencils. It always amazes me what comes out sometimes. There was a rough sketch of a man. A scar on his shoulder.

I thought of packing my bags and heading over to the station. But then how would I explain coming home so unexpectedly? But deep down inside I knew this couldn't be over. After all these years, it couldn't end this way.

It was after midnight when I went downstairs to the lobby. There was a circular bar in the corner. I hadn't noticed it before. In the morning, the bar served breakfast. I looked inside. There were a group of men sitting around a table. A local union number for autoworkers was printed on their shirts. They glanced over at me. What did they think I was looking for? At the end of the bar a couple sat facing each other. He had his hands on her thighs. Her hands were around his neck. Stroking the back of his head. Half-drunk beer in tall glasses sat in front of them. The beers looked warm to me. Flat. I imagined they had been that way for a while. They were too engrossed in each other to be drinking.

For some reason I thought Jim would be in the bar. I pictured him sitting alone in a corner. I fantasized that he would look up and I would just sit down next to him and everything would be all right.

I don't know what made me take the cab to the Memorial that night. I think it was because I wanted to be somewhere close to him. Where he had been before. Had I been back in Connecticut, I would have driven to Tod's. It was a ruse, but I went upstairs and took my sketch pad and my pencils. Maybe this way it would look like I was working.

The doorman reluctantly got me a taxi, telling me it was awfully late to be out alone at night.

"It's after midnight, you know," he said. "Everything is closed."

I told him that I knew. That I would be okay.

"I need to draw," I said. Then I managed a laugh. "I'm an artist. Inspired, you know?"

The Memorial is lighted all night long. I was uneasy when I walked up the hill to the bench where Jim and I had sat the day before. The driver asked if I wanted him to wait.

"No, don't wait," I said and then shaking sense into myself I asked him to come back in a half hour. He said he'd come back. He'd be where he dropped me off.

I didn't see Jim at first. He was standing by the wall. I sat down on the bench. Then I saw him. His hand touched the wall. His head was bent down. Later, he said he had a sense that I was there. He turned around and glanced up the hill. I raised my hand. As if to stop him. As if to tell him to stay there. Wait for me. I walked toward him.

We stood by the statues of the soldiers. We were a distance apart. Maybe a few feet when we stopped.

"How could you not have seen past the Marine?" he said, so simply.

"How could you have not seen past the girl?" I asked.

"You were no better than anyone else," he said.

"You acted like a Marine," I said.

"I was a Marine."

"But I still loved you," I said.

"So, there was no one else," he said.

"Not for years to come," I said.

"I wish I had known," he said.

"Oh God, Jim, I wish I had told you."

The taxi honked its horn and we walked down the hill. Driving back to the hotel I felt like I couldn't sit close enough to him. The doorman smiled broadly when we got out of the cab. We took the elevator to the sixth floor.

"Will you come with me?" I asked. The elevator door had opened.

"Maybe if one of us had dialed the phone that night in October, life would be entirely different," he said.

We walked down the corridor to my room.

"I wrote in my diary the day you left for boot camp. I said that loving you and having you leave took away my innocence," I said. "I guess that sounds silly, doesn't it?"

He leaned against the wall in the hallway. Pulled me to him and put his arms around me.

"Give me the key," he said.

Jim sat down in the chair by the window, bent over to untie his shoelaces. His shoes were the same kind he wore that October day. Man's shoes. I knelt next to him. Reached my hands up to his face.

"We have to leave tomorrow," he said.

"I know," I said. "Another thing I don't want to talk about."

"I don't want to sleep tonight. I want to be with you every moment," he said.

"I never stopped loving you," I said.

"Emily, why do things happen this way?"

And I said that maybe it was because although I always thought that youth had courage maybe it wasn't quite the right kind. Maybe it was because no matter how I could stand up to my mother, her words reeked of gospel. Maybe it's because youth never really looks ahead.

He reached behind me and unzipped my dress, rubbed his hands along my back.

"Your hands are rough," I said.

"One time that scared you," he said.

He made love to me that night as though he would never see me again. And it crossed my mind that maybe, just maybe, had we been together for the last thirty years it wouldn't have been like that. He must have been reading my mind.

"I would always have loved you like this," he said. "I always want to love you like this."

The morning came too soon. He was lying next to me when Peter called.

"Hi," he said. "We'll pick you up at the train. When do you get in? Around four o'clock? How was dinner?"

I tried not to sound stilted. I just woke up, I said. Dinner was productive. Productive. Let me shower and pack and I'll call you from the station.

Jim got up from the bed when the phone rang.

"I'll go pack my bags," Jim said, after I hung up. "I'll come back in a half hour. I'll take the key."

I held the pillow to my face where his head had been. I got up and took a shower, packed my bags. Put the ring back in tissue. Placed the book in between the clothes in my suitcase. Packed up my sketch pad and pencils. I ordered coffee for two. A basket of rolls.

When Jim came back, we sat across from each other at the small round table at the end of the room. I poured his coffee and he smiled at me.

"Oh, those things you do," he said.

"You're awfully easy," I said.

"Actually, I'm a really tough customer," he said.

His flight was at eleven o'clock. We took a taxi to the airport. It was a beautiful day. The sky was clear and blue. The taxi pulled into the airport too soon. And I remembered how long it took me to get there when he first arrived. They weren't going to let me wait with him at the gate. But then he took the woman official aside and spoke to her, pointing at me as he spoke. I saw her nod her head. I had to show her my driver's license and she let me go with him.

"What did you tell her?" I asked.

"I said I wanted you with me," he said.

"As simple as that?"

"As simple as that," he said.

We took two chairs side-by-side by the window where the Delta jet sat on the runway. We watched them load on the baggage. We heard them call the flight. I almost wanted him to get on the plane at first call. I didn't want to prolong the leaving anymore since I knew it was inevitable. But he waited until last call.

"You have to go," I said. "You know you have to go."

We stood up and that's when I began to cry. Suddenly I was back at the depot. He held me in his arms and told me not to cry.

"Don't do this," he said. "You're killing me."

"I love you, Jim," I said.

"I love you, Emily," he said.

"Tell me everything will be okay," I said. "Promise me."

"Promise you."

He took my face in both his hands and kissed my lips, my cheeks, my neck. He put on his Ray•Bans, hefted his carry-on over his shoulder. And then he turned and walked away. His back was stiff and straight. He never looked back.

I didn't go after him. I stood motionless until I walked over to the large-pane glass window. I stood at the window and watched until the plane turned and taxied down the runway. My hand was pressed against the glass. I waved a few times, hoping he would see me. Then I remembered that he didn't like window seats. I left when I could no longer see his plane. I pulled my suitcase through the airport, headed out to the taxi line at arrivals. I don't even remember getting to Union Station. I don't know how I found the track. I barely remember the ride home. My heart was hollow.

# 24

Sunday morning came too soon. My flight was leaving at eleven. Her train at twelve-thirty. We stayed up all night. Making love. Talking about the years we missed. She and Jennie were handing out carnations when I was robbing the Esso. She was at Skidmore College while I was in Chou Lai. How was it possible for lives to take such different turns when we thought they were destined together? She told me about the night with Steve.

"I'm going to tell you something," she said. "But promise me you won't walk away again."

And I told her I would never walk away again and held her in my arms. I was sitting in the bed, leaning against the pillows. She was leaning on me, her back against my chest. It was easier not to see each other's face.

"Why Steve?" I asked when she finished the story.

"Because, I think, at the time he was one of the closest things to you," she said.

She told me about the day the letter came with my

graduation picture. How her mother warned her about me. How they still called her "Jimmy's girl" for months after I left. She told me about Jennie and Shade. The guy at Columbia. The night she met Peter at a bar called Maxwell's Plum. She said he was drinking beer from a glass and she was sipping one from a bottle . . . . And then I stopped her.

"I don't want to hear about you and Peter," I said.

"He exists, Jim," she said.

"That's the problem," I said.

"Do you love her?" she asked.

"Love who?"

"Love Mary."

And I said that there were so many different kinds of love.

"I love her," I said, not wanting to lie. "She's put up with me for twenty-five years. She's a good woman."

"Would you ever leave her?" she asked.

"Would you ever leave Peter?" I answered.

Both of us knew the answers without saying a word.

"I shouldn't have asked," she said.

"You know it's not the same," I said.

"Maybe it's just easier to love someone in Washington where the only baggage is a suitcase," she said.

"You think we don't have baggage?" I said. "We have a fucking steamer trunk."

"It's filled with different things," she said.

And I knew what she meant. But I didn't know how I would live without her.

She took her suitcase from the corner of the room and I helped her lift it onto the bed. She looked tired. Circles under her eyes. And I thought of the circles under Mary's eyes and wondered why Emily looked so beautiful to me in spite of them. She was putting the soda cans back in the bar, the ones displaced by the champagne that first night, when suddenly she kneeled down on the floor. She covered her face with her hands, the way people do when they see something they don't want to see.

"I don't know how I'm going to be able to stand missing you this time," she said, looking up at me as if I could say something to calm her.

"We'll figure something out," I said. But I wasn't sure if we could.

She asked me if I ever had to travel to buy and sell the wines.

"Aren't there conventions? Things like that? Wine shows in New York?" she asked, as though she'd just thought of something we might have overlooked.

And then I told her about Long's. Hefting the bottles onto the shelves. Unloading the crates from the trucks. The red shirt with the plastic name tag. The way I kept it in my car so Clancy wouldn't see it.

"Why didn't you tell me this before?" she asked. "Why did you think it would matter?"

I didn't tell her that at sixteen she loved me for what I was and what I wasn't. I wasn't sure if those ideals could transcend time.

"I told you what I wanted to be instead of what I was," I said.

I went back to my room, carrying my razor and shave cream in my hand. Packed up my things. The room was so untouched. I turned down the bedspread, rumpled the blanket and the sheet. Punched the pillow with my fist. I felt so foolish. Like the maid would really care. They were the actions of a married man. I had a child. A house by a stream. I was going home. I called Mary and Clancy. Clancy was wailing in the background when Mary picked up the phone.

"One of the fish died," Mary said. "We had a burial at sea."

"Put her on the phone," I said.

"Daddy! Daddy! He was just floating upside down when I went in this morning. It was horrible," Clancy said.

"I'll buy you another when I get home," I said. "It's just a few hours now."

"Mommy and I are making you a welcome home sign but I'm not supposed to tell," she said. "We used silver glitter."

"I love you, baby," I said. "Kiss Mommy for me."

And suddenly I felt as though I didn't know where I belonged. It was the same feeling that came over me the day I came home from Chou Lai. I almost didn't know who I was anymore.

Emily and I took a taxi to National Airport. We barely spoke on the way. I asked if she had the ring. She asked if I had the photographs. Send me copies, she said. She wrote her name and address on a piece of paper.

"You wrote your name?" I laughed. "Did you think I would forget? Why didn't you take Peter's name, Emily?"

"Because it's his," she said.

"Would you have used mine?" I asked.

But she didn't answer me. I shouldn't have asked.

It was the first truly sunny day we'd had since we got to Washington. The streets were empty. The traffic was light. It seemed that the cab got to the airport too quickly. Emily waited beside me while I checked my suitcase through. We walked to the gate. There was a sign that said only persons traveling could wait at the gate. I took the woman aside who stood at the metal detector, turned on the charm, and she let Emily come through with me.

They called the flight four times before I was able to get the courage to walk on. We didn't say much while we waited. Emily sat beside me, leaning on my chest, my arm around her. She was the one who said I had to go. You'll miss your plane, she said.

It took everything I had to walk away from her and get on that plane. I was hoping she wouldn't cry and, naturally, she did. I remembered that day at the depot when she clung to my neck behind the ticket booth. It was the same sort of feeling. The feeling where I had no choice. I had to leave her. And my heart was broken.

I never told her that I put on my Ray•Bans to hide my eyes. I never told her that I walked straight ahead and didn't look back because I was afraid if I saw her standing there I wouldn't be able to leave. I had reserved an aisle seat but when I got on the plane I asked the woman by the window to switch with me.

"Just until the plane takes off," I said. "There's something I want to see."

And I saw Emily with her hand pressed up against the window. She waved now and then. I waved back. But I knew she couldn't see me. I moved back to the aisle as the plane turned and taxied down the runway. The engines came to a hum before they revved up again. I tipped my head back in my seat. Shut my eyes. I could still feel myself inside her. I could taste her. I could feel my face pressed next to hers. I could see the way her eyes looked up at me as I lay on top of her. I felt her hand on my back, her fingers in my hair.

The plane turned and I stretched my neck to see the Monument through the window.

"Would you like to change seats again?" the woman in the window seat asked. "I don't mind at all."

But I told her there was nothing left to see.

Promise me, I thought. Promise you.

# 25

The train pulled into the Stamford station. It was an effort to change the expression on my face as I stepped onto the platform. Get out the sponge. Rub off the charcoal. Change the expression. Shadow the features. Exchange the face of sorrow for one that said I was glad to be home.

Peter sat at the wheel of the Volvo. I could see the cardboard cartons peeking from the back. Julie hopped out of the backseat when she saw me.

"Did you have fun?" she asked. "We all missed you. Daddy bleached my shirt by accident. Where do you keep the lightbulbs?"

I kissed the top of her head and hugged her.

"I had a very good time," I said.

"Does he look old, Mom?" Julie asked.

"Old?" I said.

"Mr. Moran. Did he look old?"

"Older," I smiled. "Not old. Hop back in the car."

Peter walked around the side of the car and met me

as I started to lift my suitcase into the gate. He took the suitcase from my hand.

He kissed my cheek because I turned my head.

"You look tired," he said. "Did you get much sleep?"

I avoided his eyes. "It's not the same when you're in a strange bed."

Peter lifted the bag into the car. He walked to his side. I walked to mine. Julie leaned over the seat.

"Where are your brothers?" I asked. "Put on your seat belt."

"Home. Playing basketball," she said. "Dad said we're taking you out to dinner. To celebrate."

The boys ran up the driveway when the car pulled in. Except for Jack. Maybe it was my imagination but I thought that Jack looked at me strangely. Peter carried my bag into the house. Carried it up the stairs.

"How was the train?" he asked, setting my suitcase down on the bed.

"Endless," I said. "And boring. I read a little. Went over my notes." I lied. All I did was stare out the window.

He walked over to his dresser and set down his car keys. He sat on the edge of the bed as I unpacked.

"So, what was it like to see him after all these years?" he said.

I stopped and held a sweater that I was refolding. I wondered whether the silence that ensued was as long as it felt.

"Odd," I said. "We all change. We all grow up."

"Everyone missed you, you know," he said. "The house is not quite the same without you."

I tried to joke. Not wanting to be serious or senti-mental.

"That's probably because it was a mess," I teased. "What time did you all get up this morning to clean?"

And Peter laughed and said they were up at the crack of dawn. And I thought of dawn and how I was lying in Jim's arms.

That night we drove to a restaurant that sits on the edge of the Saugatuck River. The six of us sat at a table outside under an umbrella. Everyone was fairly animated. Talking about how school was going to end soon. Jack got his old summer job back: lifeguard at Compo Beach. Sam was going to work at the snack bar. Charlie was playing Little League. Julie would go to camp in the morning and be a mother's helper for the family who moved in next door.

"They finally moved in yesterday," she said. "They have a little girl who's three. She's really cute."

And I pictured the little girl riding the school bus one day while Julie was off at college. Peter must have caught a look on my face because he said he remembered when we moved into the house.

"Jack was only two," he said. "The other three babies came home to this house. I remember when your studio was a playroom. Before we could afford to finish the basement."

It struck me odd that Peter would know or remember those things. It always seemed to me that Peter was removed. Not paying attention. Not knowing where I kept the lightbulbs.

"Sometimes I think about how empty the house will be when all of you are off at school," I said.

Everyone grew quiet at the table.

"You and I could move back to the city," Peter said. "Sell the house and hightail it out of here."

Julie protested with almost a cry, "But you always have to stay in our house," she said. "It's where we all grew up. It has to be ours. Forever and ever."

We got back home later than we should have that night. Julie fell asleep in the car. Charlie had homework he had forgotten to do. Jack and Sam played a video game in the den. Peter made himself a Scotch and sat on the porch swing. I was cleaning out the refrigerator, throwing out old cartons of Chinese food from the weekend, when I heard the porch swing creaking.

"Why are you out here?" I said, sitting down next to him. "This isn't like you."

"It was strange being with the kids all weekend without you," he said. "I don't think I ever realized before how taxing they can be. You're like the glue, Emily. When you're away, it's just not quite the same. I bleached out Julie's red shirt."

"So? She likes pink," I smiled. "Seems to me you did a good job."

"I enjoyed them, you know?" he said. "They're nice kids. I've missed out on a lot over the years."

A wave of sadness swept over me. Lately it felt like too many things were coming too late.

Then out of the blue, he said, "Does Moran love his wife?"

It was a strange question for Peter to ask, but then again, it wasn't strange at all. Peter rarely comes right out and asks what he wants to ask. He rarely says what he wants to say. In the last several years, I have avoided being the translator for his emotions. This time I had to help him.

"He loves his wife very much," I said softly. "And he loves his child."

"Do they know?" he asked. "Does he tell them?"

"I hope so," I said.

If I had let him, Peter probably would have made love to me that night. He sat up against the pillows,

reading a magazine, while I washed up in the bathroom. Usually his light is out. Usually he's half-sleeping
or pretending to be before I even get in the bed. I sat
on the bed. My back to him as I set the alarm for Monday morning. He reached up and touched my back. I
turned and smiled at him. Kissed the top of his head.
Good night, Peter, I said. I really am so tired. It just
wasn't possible that night. I'm not sure how Peter felt.
He wasn't angry. He turned off the lamp by his bed
and turned over facing away from me. I turned off my
lamp and faced away from him.

"We used to sleep like spoons," he said.

I didn't know what to say. I wanted to stroke his
back as one might a child who was restless, but I
didn't.

When the alarm went off at six in the morning, Peter
was already in the kitchen. He was sitting at the
counter drinking his coffee. The newspaper, still in the
plastic bag, lay next to him. He was looking out the
window.

"I couldn't sleep last night," he said.

Peter went to work and the children left for school
that Monday morning. I finished up the breakfast
dishes. Ran the mop along the kitchen floor. I thought
of Jim and where I was that same time the morning before. The bag of Peter's shirts for the French laundry
was on the kitchen table. I remembered how handsome Jim looked the night he wore the shirt and tie.
Peter's half-drunk cup of coffee with cream sat in the
kitchen sink. I thought of Jim and how he drank his
black.

I went down to the basement. The now pink shirt of
Julie's hung on the clothesline. A pile of wash sat on
the floor by the machine. Peter's striped pajamas lay

on top. I thought of Jim and how we slept naked. I wondered whether I should have taken the nightgown out of my suitcase and put it with the laundry even though it was untouched. I wondered if Peter had noticed. I separated the whites, the darks. Put the top back on the bleach that Peter left on the shelf.

Months before, Peter and I had cleaned out the basement. It is dank in our basement. The walls are made of stone and the floor is sprinkled with a faint coat of stone dust. The stairs leading to the basement are steep and, if you're not surefooted, you can easily miss a step and tumble down. It was one of those rare Sundays in winter when Peter wasn't buried under legal briefs. Actually, it was the day after Christmas. We were throwing things away. Get rid of the old. Make way for the new. We were planning to part with many things that day. The crib that had seen all four children through infancy. The old stereo with the turntable that we had in our first apartment. We looked through plastic crates of the children's old report cards, favorite pull toys, the clothing each child wore home from the hospital. But all we did was rearrange the boxes. Propped the crib up on its side against the wall. Covered the old stereo with an even older blanket. As cluttered as it was, everything had some memory, some meaning. Nothing was thrown away.

I stopped and looked around me before heading back up the steps. Taking stock. Thinking how all the memories were the way Peter and I had left them that Sunday in winter. Yet, I knew, at least for me, that nothing would be the same. I pulled the string on the lightbulb on the top of the stairs and shut the basement door. I stopped in the kitchen and put on the kettle, figuring I'd straighten out the studio while it came to a boil.

I was putting the sketch pad and pencils away when the kettle whistled and the phone rang at the same time. Unlike the first time when he called, I knew just by the ring that it was Jim.

"I couldn't sleep last night," he said.

A few days later, he sent a copy of the photo. The one of the two of us on the beach. I put it in the pages of *Listen to the Warm*. I put the book on the shelf in my studio. Then I took the book and put it in my keepsake trunk in the basement.

# 26

I slept through most of the flight from Washington to Atlanta. From Atlanta to Mobile, I sat by the window. As I walked to the baggage claim I was aware of her absence. Wishing she was by my side. Remembering what it was like those first few moments when I arrived in Washington and held her next to me. Not wanting to let go even for a moment while I bent down to get my bag. It was so right. So easy.

The jitney drove me to long-term parking. There was the El Camino, just where I left it. Coated with a dusting of yellow but otherwise the same. I didn't listen to the radio on the drive home. I didn't want to hear anything that could possibly remind me of her. It was as though every shift of the stick was a transition. Downshift. Go home. Dream over.

Mary was tending the flower barrels when I drove up to the house. She was wearing a summer dress instead of the usual khaki shorts. She had on white sandals. She turned around, held her hand up to her eyes to block the sun, waved as I pulled in the driveway.

Clancy came running up from the stream and jumped on me, full force, straddling her legs around my waist. Her red sneakers muddied my jeans. There was the sign, hanging over the front door: WELCOME HOME, DADDY. Lots of hearts and flowers. Sprinkled with silver glitter.

"I am very surprised," I said, looking at the sign, winking at Clancy.

"It was my idea," Clancy said. "But Mommy helped me. We're having ribs for dinner. Mommy says it's your favorite and she's making me a hot dog."

"She missed you," said Mary.

I opened the door. Clancy took the carry-on and walked ahead of me up the stairs.

"Daddy! Daddy! You forgot to kiss Mommy hello," she said.

"No, you just weren't looking," I said.

Mary sat on the chair in the bedroom while I unpacked. Clancy sat in the middle of the bed.

"Did you bring me anything?" Clancy asked, peering over into the suitcase.

I handed her the T-shirt. Remembering where I bought it by the steps of the Lincoln Memorial. Remembering how Emily and I drank our coffee that morning.

"I hope it fits," I said.

"We'll have to wash it first," said Mary. And then to me, "So, how was it?"

"It was all right," I said.

"I tried to call you a couple of times," Mary said. "One time it was sort of late at night."

"I turned the phone off," I said. "By the end of the day I was exhausted. You didn't leave a message."

"There was no message," she said.

The three of us sat outside on the deck that night. Mary had bought these little citronella candles in purple glass jars. She put them on the table next to an ice bucket filled with four Coronas. I was the one who actually cooked the ribs on the barbecue while Mary sat in a chaise lounge, Clancy curled by her side. They were reading a *Madeline* book. Clancy stumbling through the words while Mary pointed with her finger.

"Sound it out, now," Mary would say and smile when Clancy got it.

After dinner, Parker came by and he and Clancy went inside to play.

"I'm glad you're back, Daddy," Clancy said before she and Parker took off. "I hope you liked your party."

And I told her it was the best party I ever had.

I opened a second Corona for Mary and me. She was sitting at the table, her feet resting on the chair next to her.

"You never sit with your feet hanging down," I said.

"Oh, but they're always on the ground," she said.

"What's that supposed to mean?" I said, trying not to sound defensive.

"You look mighty tired for someone who turned his phone off at night, Jimmy," she said.

"I'm not used to traveling," I said. "You know, I'm not crazy about flying."

"Is she pretty?"

"Yes. Yes. She is pretty," I said. "What does that have to do with anything?"

"We all chase our youth, Jimmy," she said. "We all remember what it's like to be seventeen."

"I don't know what you're talking about," I said.

"I can look at your face after twenty-five years," she said.

"This is crazy. She's married. She has children," I said.

"You're married, too. You have a child. It has nothing to do with it."

It bothered me that Mary saw right through me.

"I think you're just not accustomed to me being away," I said. "You look nice tonight, Mary."

Mary looked away. A breeze made the citronella candles flicker and one of them went out.

"Clancy missed you something awful," she said. "She slept in the bed with me at night. She said the house wasn't safe without you here. I told her that was silly."

"I'm home now, Mary," I said. "Why don't we just leave it alone now?"

We cleared the dishes from the table. Covered the leftovers with foil. Wiped down the stove. Sacked the trash. All in silence.

"That was a good dinner," I said, trying. "Nice party."

"Glad you liked it," she said and walked away.

I didn't sleep that night. I went to the living room and sat in the armchair. There were a few times I must have dozed off because I was dreaming. I couldn't remember any of the dreams. But when I startled awake I was surprised to see where I was. I got back into the bed before the alarm went off. Mary was sleeping. I'm not sure if she heard me tiptoe into the room.

It was the same that Monday morning as it always was when I came downstairs. The smell of bacon and pancakes from the kitchen. Clancy's cartoons playing on the television that sits on the kitchen counter. Mary, drinking her coffee, leafing through the paper, before setting out to The Stitching Post. Mary was telling

Clancy to eat her breakfast. Don't just watch TV, she said. Eat your breakfast or I'll turn it off.

As soon as Mary's car pulled down the driveway, I drove Clancy to school. I stopped at the Photo Spot and asked them to make copies of the picture on the beach.

"This picture must be thirty years old," the clerk said. "Since you don't have a negative, we can't guarantee the quality."

"You'd be surprised how good things can turn out after thirty years," I said.

"Well, it might be a little blurry."

"Yeah?" I said. "We'll see."

Emily was in her studio when I called that morning. I told her I hadn't slept. How much I missed her. When we hung up the phone, I sat there for a few moments.

Emily had said, "I'll always love you, Jim."

It was all too apparent that we were both home.

Mary and I never talked about that weekend again. A month later, the bill came for the dinner at Calvin's. Mary never said a word. She never mentioned the money from the jelly jar. Clancy wore her T-shirt to bed every night for a week and then went back to her butterfly pajamas. I remembered what Mary had said about marriage and children: "It has nothing to do with it." The problem is, it does.

# 27

It wasn't until July that I got the courage to go back to the beach. The beach was crowded, strewn with beach blankets, dotted with striped umbrellas, mesh playpens. You could smell the cotton candy, the hot dogs on the grill, the coconut scent of suntan oil.

I found a spot near the rocks for my easel. Jim never brought me photographs from the Marine Corps. He never gave me a picture of his father. The photo he sent of the two of us on the beach remained between the pages of the book. I relied on my memory and his words.

For the first week or so when we got back from Washington, Jim and I spoke every day. But after a while it became too difficult. Too painful. We began to speak less frequently, maybe once a month. There were too many long silences on the phone. Things to say that shouldn't be said. Reality clouded the desire to see one another again. We joked that the ideal relationship would be one of *"Same Time, Next Year"* but it always ended up with one of us saying that once a year would never be enough.

In the beginning, we reminisced about Washington. The breakfast at the Lincoln Memorial. The first time we made love. The evening we sat in the rain at the Vietnam Memorial. I sent him a copy of *Listen to the Warm*. It took seven weeks to get it since it was out of print. I wanted to inscribe it but I was afraid to put anything in writing. The only thing we never talked about again was that day in October. We talked only once about the night I found him standing at the wall. He told me he was touching Quinn's name.

That fall Peter and I took Jack around to look at colleges. One weekend in October we all found ourselves in Washington at Georgetown. We stayed at the L'Enfant Plaza. Peter said the concierge recommended that we have dinner at a place called Calvin's.

"I ate there with Jim," I said. "The service was rotten. Food was lousy."

"Are those the only reasons not to go, Emily?" Peter asked. The remark was caustic and penetrating. I pretended not to hear him.

Peter and the kids went to the Vietnam Memorial. Peter said they should see it again now that they were older. I went to the National Gallery that day instead. I've had enough of that Memorial, I said. But I did go with everyone to the Lincoln Memorial. We all sat on the steps for a while because Julie's new shoes were giving her blisters. Peter drank a cup of coffee. He took it from the same coffee shop where Jim and I had bought our breakfast. It was wrenching.

In November, the paintings were exhibited at a local gallery in New Canaan. Though I'd hoped to have been more prolific, I had done only six. I joined a group exhibition called Sense of the Sixties. There were black-and-white photographs from Woodstock taken by an artist, an old hippie who still wore his hair in a braid. Two charcoal renditions of the moon landing. A massive collage called *Spanning Decades: The Rise and Fall of the Berlin Wall.* A portrait artist exhibited commissioned oils of John F. Kennedy, Martin Luther King and Marilyn Monroe. My work, obviously, focused on Vietnam. I never wrote the texts to run along the sides of my paintings. I tried, but my words became too personal, too subjective.

Sara, Catherine and Robbie came to the opening. My father was recuperating from a knee replacement so my parents stayed in Florida. I had sent Jim an invitation addressed to Mr. and Mrs. James Moran and Clancy. It was Mary who called in the RSVP. The opening conflicted with their niece's wedding that Saturday, she said, but they'd come the next day. They wouldn't be far, she said. Just outside of Boston.

"I'm looking forward to meeting you," I said. I could feel my heart pounding.

"I've heard so much about you," Mary said.

"All good things, I hope," I said, trying to be light, to make a joke.

But Mary answered only by saying that Clancy would be with them if that was all right. I wanted to ask if Jim was there. Tried to muster up the nerve to say, Oh, I'd love to say hello. But I didn't ask for him. It didn't feel right.

It was three weeks later that I saw him. The Sunday right before Thanksgiving. My boys were at a high school basketball game but Peter and Julie were at the gallery. Peter was sitting at a table by the entrance, manning the sign-in book, when Jim came in. I was standing by a painting of Jim, talking to a reporter from the local paper. The painting showed a man standing alone at the Vietnam Memorial. It was night. He was facing the names, his hand raised against the wall. I saw Jim walk through the door.

"Excuse me," I said to the reporter. "I have to greet someone."

Mary was standing by Jim's side as they stood in the vestibule. Clancy was holding Jim's hand.

"I'm so glad you could come," I said not knowing where to put my eyes. "You must be Mary." And then I thought how stupid I sounded.

I shook her hand.

"This is our daughter, Clancy," Mary said.

I leaned over and Clancy said, properly trained, How do you do.

"You're even prettier than your picture," I said to Clancy. "I saw one of you on a pony. I bet you've gotten taller since that picture was taken."

I stood up and looked at Jim. He reached out and took my hand. Kissed me on the cheek the way you say hello at cocktail parties.

"Quite a show, Emily," he said.

For a moment I forgot about the gallery and wondered what he meant. Peter got up from his seat and walked around the table. He stood next to me, placed his hand on my shoulder.

"This is my husband, Peter," I said.

There were introductions all around. Everyone shaking hands. Smiling. It was so civilized.

Julie appeared from the back of the gallery where she was playing checkers with some bored children. Children of the gallery-goers. Julie had become very maternal since her job over the summer.

More handshaking. More greeting. Julie asked

Clancy to join the other kids in the back. Clancy ran off happily. The four of us stood there awkwardly.

"Would you like the tour?" I said. "Mine is not the only work here. It's a potpourri of the sixties."

Peter and I walked a few steps behind Jim and Mary. The six paintings in my series had no titles. Only months and years. *June 1967:* A boy on a windswept beach, his dark hair blowing as he looked to sea. *July 1967:* A boy stepping off the bus at Parris Island. *October 1967:* The same boy, a boot camp graduate now, hair shorn, full uniform. *December 1969:* A group of Marines in a bunker. *February 1970:* The Marine stepping off the plane at an empty airport in winter. *May 1997:* The Marine, now a civilian, mourning at the Vietnam Memorial, facing the wall.

"You're talented," Mary said.

"I had good subject matter," I said. "It feels like they painted themselves."

The reporter was still there. I introduced her to Jim and Mary. I guessed she wasn't more than twenty-five. The sixties to her was merely tie-dyed history.

"What did you think of the Vietnam Memorial?" she asked, cornering Jim, pen poised.

"My friend's name was on the wall," Jim said.

"What did you do?" she asked.

"I cried," he said and then he excused himself and walked away.

Mary walked over to where Clancy and Julie were playing checkers. Peter went back at his post behind the sign-in table.

"Want to take a walk with me, Emily Hudson?" Jim whispered.

We never bothered to get our coats. He wore a black wool sweater under the same tweed sport coat he'd worn last May in Washington. I was wearing a long, straight skirt and a turtleneck. The November air was cold. I thought, we'd never been together in the cold before.

"There's a path down there to a gazebo," I said. "There's a place where we can sit and talk."

He glanced back to the gallery.

"Will she mind?" I asked.

"Don't worry," he said. "She's fine."

We walked side-by-side down the stone path. Parts of it were icy. He held my arm to steady me but not until the gallery was no longer in sight.

A circular stone bench wrapped around inside the gazebo. As we stepped inside, it started to flurry. We sat down. He leaned his elbows on his knees, rested his chin on inverted hands.

Without looking up he said, "Sometimes I ache inside, you know. Sometimes it's unbearable to be away from you."

I put my hand behind his head. Stroked his hair. Brushed my fingers down his back.

"I know," I said. "I miss you. All the time. At night, as I fall asleep, I remember what it was like to hold you. Be held by you."

"What are we going to do?" he said, sitting up straight, turning to me, taking my hands in his.

"We promised not to ask that anymore," I said. "It used to be only about us. We were out there and in love. The world had to deal with us. Now it's different."

"Too many casualties," he said.

"Did Mary want to come here?" I asked.

"I think part of her did and part of her didn't. I think she needed to meet you. Maybe it was some sort of closure."

"With Peter, sometimes it's hard to tell. Meeting you removed the enigma," I said. "You became real to him with a wife, a child."

There was little else to say. He put his arms around me and kissed me. My neck, my face, my mouth. The snow was falling harder. It was time to go back.

"I want you so much," he whispered.

"I will always love you," I said. "Always."

When Jim left the gallery that afternoon the snow was coming down in big lacy flakes. I watched him through the plate glass window as he walked away with his wife and child. Mary folded a scarf under Clancy's chin. Clancy was mesmerized, staring at the sky, catching the snowflakes on her tongue. I saw Jim touch Clancy's cheek with the back of his hand. She leaned her head on his arm and smiled at him.

# 28

The invitation to the gallery opening arrived in October on a Saturday morning. Emily said it would be coming. Mary had picked up the mail.

"That woman sent us an invitation to her art show," Mary said. "I suppose you want to go."

Emily's name had dropped from our conversations. Emily was a topic we avoided. For Mary, she was forbidden territory.

"Come on, Mary," I said. "Her name is Emily Hudson. Why don't you stop calling her 'that woman'?"

"There's an RSVP to call," Mary said, ignoring me. "We'll be up for Ellen's wedding then. We'll have to miss the opening but we can go by on Sunday. Fly out of New York."

I think Mary was curious to meet Emily at that point. To see her in the flesh. To get to know the devil.

"I'll call and tell her," I said.

"No, that's all right," Mary said, disappearing into the kitchen. "I'll call."

I heard Mary's voice talking to Emily. She was polite. Restrained.

"How'd it go?" I asked when Mary reappeared.

"Just fine," she said. "Just fine."

I'm not sure if it's Mary who's changed in the last year or if it's me. I tend to think we've both changed. Words unsaid are probably more significant than any words we've ever spoken. Mary wears more sundresses now. She goes to the hair salon and gets the gray washed out of her hair so it's nearly as black as the day I met her. She cut back her hours to part-time at The Stitching Post. She's the one riding the exercise bike. And she wears a perfume, something French. I can't pronounce the name.

I have a new job managing a liquor store in downtown Mobile. I wear a coat and tie. There are wooden wine racks and a glass display with expensive corkscrews and fine crystal. Prices written in gilded script on dark background. It was me who got the idea for the script. I went and bought the gold felt-tip pens and ordered the black oaktag. At night, when I come home, Mary's already started dinner. I pour us a glass of wine and if the weather's good, we sit outside on the deck. Clancy still plays by the stream. Clancy's gotten taller and her red hair flows down her back. And Mary and I just sit and watch her.

I still shudder when the tornadoes blow through town and I remain inconsolable. Sometimes when I look into Mary's eyes, I wish I was seeing my reflection in Emily's eyes. But Mary's eyes are filled with a tenacity I probably need or maybe I'd be long gone. But there are still too many times I spend the hours before I'm able to fall asleep thinking about Emily. I think about how she throws her head back when she laughs.

I think about her arms holding me. And I remember her as a girl on the beach and as a woman. Sometimes it kills me to think about her. But I no longer want to erase the past. I'm no longer in fear of it.

So Mary and I rented a car and drove from Boston to New Canaan for Emily's show. It was snowing on and off. Clancy slept in the backseat, overbundled by Mary. Mary stared straight ahead the whole time. She barely uttered a word except to tell me to slow down.

"The roads are slick, Jimmy," she said. "You're not used to driving in New England anymore."

I hadn't seen Emily since the May before. Six months. Long months. In the beginning, we spoke to each other every day but then the calls became too painful. It was always more of the same. Figuring out a way to see each other again. Telling each other we missed each other. Remembering and almost wishing we could forget.

I knew it was Peter sitting at the reception table at the gallery. I should probably have just introduced myself and said hello but I was worried that he would wonder why I knew that it was him. He's a handsome man, Peter Walters, and for a moment I had the same feeling come over me that I did on the day that Emily said there was someone else. I pictured Peter with Emily and I turned my head away.

Emily walked over from across the room. The arms that had held me were covered in a long-sleeved turtleneck. She wore a long, narrow skirt and I thought she looked thinner than she had in Washington. She'd cut her hair so that it just touched the edge of her chin. She looked so beautiful. Jimmy's girl.

I think that Mary was taken aback when Emily greeted her. I don't know how she managed but Emily was so warm to Mary. Better than I was with Peter. She clasped Mary's hand in hers and said she was happy to finally meet her. Clancy told me later that Emily was a pretty lady. She said that in front of Mary and I don't think Mary was too pleased. But then Clancy, in that inimitable way of hers, added, "Not as pretty as Mommy, though." And Mary smiled at her.

Peter walked over and before Emily could introduce him, he reached his hand out to me.

"I'm Emily's husband," he said. "Peter Walters. Good to meet you, Jim."

"This is my wife, Mary," I said.

Julie came bounding out of nowhere. She is much like her mother though she looks like her father. She is warm and open.

"Hi, Mr. Moran! I recognize you from Mom's paintings," she said.

Then she took Clancy right by the hand and led her off to play. Mary and I walked the gallery with Emily and Peter a few steps behind us.

That day at the gallery was an exercise in self-control. It took everything I had to kiss her so simply on the cheek after all those months. To shake Peter's hand. To introduce my wife.

I remembered that day at the airport when I first saw her last May. How easy it was to hold her, press my cheek against hers, and here I was greeting her the way you might someone's wife at a dinner party. But that was just it. She was someone's wife. And my wife was standing next to me.

It was quite amazing how Emily captured me in the paintings. Her art was a side of her I never knew about. Until I saw the paintings, I only knew the side of Emily that loved me. She had told me about painting on the beach at Tod's but I never expected it to be, well, so touching. To capture the spirit of the boy. I was awed by the painting of the young Marine. It could have been my graduation picture. How did she remember so well? I wished my father was alive to see the paintings.

"They're really very good," Mary said to Emily. "I guess you really are an artist."

"I try," Emily said.

I'm not sure what it was that made Mary decide to check on Clancy. I think she probably felt self-conscious standing there. Maybe she figured I would follow her. I thought about it for a moment, thought about trailing after her. Maybe it was because Peter walked back to his post at the table and Mary took it as a safe cue. And as soon as Peter and Mary were out of earshot I whispered, Want to take a walk with me, Emily Hudson?

It was freezing outside. We had no coats. The gallery was mostly glass. I walked a good distance apart from Emily until we got to the bottom of the path where I could no longer see the building. There was a gazebo at the end of the trail. We sat inside, away from the wind, but it was still cold.

I realized while we sat there that I'd never been with her in winter. I'd been with her in spring and summer when the air was warm and the flowers bloomed. It almost scared me to sit there with her under the bare trees and the white sky. It seemed like almost a portent. Everything around us was bare and dying if it wasn't dead already. I was leaning over with my face in my hands when she touched the back of my head.

"It's so cold outside," I said. "Your hand is so warm."

And I sat up and put my arms around her. I kissed her face and her mouth.

"You cut your hair," I said, pulling back for a moment to look at her eyes. "You look wonderful."

"So do you, Jim," she said. "I've missed you."

"What are we going to do, Emily?" I asked.

But I knew she had no answer.

"I'm glad you're here," she said.

"But what about us?" I asked. And as I asked, I closed my eyes.

A long time ago, there was just the two of us. In Washington, it was just the two of us. But there were seven other lives. There could be too much fallout.

I took her in my arms. I wanted her so badly. I kissed her and I never wanted to let her go.

We walked back along the path to the gallery and let go of each other's hand when the building came in sight.

"I'll always love you, Emily Hudson," I whispered.

# 29

It is May again. The May before, a year ago to this day, I was in Washington with Jim Moran. It's been six months now since I've seen him. But I feel as though it's been a year. Seeing him at the gallery last November was not the same.

Two of the paintings sold the day Jim was at the gallery.

*May 1997* was bought by a wealthy businessman whose son was killed in Vietnam. His son, a medic, chose to enlist. He was killed as he tried to save someone else. He was killed in the massacre at Khe Sanh. Jim wondered if the man he tried to save, in vain, was Quinn McBride.

*December 1969* was bought by a woman named Rose whose husband won a Purple Heart for valor during the Tet Offensive. Rose said the painting was for her husband's birthday. Jim questioned if the gift was wise.

*June 1967*, the boy on the beach, hangs in my studio. That one was never for sale. I sent the one of the boot camp graduate, *October 1967*, to Jim and Mary. Jim said that was the one he wished his father could have seen.

The others sit wrapped in brown paper, tied with string, in the corner of my studio. It is hard for me to look at them.

Sometimes it amazes me how life has gone on. Jack bought himself a car with the money he earned as a lifeguard last summer. A 1966, navy blue, fastback Mustang. Right now, Jack is over at his girlfriend's house. Her name is Jill. Her name is something Sam and Charlie are teasing Jack about relentlessly but Jack is too in love to pay attention. Sam and Charlie are working after school at the ice cream parlor. Julie is in her room, giggling, talking on the phone to her friend Amanda. But unlike last year, now her door is closed. I eavesdropped for a few minutes and I know they're talking about a boy named Tommy. Julie says that Tommy is cute. She asks Amanda if Amanda thinks Tommy likes her. I think to myself, Ah, it's only just beginning.

Everyone is growing up and yet there is a sameness, a sense of comfort in the growth.

There were Christmas cards exchanged last December. A photograph of Clancy wearing a red dress, holding her new kitten. A photograph of my children sitting on the grass in the backyard. The leaves were brilliant colors on the trees behind them. The boys wore white T-shirts against the leaves. Julie wore jeans and a peasant blouse. Julie said the sixties are "in" again. The latest style. She wanted a silver peace sign for Christmas.

Jim and I spoke the day of New Year's Eve. Peter and I were having a party at home that night. The kids, their friends, our friends. Jim and Mary were going to a neighbor's house. I said it was cold here in New England. We expected a snowstorm for the New Year. He said it was still warm in Mobile. Almost warm enough for azaleas.

He called me on my birthday in January. I called him on his in March. It's hard to believe he is almost fifty. Last month, Jim called to say he got a new job. "I'm managing a real liquor store in Mobile," he said. "It's a lot like Sherry-Lehman. No more plastic name tag. Mary cut back her hours to part-time. She only works three days a week now," he said. Clancy had the chickenpox. His cholesterol was high. Mary wants to adopt another baby. Jim says he'd like to have a son.

I told him I found my first gray hair.

You know I'm lousy with the grays, he said.

I told him Jack was going off to college in the fall. Georgetown in Washington, D.C. The first of my children to fledge the nest.

I guess you'll be visiting Washington next year, he said.

I said, I guessed I would. I started to say something else.

Don't say it, he said.

No, I said. I won't.

Peter still works long hours. But lately he's taken to coming home early at least one or two nights a week. We let the answering machine pick up calls during dinner. Peter steels himself from picking up the phone. We laugh at his efforts.

I go to Tod's only occasionally now. It doesn't feel as necessary to be there anymore. Mostly I paint in the studio. I've switched from oils to watercolors. I'm taking classes in ceramics at the gallery in town. Keeping busy. Though I'm never quite busy enough to stop remembering.

There isn't a day that goes by when I don't think of him. For many months there wasn't a phone call that didn't end with both of us saying I'll always love you. But the calls have become less and less frequent. We've stopped asking, What are we going to do? We haven't asked since that day at the gallery. We both know the answer.

It makes me angry sometimes to think that he is there and I am here. I think of my children and his daughter and how one day they will all be off with lives of their own. Lovers, husbands, wives. I think of how it would be to lie in his arms at night. Bring him black coffee in the morning. Have him wait for me at the end of the day when I return from the beach. Talk to him over glasses of tepid wine.

But then I think of how it would be to walk my daughter down the aisle apart from her father. How Jack's graduation would be if Peter and I sat on either side of the auditorium. How my children would never forgive me if I tore this home apart. How Clancy was adopted by two people who promised to give her a home. Parents. Together. Forever.

For years I thought there was a sixteen-year-old girl trapped somewhere inside me. A girl whose first love was, perhaps, fantasized and romanticized. I thought perhaps it would have been dissuaded by the reappearance of a boy who was not the man she thought he would be. It was unfortunate that it didn't happen that way. That it wasn't so simple. The boy grew up to be a man and I still loved him. The sixteen-year-old girl still lingers. She's stepped aside but she remains. For a weekend she was real. Now she's but a shadow. This is, I suppose, the stuff I explain to Julie about growing up.

This is not to say I do not love my husband. I am neither delusional nor egotistical: I know how deeply Jim loves Mary. Perhaps even more than he cares to realize. I believe that Jim loves Mary for her strength, for her ability to deal with the grays. I would like to think each of us loves the other for what we are and what we are not.

Speaking as I can only for myself, my love for Peter is a very gentle love. He is a good man. A decent man, I have come to realize that he loves me the best way he knows how. The only way he knows how. Perhaps the only way I have allowed him to love me.

I suppose that one day I will see Jim again. It's just not possible right now. There are no valid reasons to be together. Less valid reasons for us to be alone. Yet there are days I long to be with him. To fall asleep on his chest. Wake up in his arms. I worry that he drives his car carefully, that he eats properly, that he is happy.

Always the mom, he would say.

The sun is beginning to set outside the bay window in the kitchen and I know that soon I will hear the crackle of gravel in the driveway and Peter will be home. I will hear his car door open and shut and I will embrace the familiarity and yet something will never quite be the same. Tonight I took out the chopping board, the paring knife, set the paper towel where I could grab a sheet to dry my hands. I even set the table. But I did not make dinner. There is something about this night as the warm breeze comes through the kitchen window. My heart feels heavy. Tonight I want to gather up the kids and head to a restaurant in Compo Beach. I want to be where I can smell the salt air and look out at the water. Peter will balk and offer to boil up some pasta or bring something in. Sam and

Charlie will say they're tired from working at the ice cream parlor. Julie will want to stay home so she can wash her hair. Jack will prefer to spend the evening with Jill.

So maybe I will order pizza for the kids and go alone with Peter. We can sit by the Sound and talk about the coming summer. The fall when Jack leaves for Georgetown. And Peter will take my hand in his and I will heave a sigh. And I will wonder if he knows all the meaning behind the inhalation.

My heart will ache to remember but refuse to forget. I remember as clear as water the day Jimmy said, "Take a walk with me, Emily Hudson." You see, this love was ours. This love is mine. And despite everything else, it still is.

And as I gaze at the Sound I will know that a part of me is still on the beach with Jimmy Moran. A part of me will always be Jimmy's girl.

**Coming from Dutton
in July 2002
*The Puzzle Bark Tree*
by Stephanie Gertler**

One night, before Grace went to sleep, she asked her. Sit down on my bed, Grace said. Sit down just this once. I have the same kind of dream all the time, Mom. Melanie and I are on a ship and the ship is tossing in the night. A hole is gaping through the hull and icy water is pouring in and coming up to our knees and then rushing past our waists. Faster and faster. And I scream for someone to help us. You're there but you won't save us and you swim away. I need to ask you, Mom, if Melanie and I were on a ship, and the ship was tossing in the night and there was a hole gaping through the hull and water was pouring in so that it came up to our knees faster and faster, couldn't you save us? Wouldn't you save us both?

Her mother looked at Grace as she lay in her bed, the covers pulled up to her chin. Her mother's eyes became wide. She looked almost startled, blinking in what appeared to be disbelief. Looking into her mother's eyes frightened Grace more than the dream of the ship sinking in the darkness. When her mother finally spoke, her voice was raised and trembling. What a foolish question, her mother said. Stupid question. That is a cruel and selfish question, Grace Hammond. Why would you *think* about such things? How could you *ask* such a thing? her mother moaned. She inhaled a breath so rasping and deep Grace wasn't sure what would happen when she let it go. Her mother clasped her hands, then released them, wrung them and twisted them in a way that frightened Grace and made her wonder if her mother would tear them off her wrists.

Grace wailed that she didn't mean anything by her question.

I was only wondering, Grace apologized, pleading for mercy.

Her mother left her seat at the edge of Grace's bed and flipped off the bathroom light.

Please, please, leave it on and leave the door cracked open, Grace begged. But her mother just walked away, as though she were an apparition in the darkness.

There were so many nights, when Grace was a child, that she dreamed of ships and boats rocking to and fro on metal gray waves. She was probably around six years old the first time she had the dream. It wasn't until she was ten that Grace found the courage to confess the dream to her mother. The dream recurred over and over again after that. A boat, sometimes a ship, rocking violently on steely dun water that splashed over the deck and soaked Grace's clothes so they clung to her like onion skin. And, in all the dreams, Grace and Melanie would call out for help, their cries trapped somewhere deep inside their throats, down to their chests, though their mouths were poised to cry.

Grace's daughter, Kate, asked the same sort of thing when she was a little girl. Her question, however, did

not come from a dream. It was simply one of those
questions that children ask like why is the sky blue and
is there really a man on the moon and why don't we fall
off the edge of the earth as it spins? Kate called Grace
back to her bed one night after Grace had tucked her in
and read *Anne of Green Gables* for the umpteenth time.

If you and Daddy and I were on a desert island and
you could save only one, who would you rescue? Kate
asked, her eyes imploring.

And Grace answered, ignoring her own sense of something arcane as Kate posed her question, I would save us
all, Grace said matter-of-factly. I would save us all.

But you can save only one, Kate said. That's the rule.

I would break the rule. Grace smiled, lifting her chin
triumphantly. She enveloped her daughter so tightly
that Kate laughed and said she was squeezing her too
hard.

They fell asleep together that night and, in the
morning, just like so many mornings, Grace wondered
why it never occurred to her own mother to simply
gather Grace up in her arms and say she would save
them both. . . .

It was Jemma who called Melanie to say she couldn't
awaken her parents that Sunday morning. Jemma, who
had lived with the Hammond family for the first
twenty years of her employ and, for the last twenty,
loyally took the train up from the Bronx every morning
and then a cab to their house in Purchase, New York.
She did this every morning save an occasional Saturday and Sunday when there was a church function or
one of her friends or neighbors needed her assistance
but, what with the snowstorm, she decided to check
when the Hammonds hadn't answered their phone.

*     *     *

The throbbing in Grace's temples was palpable. . . . A blue-and-white patrol car sat in the driveway of her parents' house behind her brother-in-law's old orange BMW. Yellow banners with black lettering, CRIME SCENE DO NOT CROSS, stretched from branch to branch of leafless brittle bushes crusted with iced-over snow. Strange tinsel this time of year, Grace thought. Neighbors huddled behind blue police sawhorses, bundled in down jackets and wool scarves, some still in pajamas, straining their necks, holding mugs of steaming coffee as though they awaited a parade.

No one behind the sawhorses spoke as Grace and Kate got out of the car. They watched them walk up the stone path. Their eyes, in unison, followed Grace's hand as it ripped away a yellow banner, ignoring the command not to cross. They moved their eyes away from hers as Grace scanned the strange faces behind the barriers. Strangers. There wasn't one who could step forward and take her arm. Not one who could call out her name or comfort her. Not even someone who might say they knew, or once knew, her parents.

It had been years since Grace knew the residents on Harvest Lane. There was Mr. And Mrs. Connelly whose son Brian had been the first boy Grace had ever kissed. Mr. and Mrs. Rinaldi, whose daughter Angela still sent Grace a birthday card every year. The Millers, the Howards, the Schroeders. They all had kids who played with Grace and let Melanie tag along. Grace remembered every nook and cranny of their basements, attics, kitchens, the kinds of cookies they kept in their cookie jars, the creak of every stair in their homes. But the kids never played at Grace's house. Grace and Melanie knew better than to ask them. It was too much noise, their mother would say. Something might get broken. But Grace always thought it was because things broke too easily in a house of cards. . . .

Her parents had become the eccentric old couple on the street, a reputation not far removed from the one they held as the reclusive young couple forty years before, who had not joined neighborhood organizations or gone to garage sales or watched the fireworks on the Fourth of July. The ones who simply stayed to themselves. And then there was the "old" house. . . . Shingles, fallen from the roof, lay on top of the snow. The window panes were cracked. The paint on the chimney was peeling. Even in spring, the house looked abandoned. The lilac tree no longer bloomed; the magnolia's branches were half dead. Rusty gutters overflowed with debris. But then, the house had always looked a bit abandoned, Grace thought, even when she was a child. . . .

"I bet it was the old man," a young woman whispered to a newcomer who had a child in a stroller, bundled in a snowsuit.

"No, the old lady was pretty frail. She rarely saw the light of day," said another neighbor, tightening his collar around his neck. "The old man's been wandering lately. Saw him the other day, strolling around the backyard in his bathrobe."

"Real oddballs," the young woman said. "They never even had candy for the kids at Halloween."

"I heard they were always a little crazy," the man said. "Real kooks."

A white van stenciled with blue lettering, MEDICAL EXAMINER, was parked in front of the house next to several black unmarked cars whose only indication of something official were the half-dozen spiraled, thick antennas stuck to their rear windows. Blue-and-white squad cars were parked up and down the street with red dome lights turning and glistening, casting scarlet blazes on the snow. Everything seemed surreal and muted, cushioned by the snowfall. The silence was broken only by the crackle of the two-way radio on the hip of the police officer who stood by the front door. Unintelligible conversation broke through the radio in spurts of static that the officer pressed on and off. . . . Grace drew her breath through her nose, held it for a moment, and stopped in front of the police officer who guarded the front door.

"Officer, I'm their daughter," Grace said, her breath letting out like smoke. "Their other daughter. My sister is inside. This is my daughter, Kate."

"I'm sorry, ma'am," he said. "I'm afraid I can't let you in." He blocked them, placing his arm out, though he never touched them, as Grace started through the door. "You'll have to wait here until I can get someone to clear you through."

"My parents live here," Grace said. "I need to go inside."

"Give me a moment, ma'am," the officer said.

The police officer was unhooking the walkie-talkie from his belt when the door opened. A plainclothes detective stepped out. He was wearing jeans and a green turtleneck.

"What's going on, Jack?" the man said to the uniformed officer.

"She says she's the daughter, sir," the officer said, rehooking the walkie-talkie. "Says the girl is the granddaughter."

"I'm Grace Barnett and this is my daughter, Kate," Grace said.

"I'm Detective Douglas Bush. I need to see some identification, ma'am," the detective said gently.

Grace's hands trembled as she reached into the caverns of her purse for her wallet. She handed him her driver's license. Credit cards, loose change, a stick of gum, a small hairbrush fell to the ground. Kate reached down to retrieve everything, placing them back into her mother's bag.

"Let them in, Jack," the detective said to the officer as he looked at the driver's license and then back to Grace. "It's okay." Then, turning to Grace, he held the door open. "Please come in."

Melanie had been sitting on the couch between Jemma and Mike when Grace came in the door. She threw her arms around her sister's shoulders, hugging her tightly. Jemma was standing to the side of them until Grace managed to stretch out her hand, pulling Jemma into the embrace. The three stood there, huddled, heads down, as though in prayer, wrapped around each other. There was barely a sound except for Jemma's muffled sobs. Muted words of comfort murmured as though they were in church. As though the funeral had already begun, Grace thought, or perhaps was over. . . .

"Please sit down, Mrs. Barnett," said Detective Bush, breaking up the women's embrace. "I'm very sorry but we have to ask you some questions."

"I'm their other daughter," Grace repeated as she gazed up the stairs. She felt empty. Flat. As though she were floating above the room. Her voice came from somewhere else. She tried to make a fist but she couldn't feel her hands.

"Yes, I know, ma'am," the detective said patiently. "First of all, I'm sorry for your loss, Mrs. Barnett."

"Can I see my parents?" Grace asked. "What happened? How did this happen?"

"They won't let us upstairs," said Melanie.

"What do you mean? Why not?" Grace asked, turning to the detective.

"Please, ladies, we're doing what we have to do," Detective Bush said. "Until we know exactly what happened here, we have to treat this as a crime scene. I cannot permit you to go upstairs. We're collecting evidence."

"Evidence? For God's sake, they died," Melanie said. "They killed themselves. This was no crime!"

"It was that, wasn't it, Mel?" Grace said, turning to her sister. "I knew it, I swear. I felt it."

"In my heart, I knew it was," Melanie said. "From the moment I heard Jemma's voice, I knew. I think even Jemma knew."

"Did you know, Jemma?" they asked, not surprised by their chorus.

Jemma didn't answer. She looked from Grace to Melanie, her lips pressed together but not quite firmly enough to stop quivering. Jemma didn't have to answer. They all knew. Grace and Melanie knew even as children. Grace and Melanie could feel it coming when they would tap on their mother's bedroom door and there would be no answer. They would come home from school and jiggle the doorknob to their parents' room and rap furiously.

She's in there, they would whisper to each other. You know she's in there. Do you hear anything? Put your ear to the door. . . .

And then the day came when they knew that it wasn't just that something wasn't right, something was terribly wrong. They discovered that other families went to church on Sundays and ate their meals together. That mothers took their daughters shopping and fathers held them while they learned to ride their bicycles. They realized that even when they saw their mother, she did not see them. She didn't want to see them. And their father closed his eyes as if he were blind. Or perhaps he was simply afraid to look. They asked Jemma why it seemed their house was so different from the others and Jemma said it was different strokes for different folks. Your parents are reserved, is all, she said. And perhaps because they didn't want Jemma to feel that she wasn't enough to anchor their lives and make them a home, they simply let it go. Perhaps because they knew it wasn't that Jemma was lying so much as she, herself, was uncertain of the truth.

"This is rather unusual," the detective said quietly, aware that he was breaking Grace's thoughts. He turned to Melanie. "Mrs. Peterson, why didn't you say this to me before? Why didn't you say that you thought your parents' deaths were suicides?"

"I needed to wait for my sister," Melanie said, her eyes down.

"Anything else?" he asked.

"My mother was wearing lipstick. She never wore lipstick," Melanie said.

"Did your parents tell you they were planning this?" the detective asked, looking back and forth from Grace to Melanie. Like Jemma, Grace thought, looking from one of us to the other for an answer outside her bedroom door.

"I don't know what to make of the lipstick," Grace said. "Our parents didn't indicate that anything was planned. It's an awfully long story, Detective. Nothing was ever quite right here."

\*      \*      \*

"I have here your parents' last wills and testaments," Thompson said, clearing his throat. "They were recorded just three weeks ago, updated for what, of course, became the final time. In fact, your parents had what are called reciprocal wills, wills that can be interpreted as one since the documents are mirror images of one another. Often the deceased leave notes or letters within the will to accompany the document. Just so you know, right off the bat, there was nothing of that nature left within for any of you. It's pretty straightforward. I know this is hard for all of you. Before I begin, again, Grace and Melanie, if there is anything at all that I can do, please let me know."

"For Jemma, too," Grace said.

Thompson nodded to Jemma. "Forgive me. You, too, Mrs. Polk. I am aware of your devotion and loyalty to Mr. and Mrs. Hammond," he said stiffly as he dunked an herbal tea bag in a mug of boiled water.

"They were my family," Jemma said.

But Thompson just went on. He wasn't one for sentiment. "You'll all get your copies. In the meantime, I will paraphrase a bit. You don't need to be bogged down with legal mumbo jumbo. I assume we're all comfortable?"

"We're ready now," Grace said.

"They've left things quite clean, as it were," said Thompson, lifting his teacup with a pretentious pinky up as he continued. "All succession, estate, or inheritance taxes which might be levied against the estate will be paid out of the residuary estate. There should be no surprises for any of you.

"For Jeremy and Matthew Peterson and Katherine Barnett: The net proceeds sale from the Purchase house is to be divided equally among the three grand-children. Proceeds from the aforementioned sale will be held in trust for the benefit of each child with John Glass, your parents' accountant for the last ten years, as trustee and myself as alternate trustee. Mr. Glass is also the executor of the will.

"The furnishings of the house as well as vases, dishes, household appliances, books, records, and all personal effects are to be sold at auction. Additionally, net proceeds from said auction should be divided equally among the grandchildren and held in trust as set up in Article IX.

"Your mother's jewelry, consisting of a diamond engagement ring (total one carat in a platinum setting valued at seven thousand dollars), one sixteen-inch strand of pearls with an amethyst clasp (valued at two thousand dollars), a gold seashell necklace with matching earrings (valued at three thousand five hundred dollars), and a diamond and sapphire bracelet (valued at two thousand five hundred dollars) has been left to Melanie."

"And to Grace, I assume?" Melanie asked, interrupting him. "I assume that Grace shares in the jewelry as well?"

"No. Your mother left the jewelry to you alone, Melanie," Thompson said. "Just to you. It is rather irregular, I know, seeing that there are two daughters. For you, Mrs. Polk, in appreciation of what is termed a lifetime of devotion and service, the Hammonds left a flat sum of twenty-five thousand dollars."

"And to Grace?" Melanie asked again angrily. "What about Grace?"

"Melanie, it's okay," Grace said. "They provided for Kate. That's all that matters."

"Now, now, now. They actually saved the best for last. The residuary estate does not include the following, Grace. They most certainly have not forgotten you, my dear. It says right here that Grace Hammond Barnett is the beneficiary of their house at Sabbath Landing," Thompson said, smiling broadly.

"A house?" Grace asked. "What house? What is Sabbath Landing?"

"I never heard them mention a house," Jemma said. "What on earth—"

"Well, I must say I am rather surprised. I don't quite understand. You are not familiar with this house?" Thompson said, interrupting Jemma.

He pulled the deed out of the folder in his briefcase.

"Says right here that in 1950, your parents purchased a twenty-five-hundred-square-foot dwelling in Sabbath Landing, New York. Let me paraphrase: said dwelling rests on four acres with southeast view of Pilot Mount, northwest view of Hester's Peak."

"They own another house?" Grace asked. "Are you sure it's not a mistake?"

"Oh, no. There's no mistake. They most certainly do own another house," said Thompson. "And in a magnificent area. There's a grand old hotel in Sabbath Landing. The Alpine. Marge and I have spent many fine weekends there. Of course, come the end of September it gets pretty darn cold. Must be frigid there now. Doesn't really warm up after that until June."

"Have you been to the house?" Grace asked, a shiver running up her spine so vividly she shuddered.

"Well, no," said Thompson. "I admit, it's a bit odd that your father never mentioned it since he knew that Marge and I often went up there. But then again, your father, may he rest in peace, was not, well, loquacious, shall we say. Oh, it's a gorgeous spot. Way back in the 1930s and 1940s, people snatched up property for a song up there. Before the DEC came in and started to say you couldn't do this and you couldn't do that. Your parents' house was built in 1868. Sounds like it's quite special. Built of cypress. They say that cypress never rots, you know."

"Why me? Why would they have wanted me to have that house?" Grace asked.

"That I can't answer," said Thompson. "I'm a bit dumbstruck, to tell you the truth. I would have thought you girls knew the place."

"Well, we don't. We've never been there nor have we been aware that they owned it," Grace said. She was becoming irritated. "*Where* exactly is this house? How do you get there?"

"Oh, it's easy," Thompson said. "About a five-hour drive from here right up the thruway. But you don't want to go there now. As I said, it's too damn cold there now. You couldn't even get out to the house."

"Well, there must be roads," Grace said. "I mean, people live there, don't they? They probably all have four-wheel drives."

"People live there all right, but not where this house is," Thompson said, pulling an aerial photograph from a worn brown envelope. "It's a beauty, isn't it?" He held the photo in front of Grace. "There it is. A real log cabin on Canterbury Island. About a mile and a half off the coast. Right smack dab in the middle of Diamond Lake."

Thompson finished his tea. He dabbed his mouth too delicately with the corner of a calico napkin and handed the deed and the photograph in the worn brown envelope folder to Grace. Grace never rose from the sofa when she took the envelope in her hands. She lifted her head to Thompson and thanked him, trying to look him directly in the eyes, hoping she might see a hint of something that he wasn't telling her but knew. Something he might have been keeping from her or waiting for her to ask about. There was nothing. He nodded his head. Smiled at her. Wished her well.

Jemma picked up the tray of cups and saucers and carried them to the kitchen while Melanie ushered Thompson out the door. He sputtered more amenities, the banal recitation Grace had tired of hearing over the last week. Sorry for your loss. My deepest sympathies. Marge sends her condolences. Once again, let me reiterate, if there is anything you need . . . Grace heard the low drone of Thompson's voice, the empty yet appropriate words, trailing on and on until she heard Melanie shut the door behind him.

"What do you think this is about?" Grace asked, waving the aerial photograph at Melanie as she walked into the living room.

Jemma was wiping her hands on a dish towel. She sat down next to Grace, peering over her shoulder at the picture.

"I have no idea," Melanie said. "You would think that as bizarre as this last week has been, things couldn't get stranger. And now this. Jemma, do you know? Did they ever go to that house? Had you ever heard them mention Diamond Lake?"

Jemma shook her head. "What I find so odd is that if they had a house in the middle of a lake, why didn't we ever go there? I bet it's beautiful there in the summer. I couldn't even get your folks to take you girls swimming when you were kids. Remember? I was the one who took you for those swim lessons. For the life of me, I can't understand why they'd have a house by a lake and not even tell us."

"What are you going to do with it?" Melanie asked, turning to her sister.

But Grace didn't answer. She had opened the envelope. She was studying the aerial view. The house was all but hidden in a layer of trees. The deed said it was twenty-five hundred square feet but it was hard to make out the size or the shape from the photograph. There appeared to be dirt paths leading around the island, what looked like a patio of sorts high above the lake on one side, dots that looked like a table and six chairs. Lower, at water level, there was a dock with what looked like a boat tied to a rafter. The island was not flat the way one might imagine an island. It was hilly, rising sixty feet above the lake's surface according to the deed's speculations. The house stood center, a good hike uphill from the lake below. But the age of the yellow-tinged photograph, the distance from which it was taken, obscured the details.

"It doesn't look like the kind of place that Mother and Dad would have gone," Grace said. "It seems so remote. But then again, maybe that was so much like them. Maybe it was a place they went to by themselves. Or maybe it was just an investment." She slipped the photo back into the envelope. "I don't understand. I don't understand any of this at all. Most of all, I don't understand why they left it to me. Why leave an island to someone who has a fear of water?"